COLLOQUIUM

CHARLES D'AMICO

NEIL BAGGIO
EST. 1996

COLLOQUIUM

Cover & Interior Design: Blue Handle Publishing, LLC

ISBN: 978-1-7347727-4-6

Thank You Bryan, Mike and Joe. Without your early support, none of this would have happened.

To
My loving, supportive wife.
My mother, looking down on me.
And the literary inspiration for whom I wish to write a hundred books, my sister.
Simply, thank you!

1

Neil, it's about time you took time and admitted to yourself and others that I am a driving factor in your overall success.

It's a bit frustrating to think that after all these years, I'm still tied to this asshole. He can take credit for my greatest success; my growth as a person; and, most notably, celebrity. That's the life of an investigator when chasing someone as prominent as Cappelano. You will always be tied to him, especially if you let the asshole live. I know I should have killed him back then, that day in Mexico, I was so close. I pulled that trigger back, was ready to shoot him, put a bullet in his head, but the gun jammed. I guess it's what you get for buying your gun in Mexico from a liquor store.

"Neil, I understand why you come here, but it's getting tiresome. You come here, we talk, and I go back to my room."

"It's not like you have anything better to do. Do you have some license plates to stamp? Maybe you can make me one for my new ride. I finally upgraded."

"Your wit, though tiresome, is getting better. All these visits must be improving something."

I have visited Frank in the past, continued some form of a relationship with him. In the beginning, I had some semblance of hatred. Then I realized it was my issue with the weight of it all. I was struggling with the fact that he was just as much of a celebrity as I was. I mean, I'm the good guy. Why is the bad guy just as popular as the guy that got him caught? Then I remember, there is no need for Batman without Robin. That's when I started to look into him more—spend more time looking into our relationship; what he saw in me, what he was doing to me, with me, and how he saw me. I started going to him, interviewing him, and talking to him in depth about our past. About the interactions we had, the crimes he had committed, and what he had done. Why he did them, his reasoning, his motivation behind them.

"I guess you could say that being aware of your craziness, as well as your impact in my life, and merely accepting it's there, not ignoring it anymore, have helped me."

"Neil, it's about time you took time and admitted to yourself and others that I am a driving factor in your overall success."

His ego is consuming him, but there is nothing I can do at this point. I'm intrigued by him, but the transition from when I met him back in the nineties as a fresh recruit, and he was a top- tier agent, messed me up. He can explain away his behavior to extreme levels, its Olympic-level shit. I must deal with it. I internalize and overthink everything, which is great as an investigator, but it's brutal to live inside your own thoughts.

"Frank, you believe I wipe my ass because you willed it. Your ego is insane. I enjoy our talks and feel that I am growing and learning. Overall, we at the bureau are gaining knowledge from you. However, I think your ego is consuming yourself three times over."

"Neil, there you go again, pushing things to the extreme. We were having a perfectly good conversation, and you had to get testy about it."

"I can see our conversation today is going to be a rough one. When you are feeling self-righteous, I might as well call it a day. There is no point in talking to you because you are going to bring everything back to some lesson you taught me."

"But I did teach you so much, Neil. You don't give me nearly enough credit."

"I'm not sure what you expect of me, what you plan on having me do with this conversation. I came here to talk to you about a specific case we worked together back in the day, a case we cracked together before you disappeared. You know, before you killed your family member who learned too much about you."

"Please don't remind me of all the things I have done. That is the only one that I have regretted, the only one I feel I had no justice in, I feel vindicated, that I deserve to be back here merely for that one murder. All the others I feel were deserving."

"Frank, the problem is you don't see the parents you destroyed, the spouses whose lives you condemned because of your actions."

"Why don't you enlighten me as to something I don't seem to understand, give me some insight into this path of destruction I created?"

"Okay, I can do that. Tell you what, when I come back, we'll sit down, and I'll map it out for you. You have to get back to doing your life sentence, and I have to get back to the office. We have some items to review for a big case we're working on."

"Did you guys finally get called in on that missing girl case?"

"Yes. I only wish they would have done it sooner. Now we're behind the ball, but we have a good team working on it. I'm just supervising, working from the office, not doing any fieldwork on this one."

"Look at Neil moving up in his own company. I wasn't sure you had it in you."

"You wore me out, and this last case that didn't seem to have an end or a point wore me out too."

"Have a great day, Neil."

I just turned around and walked away, not sure why I didn't say good-bye. I knew it was odd, but I've been doing that lately. I think it's because I want to keep some semblance of distance despite my curiosity. That's what is driving me to keep coming back. Trying to understand the mind of a psychopath isn't easy; it's what led Cappelano down this path of destruction in the first place.

I can't believe it has been more than ten years since Cappelano and I met and since this whole dance started. It's about to be the new year, and the Detroit winter is the usual mix of wet, temps in the cool twenties, and dirty black air. You're reminded of how dirty it is quickly after it snows. Within a day, all the white snow alongside the roads are as black as the smog-filled air. I know people are trying to make a difference, but it's hard to see with this crap all over. Pulling into the office, I noticed Ken was standing there talking to Christian. He is one of our leads and we are helping a joint investigation with local and federal employees.

"Hey Neil, Christian and I were going over the Monroe case. How was everything this morning at your Tuesday chat?"

"The usual. I think he is finally ready to start digging into the shit with more detail. I want to know what is going on, how he saw me, saw his victims, and what his purpose was, not just to use going forward, but also out of curiosity, I guess."

"Be careful, Neil. You know the adage stare at the fire long enough and you can fall in."

"Thanks, Ken, I'll keep that in mind. I think I have so much disdain and hatred for him that it will keep me far back enough."

"Neil, you've been burned so many times you're a little afraid of the fire." Ken has a good point.

"Exactly. How about we go into the conference room? It looks like you have a command center of sorts set up, and you guys give me the rundown."

Ken, Christian, and I made our way across the warehouse to the conference room, where they had set everything that pertains to the case. The case involves Erin Beddington, an activist in the community. She worked with a local newspaper while protesting Gaines Chemical, in Detroit. They had just gotten a big contract that was a bit dirty. Erin brought it to light, got lots of press, and got the contract scrapped. It cost Gaines Chemical millions, then suddenly, she's missing. The local authorities figured it wouldn't be hard to track her down. It's not the first time she went into hiding after causing a stir. They sat on the case. Then the feds were brought in when evidence was found linking her to another plant in Ohio and perhaps Canada.

After six weeks of hitting dead ends and chasing a ghost, the bureau reached out to my team and me. They knew with all the potential roadblocks going into and out of the country, and even if it is Canada, that it would be simpler for us to go over and investigate the simple stuff. We put Christian as lead with Nicolette and a few others. They have already made some headway and that's what this meeting is about.

"Christian, since this is your case, why don't you give me the rundown of what you have found so far."

"From what we can tell after looking at the history of Erin's protests, it looks like she has a partner or a copycat. We're almost certain the other protests in Ohio aren't her, and definitely not the one in Canada. Her passport was never flagged going into Canada, and chances of her using an alias for the first time are slim. She has traveled plenty in the past."

"Do you have any theories yet, anything you think it might be?"

"We're thinking someone might be trying to set her up, get this turned into a federal case to bring her down. She's always been careful in the past to minimize risk and get maximum exposure to the cause."

"Ever think maybe something happened, maybe someone killed her, then decided to keep the ghost of Erin alive to throw everyone off the trail?"

"No, we haven't gone that far down the rabbit hole. Then again your instincts, even if crazy sometimes, are usually on the money. I'll put some people on it just to cover our bases."

"Smart man, Christian. Keep me in the loop with emails and summaries. No need to give me updates on everything, but a nightly email from someone on the team would be nice, even if brief."

"I can do that, no problem. What are you going to be doing? This is a big case; I assumed you'd be all over it."

"I'm going to be tied up the next week or so putting together a case file on Cappelano for myself and the bureau. Trying to close out the Veritas case. I know it was years ago, but the bureau wants a complete psych eval et cetera."

"I won't let you down, boss, especially after what we went through in Warsaw. I've learned so much about patience, working through the puzzle, and seeing the whole field. Most importantly, I've learned that every case is going to test me, and I need to be open to what it's saying."

"There ya go, Christian; Neil couldn't have said it better himself," Ken chimed in.

"All right, guys, I'm going to head out of here and go home. I need to get some stuff done before I head back out to the prison to sit down with Cappelano for a full-day session."

I made my way out of the warehouse toward my house. I was taken back over the past couple of years, from finally catching Cappelano to the crazy tour all over Poland. The explosion did cause some issues that caused us to be held up at the US embassy for a few days while they looked into the event. Luckily there were a few cameras in the area, meaning none of them caught Christian and his sniper rifle. They assumed it was a gas fire from an old kitchen fire.

You may be asking yourself why I am still intrigued with Cappelano, why I am going to put myself through his mind games, the mental torture. It's simple: knowledge. I can grow more by seeing the view of myself from a psycho such as Frank. Even if it's distorted, I just need to make sure I adjust for that level of craziness when I'm reviewing the case notes. If you're wondering if I ever did make up with Maria, the answer is sort of. We are still great friends, we're great when working together, but she needed more than I can ever give her in a relationship. She actually has an amazing fiancé and they are good together. Sheila and I are still in our usual on-and-off place, and Carol Lynn is growing up too fast, but that's life. I'm fairly sure my daughter grew up by ten years when I went overseas, or maybe I just finally noticed it.

Back home, pulling into the garage, the girls started going crazy. They are getting a little bit older, though, so their crazy is more controlled than it used to be. As for me, it's time to pour a drink and sit in my chair in the front room study. On good nights, my first hour of sleep is in that chair—passing out, if you may—but it's the best sleep there is, that quick nap. As the whiskey hit my lips and Connick Jr. my ears, I began to fade away.

2

Whenever you deal with that man, it gets bad. You become a different version of yourself.

Waking up to the morning symphony of music, coffee, and dogs has me smiling. First the coffee- pot kicks on at five forty-five sharp; next the first alarm goes off ever so softly at five fifty with the local news on the radio; and that is followed by a loud-ass alarm on my phone, which gets me up to attention like a new recruit in the marines. The girls have gotten so used to it over the years that their ears don't even flinch anymore. Either that or they're going deaf. After that time they let Frank steal my safe, maybe they are slipping.

After turning off my alarm, I noticed there were a few missed messages already that early in the morning. If it's before seven, it's usually just one of three people: Ken, Shelia, or TJ, who works all the hours of the night. That kid is crazy, but we love him. These are from Sheila, though; she's just checking in on me, as she usually does. I'll give her a call after a quick—okay, let's be honest, long—shower. I'm going to be spending the day with Cappelano talking about our relationship, our history from the time we met back in '96 all the way until now, some thirteen years later, and a lot has happened since that fateful day.

With coffee in hand, the scent hits my nose, waking me up and sending a sensation reminding my frontal lobe it's time to get moving, time to get the day started. With the girls outside, I made my way into a scalding hot shower, just the way I like it, disinfecting and muscle-relaxing. With the water rushing over me, heat covering me, I'm taken back to that day, reminding myself what it was like when I met him. Being in awe of the great Frank Cappelano. Knowing what I do now, he was using me, grooming me, and manipulating me, but back then I felt special. I need to remember that going into these conversations, that is how he still sees me. Even if he feels I am learning, he sees me as a student, someone who doesn't see the whole picture. If I play into that part of his psyche, let him feel in control, still play the arrogant student, I can get him to slip a bit, but it's going to take careful steps.

Out and almost ready, I reached out to Sheila to make sure she can check in on the girls while I'm gone for the day. She usually swings by almost every day, since we just live down the street from each other, but I still like to ask, to respect her time.

"Hey Sheila, how are you this morning?"

"I would have been better with company, but you know that."

"Always playing the flirt, but that's why I still love ya, babe."

"I'll be eighty and still flirty, or at least I hope so."

"I can see that it's in your DNA. You'll be twenty-two forever, and that's what makes you so special."

"You always know how to sweet-talk a girl. You have a long day ahead of you; I just wanted to make sure you are going to be okay today. It's going to be one of those days that test you, drain you, and probably put you in a shit mood for a week."

"It probably is, but it needs to be done, and I'm tired of trying to guess what's going on in his head. It's time to go to work on him. Utilize the fact that he's in that cell at my beck and call."

"Just be safe. I don't want you getting in too deep. Whenever you deal with that man, it gets bad. You become a different version of yourself."

"I'll do my best to keep that in mind and keep the perspective that he's behind bars. He can't do any more damage out in the world anymore."

"That's the spirit, Neil. I'll let you go. Call me later if you need to talk or unwind on your way home."

"Thanks, Sheila. I'll talk to you later."

By the time I finished talking to Sheila, I had finished getting ready, was already on my second cup of coffee, and making my way out the door. I got the girls back inside and ready to go for the day. Shelia will swing by as usual for me, since I will be gone all day. I don't think I've ever had a feeling like this when dealing with Cappelano; it's not control, but it isn't chaos and anger either, for a change. It's something different. I'll have to work through it and figure it out. For now, I'm going to crank up the radio, roll down the windows with the heated seats blasting, and enjoy that crisp, cold-ass Detroit air while I drive out to the prison.

Cruising down I-94 on my way out to the federal prison Cappelano is being held at, FCI Milan, I knew it was going to be a long day. Maybe as long as the day I spent sitting in that closet, waiting for him in Mexico, plotting, thinking of killing him, ending the pain, the frustration, and letting it all go by pulling the trigger. It could have happened, it should have happened, it didn't happen. Maybe fate stepped in, maybe it was life trying to keep me from going down that same path as him.

Had I killed him, what would have stopped me from going down that rabbit hole? I would have ended a life in cold blood. There was no real reason to do it, and the guilt would have eaten me up, consumed me, and either driven me mad or made me dark. As Sheila said, Cappelano has a way of changing me. I don't like it—this trip, these sessions are about getting that power back. I'm going to check in with Ken, since I just realized by glancing at my phone that I didn't take time to review my emails, and I don't want to try to read and drive at the same time.

"Hey Ken, how's the day looking so far? Christian got anything in the hopper?"

"He has a team running down leads concerning the first protest that Erin did, to see if there are signs of foul play, maybe a death that would lead to someone faking the next couple of protests. He's learning, following your lead."

"That's good to hear, not just because it's my idea, but also because he's a great asset to our team. Christian really stepped it up in Warsaw. We wouldn't have survived there, let alone solved anything. I still don't think we solved anything in that case. It felt like a complete waste of resources."

"I wouldn't say it was a complete waste. Dealing with what felt like the Church covering up a murder was a pretty decent way to get your mind off of him for a little bit."

"Fair point. Plus I made a friend over there; if that kid ever runs for office in Ireland, I think I'll send him his first fund-raising check."

"Look at you, getting into international politics. As for the case, it's going to be a whole bunch of waiting early in the day, probably won't hear anything back before ten. Aren't you due to start around nine at the prison?"

"Yeah, I'll get there a bit early, though I'm cruising right now, and most of the cops along this route have figured out my car and don't pull me over if I keep it under ninety."

"You mean they don't pull you over anymore?"

"Fair point."

"Be safe, brother. I'll message you if anything pops up."

A solid fifteen minutes off the phone with Ken and I made my way into the prison parking lot, through the gated checkpoint to park. It was a cold, sunny day. It's always a weird feeling when you walk into a prison on a sunny day, especially in the winter. The winters in the Midwest have a way of making a prison feel that much colder, smaller, and harsher. When the sun comes out, there's a bit of hope in people's eyes; they know they aren't going anywhere, but they can't help it, human nature kicks in. They are taken back to being kids on a Saturday afternoon when the sun came out on winter break from school, and it's hard not to smile.

3

Rules are in place to ensure we're all safe; no exceptions, not even for Neil.

Walking in and working through the checkpoints are always such tasks, even for a federal agent with clearance. It's the price you pay to ensure that the people behind bars stay there. Most of it is redundant, to ensure the safety of the officers working. Still, it's needed just the same, though it just feels like a nuisance when you're an impatient prick. As I made it through the final set of secure doors to where I was going, I saw my buddy Officer Colby; we've gotten to know each other, and not just from the prison. He has done some work for us outside with a buddy of his who works for us full-time.

"Hey Neil, he's been talking shit about you all morning. As usual, it's actually quite funny. You know you're here early, and you can't get in to see him before nine. Rules are rules, they are bigger than us, and you know the warden."

"Rules are in place to ensure we're all safe; no exceptions, not even for Neil."

Colby said with a chuckle, "Exactly! You know you never told me how you got this crazy motherfucker out of Mexico and back Stateside. Did you go traditional US ops and use mules or drug tunnels?"

"Nah, you know that's not my style. We had to get a little bit creative. Cappelano was too high-profile, too much of a pain in the ass, and we didn't want to risk anything."

"Are you going to tell me, or am I going to have to beat it out of Frank? I kid, but really, how'd you do it? No one will say anything."

"All right."

There we were, the gun had just misfired. No one needs to know—okay, maybe you, but not him—that I really did try to kill Cappelano in a fit of rage and sleeplessness. Back to the story, standing there with Cappelano in front of me, pissed as all get-out, I used the butt of the gun to jack him in the head and knock him out cold. Since he was so accommodating to disarm his alarm, I had the guys come over and help me tie him up while we developed a plan. Luckily for us, Frank is a fucking psychopath and had shit stashed all over his house, including a sizable supply of pharmaceuticals. I may have skipped the part about me trying to kill Cappelano when telling the story to Officer Colby.

With him knocked out and tied up, one of the guys kept a gun on him to be safe while I ran around looking for something we could use to keep him knocked out. After a good fifteen minutes of searching, we found the mother lode of drugs and pharmaceuticals. I'm not sure what the hell—okay, I know, but I still don't understand his rationale for it.

"Hey, you think we can use this? It's propofol; I'm pretty sure it's used for surgeries. I think I had it when they took the shrapnel out of my leg."

"Yes, I would say a surgical drug made for knocking people out would be great. We just need to make sure we don't kill him. Are there any instructions? This is Cappelano. Knowing him there's a book somewhere."

"No, there isn't, but couldn't we go light and just give him small doses when he wakes up? Maybe call a medical friend back home for advice?"

"No, I got a better idea. We'll go back into the room and wake Cappelano up, plus I'm sure one of you guys can look it up back in the room on the computer."

"Good point. What are you going to ask him?"

"I'm going to ask him how much to give him without killing him. I guarantee he's tested it."

We made our way upstairs as Cappelano was coming to. I struck him again, a little lighter this time, to wake him up, as opposed to knocking him out. It got his attention, that's for sure. He was pissed when he woke up seeing two other men standing over him with me.

"What the fuck is this shit about? You think you can try and shoot me, then hit me in the head? Why didn't you just finish the job?"

"Shut up, Frank, you're just hallucinating from the hit in the head. We're about to knock your ass out with your drugs. You can either help us to ensure you're alive when we're done, or I can guess and hope I don't kill you. Your choice."

"I really don't trust you for shit, but this isn't going to come cheap. You're going to have to admit to these fine men that you tried shooting me a little while ago. Luckily, your piece-of-shit gun jammed, or I'd be dead."

"Yeah, what he said."

"Fair enough. We would have helped clean it up. It's all good, Neil. There's still time to shoot him now. My gun works just fine."

"If you guys are going to shoot me, can we just do it? I'd like to get on with my day, or end of my day."

"No. Let's just knock his ass out and get this over with."

The two guys slugged Frank one more time and knocked him out cold. They had the van in the street, close enough we could throw him in, and all we had to do was clean up and head out. As we made our way out to the van, Frank in tow, one of the guys ran back in.

"Hey, where's he going?"

"He's got a virus on a thumb drive to wipe Cappelano's security system to ensure our presence is gone."

"Smart idea. We need to get out of here quick if we're going to get to our next stop before the end of the day. I have a contact we need to meet in Altamira, an old friend of Ken's who runs the port."

"Is that how you're getting Frank out of here?"

"Yeah, we are going to throw him and my ass in a storage container for the two-day trip while you two keep an eye on us from the deck. We will be dropped off in Houston, where I'll call the local FBI office as we get into port. Maria is going to meet us and grab Cappelano."

We drove away, got to our base of operations, began packing up what items we needed, and moved out. I didn't even notice what was going on. I asked the guys their plan for what equipment we left behind.

"Hey, what are we going to do with everything we left behind?"

"It's already taken care of, the computers are wiped, and everything else is pristine. The local cartels get it and the house as payment for not killing us while there."

"Seems fair enough. Also thank you for not sharing that with me while I was there."

"We figured you had plenty on your mind. We're off to Altamira. We're getting on a freighter and heading back to the States?"

"That's the plan. It should be about a six-hour drive, and we have more than enough drugs to keep Cappelano subdued for the trip, or at least the majority of it."

As we pulled into port, it was nearly midnight. My contact, Ken's old military buddy—yes, there are a lot of them—was ready and waiting for us. We had called when we were an hour out to give him a heads up. Cappelano woke up once during the drive, allowing a small window to ask him about the meds. Luckily, he was so drugged up I was able to get some info out of him about how much to give him to ensure he stays down. The security guard saw us pulling up, had the gate already open, and waved us through. Like my guys said, money talks in Mexico. Parked and ready, our contact showed up.

"Hey, you must be Neil. Ken said to take care of you. He also said that two of your friends are ex-military, and we always take care of our own."

"Thank you. Where are we headed? We want to get all situated to ensure minimal issues. Also, when does the ship leave?"

"It leaves when you get on it. We've been waiting for you."

"How long did you hold the ship for us?"

"Just eighteen hours. We told them we lost their paperwork; turns out we just found it."

"You rock, man; I'm sure Ken will take care of you, but if you ever make it back Stateside look us up."

"Will do. Let's get you loaded up and out of here."

We made our way over to the ship. He had us pile into a shitty pickup to drive to the end of the port, where the freighter was waiting. I'm not sure what was worse, the almost two-day trip stuck inside that container with Cappelano or the fifteen-minute drive in that pickup, it was that brutal. I know I'm a little over the top, but you get my point.

"Here we are, guys. Be safe. When you get into port, it'll be a different story, but I can get you there."

"We're not worried about that. As we get closer, we're going to let the f eds know we're nearly there."

"That's your business. It was a pleasure."

I know I skipped over some details and went in on others, but this story is personal. I'm not going to give Colby everything. I'm sure it will come up when Cappelano and I are going over things. All in due time. I know you're wondering what we did in a shipping container for two days and if Cappelano stayed down for two days.

"Wait, Neil, so you sat in a shipping container for two days with this crazy fuck? You really are insane. I guess I'm lucky enough to know that much, but now I have even more unanswered questions. I'm glad you'll be coming back a lot."

"Fair point, but I can always make shit up to throw you off."

"Is that story even true?" It is; all of it.

"Oh look, it's nine, that means it's time for me to start my exposé on the FCI Milan socialite known as Cappelano."

"That's funny. Make sure you say that to him often, just to rile him up.

As they opened the door to the interview room, I saw Frank being escorted down a hallway. I began to understand how Bill Murray felt in *Groundhog Day*. Each day was going to carry some semblance of difference, but essentially they would be the same. I will need to work to find some joy in each one of them if I'm going to survive this.

"Well, here we are, Neil. I'm surprised it took this long for us to finally sit down, to go over everything. I would have thought after all the work you took to get me you would have wanted answers sooner."

"Let me stop you there, Frank. Despite what you believe, the world doesn't revolve around you. Other cases grabbed my attention. Now that you are locked up, there's less urgency. There's also that one variable you have yet to take into account."

"There isn't much I don't take into account."

"It's the annoying friend variable. I can handle only so much of you before I grow tired and need time away. You've overstayed your welcome at my house. It was time to kick you out and not invite you back for a while."

"Are you done insulting me and our friendship? I'd like to get down to business."

Frank means he wants to get back to inflating his ego, talking about himself, his prowess, and his great escapades.

How he eluded the bureau and me for so long. No one enjoys getting insulted over and over. Then again, I didn't enjoy what chasing him did to my life, my friends, and my psyche over the years.

"I didn't mean to offend, it was merely some friendly ribbing. I guess prison and a life sentence have changed your sense of humor. Which is understandable."

"You can imagine how I might not be as open to laughter these days, though I have accepted my fate. Where would you like to start?"

"The beginning I would say is the best place. Was Sarge your first kill, or had you worked your way up to him? My follow-up to that would be, had you been looking to groom me before picking your victim?"

"I guess we're jumping right in. The answer to both those questions is simple but also complicated in its detail. Yes, Sarge was my first murder in cold blood, but I had taken lives several times in the line of duty before him. As for you, I had been looking for someone to groom in the bureau for years, as I began this pursuit. You fit the bill of young, cocky, and untapped potential—immense potential."

"I guess that's a compliment of sorts, but looking back from my perspective it seemed as though you saw me as an easy mark, a person you could control and over time that drove nuts."

I know you think why give him the power in this situation, but this process is going to be about give-and-take. I'm going to have to give him some things, make him feel in power if I'm going to get anything out of him. Inflating his ego is going to be crucial in getting the truth of what he feels and how he felt during the times when he was operating freely.

"Neil, you should know better than to give up such delicate information about yourself. I taught you better; then again, our relationship is different, and this is a safe space. We are here talking, learning, and growing. I didn't look at you as a mark, you give me too much credit. I was growing in this, just as you were."

"What about Sarge? I understand the homeless draw, what made it easy, and him a target, but why a man with such great positive influence in that community?"

"You're assuming I knew that part before I did it."

That is a great point. I can tell this is going to be a long day, a walk down memory lane involving lots of coffee and bathroom breaks. I brought a recorder, notes with me for playback, and the prison has video set up, per the request of the bureau. They want to review my notes. The thing is, I can turn it off whenever I want to review something sensitive between the two of us. It was the compromise I made with them. If they wanted me in there asking all the questions, Cappelano wouldn't talk to anyone else anyway, I would get control over what they see. Here's to a long-ass day, perhaps a week. I really don't know if I have it in me to come back after today. It took me nearly three years to commit to this level of interview with him for just one day.

4

I knew there was little to no evidence left behind that would lead back to me.

"Let's start with how you picked out Sarge. How did you find him? Was it a one-off, quick moment? Was it a matter of convenience, or did you plan it out?"

"Both. I had been keeping an eye on the community around St. Pat's Church for some time. Surveying, seeing who a good target might be, but I didn't decide until the last second. It was a matter of opportunity and location. I wasn't aware of Sarge's effect on the community at that time; had I known that, I wouldn't have picked him. I actually struggled with that part of him when we investigated his death."

"How was that—I mean watching me, working with me— as I investigated your murder? I was gathering information on you, on the case of a man you killed. Weren't you the least bit worried?"

"No, but that point when I killed him, I knew there was little to no evidence left behind that would lead back to me.

Especially by the time anyone had found his body. Plus the information you were working with was from the medical examiner, who had rushed the case as a homeless homicide. I doubt they put forth any effort looking into it with their limited resources at the time."

"Then the whole reason you put me on the case was to watch me chase my tail?"

"No, I knew the case was essentially unsolvable. I was more watching you, learning from you. I could have put you on any case. I just chose that one, out of my curiosity of what it would be like being chased, I think."

"Glad I could feed your curiosity so early on. As time went on, it took its toll on me. Did you realize that your so-called teaching actually weighed on me, maybe causing more harm than good?"

"Neil, this isn't a therapy session for you to process your inner weaknesses and insecurities."

I need him to think I'm still bothered by all of this, still insecure. In truth, I overcame the majority of that shit when he went after Gracin's daughter and Hendrickson. I realized he's no different from any other crazy-ass killer I've encountered. I just happen to have a personal relationship with him before, during, and after all the killings.

"Well, I guess that's one way of putting it. I was simply asking you a question on your intent, your awareness of what you were doing. Were you simply focused on the killing aspect, and our relationship came later? Calm down there, Freud."

"My apologies, but lately I've felt you've been on edge, you have seemed a little testy, if you may. I just didn't want to go down that road if that's where you were headed."

"Don't forget, Frank, this shit is about you, not about me. I'm here to ask questions about your approach, how you viewed things, not about me. Don't get it twisted."

"I will keep that in mind; my apologies. No, Neil, I did not realize the impact I was having on you, or the toll, especially in the beginning. As time went on, I realized your potential, your talent, and your intellect, and realized I could groom you, impact you. With what I was doing, with my background and your talent, I could be the greatest mentor in law enforcement and investigation."

"Don't go all Sherlock on me, Frank. You aren't deducing anything."

We went back and forth like this getting nowhere fast for a solid twenty minutes. Eventually Colby popped his head in, asking if I needed a coffee refill and gave Frank a bathroom break. After we came back, we calmly started reviewing the case, going over in detail what it was like to work the Sarge case with him. Investigating the murder of a homeless man in Detroit who was known for being a community leader around St. Pat's Church, helping get others off the street and into homes, finding them food and beds to sleep in. Sarge was a man who found solace on the streets; his demons dissipated as he slept without walls and a roof.

Sometimes living without constraints in the alternate reality that is the life of a vagrant can be freeing. When I was doing the investigation, I found that many of the people I met on the street weren't as crazy as I expected; not all were drug addicts or drunks. I found a small group of men who just enjoyed living off the grid. It's a different reality; it's hard to explain until you're walking in it for days on end, completely cut off, you can't truly see it for what it is.

The case was open-ended and never solved, obviously. However, the biggest concern for me at the time was the illusion that someone else was putting on pressure from on high. Why put that illusion into the mix?

"Frank, let me ask you something. Why did you create the illusion that you had bosses wanting you to look into Sarge's case? You had rank, I couldn't really question you anyway, and you led with that story before I ever asked why."

"Does it really matter?" Is he really stumped, did he do it without cause?

"I think it does. For someone as calculated as you have been over the years, to do something from the hip is rare. If you're telling me that there was no reason for it, then it tells me that in the beginning you really were learning on the fly, you were growing into the full person you became."

"If you say so, this is your show, not mine. I'm just here for your viewing pleasure, and to have a change of pace for a change."

I can tell by his body language that he is losing his shit a little bit; the crazy part about it is I didn't used to catch his tics. I started to notice them as I replayed our interactions in my head. I noticed more in the way he spoke. Over the years, it was small pieces that added up. With Frank, nothing is ever obvious. It's like building a big-ass puzzle with someone, but you get only one piece a week for ten years. That shit's going to take some time before you get any idea of what you're putting together.

"I do say so. I see it regularly, I see it often. One of my favorite things about you is how hard it is to see the tells you have. Once I do, though, they are noticeable, they are like nervous tics that you can't stop."

Now he's getting visibly pissed off.

"I've had enough of this pushing and questioning. Are we going to talk about Sarge? I'm surprised you haven't asked what it was like to kill a man in cold blood. Especially since you tried to do it yourself."

"You mean when I tried to shoot you in the head in Mexico?"

"I'm surprised you're talking about that openly now. I take it you've told people about it?"

"No, not at all, but I stopped recording this part of the conversation about three minutes ago. I had a feeling you were going down this road."

"I see how it's going to be."

"Correct. You need to learn who has the leverage in this relationship. Get used to it, it's a give- and-take. You have the info, but I have the power. We need each other, as usual, so we might as well get used to it, get our shots in, and stop getting so worked up over them."

"Fair enough; maybe prison has made me soft. The lack of killing has changed me, I guess."

Jesus, did he just say what I think he did? Doesn't surprise me, though; that is something he would say, how he would look at the world. The mathematics of it all. He looked coldly at the world, even when we worked together. I remember him in a case where we investigated a serial rapist who had begun murdering their victims, and he showed no empathy for the victims. He made some comment like, "at least the perp is killing them now, less stress for the victim after such a brutal crime." I mean, who says that shit? Apparently deranged killers do.

"I guess it has. I'd offer some advice, but I don't want to get indicted when you shank someone in prison to get your mojo back."

"Okay, that was funny, I'll admit it."

"Back on track, what was it like when you murdered Sarge? If I remember the report, he was strangled, meaning you had to be close. It's not like you can rationalize it; that's a very personal way to kill."

"I wasn't trying to rationalize it. I wanted it to be close, messy, and personal. I had killed people before in the line of duty, I knew what it was like to take a life, to have those feelings. I wanted to know what it was like to do it on purpose, personally, and with conviction. I'll be honest; it felt great. That's why I accelerated down the path I did."

"What do you mean, 'accelerated'? We still worked together for almost two years!"

"I know, but I planned on trying to do both the bureau and occasionally killing for five to ten years if possible. I didn't want to give up my pension. I worked hard for that shit."

Really a rational and suburban thought from a crazed killer. I guess we all have to think about retirement. I guess it all depends on the motivation of why the person is killing. For Frank, it was about the intrigue, the need to learn, and that's what kept him partially in reality. He wanted to make sure he kept some semblance of normalcy, some routine or plan of retirement. If it's crazy when you think it, imagine how I felt as I wrote this shit. I had to look at it funny for a good two minutes.

"I guess that makes sense. A government pension is a pretty great thing, and losing it can suck."

"You get it. I might not have had my head in the game when it came to investigating all the time, but I still understood long-term stability. As for Sarge, the aftermath for me was surprisingly quick and simple."

"What do you mean by that?"

"Neither good nor bad. It was over quick, the high was over fast. I went to bed feeling alive, but woke up feeling like it was a dream. That feeling was gone, it was like having a drug that I needed another dose of."

This is the first time I feel like I'm getting close to the turning point when Frank went from FBI agent to killer. I always thought it was about me, about the lesson. In the beginning, it was simply the killing that drove him. He found a way to rationalize it, his reason to make himself feel better about what he was doing. He found a way to cover up the guilt, and the human side of him wanted a retirement plan. That's where I came in, where my teaching came in.

"If Sarge was your first kill, was your nephew your second, or were there some others mixed in there that we still don't know of?"

"Oh, you mean his college buddy that went missing? That's why I had to kill him. You guys never made that connection, and that shit has pissed me off for years."

What the fuck, there was a missing kid in connection to that case? We all missed that for years. How didn't any of us connect that, not even to this day? I mean, this shit is going to be a huge win for him, and it's going to drive me nuts for the next couple of days, trying to find out where this kid is buried or what happened to him.

"Since we are all so clueless, why not take the time to walk through this part of the story in its entirety? It's an opportunity to gloat. You can talk directly into the camera and tell the bureau and me how we all got it wrong while you were still working for them."

He took a deep breath, thought for a moment.

"Sounds great."

Frank Cappelano was in his element. He sat there smug, full of confidence, expressing no remorse. Instead, there was a level of confidence you see in athletes after winning a big game or dropping a fifty burger in an NBA game. After twenty minutes of going into the details of the story, he got up and started walking around, like he was a professor talking to a class. It was getting a bit out of hand, but the information helped me understand his process, how he looked at his victims and the people trying to solve the case, and everything between.

"Hey Frank, you need to head back for your lunch. I am heading out and making some calls. I'll be back within the hour and we can pick back up there."

"I guess we are guests in the warden's house. See you soon, Neil."

5

We're taught center mass, which I tried to explain away.

Let me take a moment to introduce myself, I'm not quite sure we've been formally introduced. My name is Franklin Cappelano. Some have known me as the Veritas killer, some as the famed Agent Cappelano. You can call me friend. Don't be worried, I mean you no harm. I simply wish to tell my story, spread the word, teach others the knowledge I have gained. What good is knowledge if not to pass it on so others can grow from it? I did all of this for a purpose. At first I wasn't quite sure, but eventually I found it. I saw where I was headed and what needed to be done.

When I killed Sarge, it was invigorating. The feeling of being in control of another person's life, watching them fade, struggling to survive. Knowing I controlled their life at that moment gave me a feeling I craved. I can only imagine it to the feeling of someone's first hit of heroin. As I had told Neil before, I had killed before in the line of duty early in my career. I remember it messing with me pretty bad, knowing I had taken a life. Eventually I had realized it was a part of the life I had chosen. It was going to be part of me, part of what I was becoming.

I remember the day that the light switch changed for me when I went from remorse to curiosity. I was sitting in a psych evaluation with Dr. Binder. She was the bureau's head manager, as I liked to call her. She hated the nickname, but this was my way of describing all the cases she dealt with. It wasn't just a few of us—she oversaw hundreds of agents across different agencies. She managed us, managed our minds, and that's how I saw it. She managed my mind throughout all my killings, too. I know, right? You didn't see that coming, but she really struggled with that one for a long time. Luckily she took her oath seriously, and no one ever connected us. Her notes were pretty weak; she was a strong memory person and didn't write much down. She liked to protect her agents, which hurt her when it came to me since she didn't have anything other than conjecture, but hey, live and learn.

There we were, I had just killed a man in the line of duty, actually two drug dealers, they had attacked another agent and me when we had raided their stash house. I killed them both, but one of them was a pretty deadly shot, head shot, and we're not taught that. We're taught center mass, which I tried to explain away, but it was hard for me mentally as well as for me at the bureau.

"Frank, it's hard to go from someone's chest to their face. Are you trying to say you aimed and they moved?"

"Doc, that's the only thing I can think of. It was all a blur, they came at us so fast. Once I saw the other agent shoot, I acted quickly. I wasn't thinking rationally."

"That's understandable and not surprising, but what do you remember? How did you aim? Where did you aim? Was it at his chest, his shoulder? Slow down, breathe, and close your eyes. Think through it."

I sat there, let my mind drift to a calm place, and thought of the scene. The beaten-down apartment complex on the East Eide of Detroit. As we ran up on the shit apartment, we knew there would be some resistance, but not like this, we didn't expect them to have automatic rifles because they were small-time. I remember seeing him, the other agent, get hit in the leg and go down quickly. For the first time, my response wasn't to respond and be safe. There was anger and rage. I think I did shoot to kill, I aimed at his head, looked down the barrel, looked him in the eye, and pulled the trigger.

"Doc, it's all a blur, I don't remember any details. I guess I just need to keep thinking about it.

I'm not about to tell the bureau shrink that I broke protocol, shot someone in the head on purpose with rage in my eyes because I watched someone get shot. They would sit me down for weeks, maybe longer.

"Keep working on the breathing exercises and trying to meditate on that day."

"Thanks, Doc."

That day was when I realized I had done it on purpose. I had looked down that barrel and killed on purpose. There was no reason to shoot them in the head. A hit in the arm or chest would have worked just fine. A bullet to the brain is personal; it's to bring gratification. It wasn't long after this that I couldn't get the thought out of my head to committing a murder, killing someone on purpose, wondering what drives someone to go from what I did to a thought-out murder.

What is the difference between what I did and someone that killed on purpose? I could have chosen not to kill, but I didn't. Because I had a decent reason, or a way to explain, I shot a man in cold blood. The excuses don't make it right. It doesn't mean I'm any less of a killer than someone who killed his wife. I just have a job that allows me to do it. I started to think about it, fixate on it, really begin to think about what it would feel like to take a life in cold blood.

One of my strengths as an agent was my ability to become fixated on a case, work it like a dog ripping through their favorite bone. In this case, though, it was a detriment to me. I'm not sure this was ever intended, or inevitable, but it does feel right. Killing for me is where I feel comfortable, alive, and peaceful. There is a moment right after I take a life that it just feels calm, like the moment a storm passes, there is a serenity to it.

I know you're thinking, *Holy shit, this guy is nuts,* and I will tell you I agree a bit. That is the interesting part of my approach. I understand both sides of the equation. I know what I'm doing is necessary, I know that many won't understand it, and even part of me still feels it's wrong. I thought I might have more time with you to tell you my side of the story. but I'm heading back to the room to interview with Neil. We will meet again, don't worry.

6

You mean the colossal blind spot you and the other agents had.

As I made my way out of the back part of the prison, there was a small area for smoke breaks and cell phone breaks for the guards to use. Besides that, there are a ton of caged entrances and exits one has to work through to get back out of the front door. I had a few missed messages from Christian and Ken. It looked promising. Christian sent out a team to investigate Erin's first protest and found some evidence of foul play. They think at a minimum there are signs of a struggle.

"Christian, what did your team find out there?"

"Well, Neil, they found a lot of different things, but most of it comes down to a few different variables. You know how she always posts her protests online after she edits them together?"

"Yes. Did we ever find her laptop?"

"We did; it was found in the woods. TJ is working on that now, but that's just part of it. The bigger part is that we found what looks like deep tracks from a van or truck around the same area, as if she was grabbed."

The call took close to twenty minutes because Christian was running through lots of details, and we were bouncing ideas back and forth. From what they found, there was plenty of evidence missed the first time around. Even the security footage they were able to pull up showed a van leaving the property shortly after Erin finished her protest at the chemical plant. Her car was still there and it wasn't moved until the following morning. They also noticed shards of broken glass in the spot where her car was parked.

It wasn't as if the police weren't looking into it, they were just looking for her usual routine. She was known to go off the grid after a protest, but this was different. The evidence was there if you were looking for it. I told him many large companies have a head of security that either is the fixer or has one. There are too many variables for them not to work on or try to adjust when problems arise.

"Stay on them, Christian, keep pushing and looking for the truth. It's out there; I know you'll find it and you'll find her."

"Thank you, boss. We won't let you down. Better yet, we won't let Erin down. We're going to find out what happened to her."

I hung up and went back inside, back to Cappelano and our interview. It was time to get back into him, push him a bit, and see if I could get him to crack a bit. I need him to show vulnerability. I know it's there, from the things he still gets upset about and works to hang onto. It shows there is still some semblance of humanity there. Even if he has lost empathy and grown with a thirst for the control in taking a life. He still craves normalcy in certain aspects of his life, and that's what I need to focus on and push.

"Frank, let's get back to where we left off with your nephew and his friend. Especially the part that we missed at the bureau."

"You mean the colossal blind spot you and the other agents had."

Frank started talking about when his nephew's best friend, Tony, went missing after they had gotten into a huge fight over a girl. According to Frank's interview, his nephew's girlfriend cheated on him with Tony. When he confronted Tony about it, he said, "She's just a girl, get over it," and it got him worked up. When he called his uncle one night, upset about it, it set it him off. Apparently enough that he said some choice words about taking care of that little shit Tony. His nephew did the quick math and figured out that Frank did something to his friend after talking to him.

"You let yourself get worked up emotionally over a family member, ended up killing for them, and then it backfires a bit because your nephew figures it out. Yet listening to you tell the story, I can tell you're leaving something out. There's something you're not telling me; I've known you long enough."

"Why don't you turn off the camera for a moment. We can have a one-on-one moment. Something between you and me."

"Okay, I can do that for you. Here you go, it's off. Now, what do you want to talk about?"

"The issue that I'm trying to gloss over has to do with my nephew. He did think I had something to do with his friend. Because of that, I killed him, but that's not the part that I want to talk about. My nephew knew I did something to his best friend, Tony. I assumed that he figured out I killed him. I just didn't know why."

"Wait a minute; you killed your nephew to cover your tracks, in an effort to try and keep your job at the bureau. Somewhere during that process, though you realized he didn't think you killed Tony but got involved and made him go away, locked him up, or something like that."

"It was right before he finally passed, he looked at me with his last breath and said that he just thought I scared Tony into hiding and he didn't know what I was doing. That really messed me up, that's why I disappeared and ran. I went to a dark place after that."

"I would say killing your nephew, someone who idolized you, would be hard, would be life-altering. I saw that change play out, but knowing more, one of the biggest questions I have is, where will we find Tony?"

"You won't find Tony at all. I disposed of his body at a crematorium. The only ones that you guys knew of were the ones I let you know about. I learned that it's much easier to get away with murder than not; people are just sloppy, lack planning, and organization. Oftentimes, passion, anger, or some emotion leads to them getting caught."

"I can see that, the motive is the defining factor. If you're simply killing without connection, it makes it incredibly hard. I remember learning that in training and school in general, not to mention it's just common sense. Random acts are the hardest to connect."

"I'm glad you did learn some things from me and our time."

I ignored his comment. "Let's get back to the moment that really turned you, pushed you past the bureau. When you realized there was no going back. When you killed your nephew and also realized it was a mistake."

"I never said it was a mistake, Neil; don't put words in my mouth. As for realizing the bureau was no longer the place for me, that was twofold."

You could tell Frank was getting physically uncomfortable talking about or even dealing with the death of his nephew. I understand the reason behind it, which is why I kept pushing on this subject. It showed the rare human part of Cappelano's psyche. There are some moments there, some parts in which he is grasping for humanity. Even when Frank was an agent and we worked together he could think in multiple lanes, similar to myself. The difference is he is cleaner about it, more mathematical. Whereas my brain functions in four, sometimes six different lanes, eventually coming to a clean lane, Frank is always running in three lanes, well thought out and organized.

It's from this that he can be a crazed killer in two of them but still seek forms of humanity in the third. It's this third lane that pulled him from the bureau, which kept him from killing my family and me but didn't keep him from threatening me. Trying to keep me and others at bay. It's this back and forth internally that drove him but also controlled him a bit. When I was chasing him down after leaving the FBI after we failed to catch him in 2000 due to Hendrickson's political bullshit, Frank got tired of the heat and threatened me. He made it known that he didn't want to kill my family or me, but he showed me that he could. It showed restraint, but also his ability to work past it if he needed to. This is what made Frank a crazed killer who was nearly impossible to catch over the years.

"You're right, Frank, I should know better than to put words in your mouth. Why don't we just end there for the day? I can come back later in the week."

"It's not even three in the afternoon, and you're going to quit on me? I thought you were down to put a day's worth of work in. The warden said as long I get my meals and psych visits in, I'm open to doing this for as many hours as needed, remember?"

COLLOQUIUM

"Okay, I just saw you getting a little agitated with the questioning about your nephew and how you exited the bureau back then, so I thought it might be a good time to stop. Then let's pick up after you left: where did you go and what did you do for that six-month span we didn't hear from you?"

7

I acted like I needed to check a tire and beat his brains in with a tire iron.

I told you not to worry, I would be back. Yes, this is Frank. I'm butting into this story, and I will continue to do so because I don't feel Neil is doing it justice, but when does he ever? Hell, he took more than a decade to bring me to justice. I was getting a bit testy when he pushed me on my nephew because it's a soft spot. It's a hard memory for me, knowing that I killed my nephew, someone who idolized me, in cold blood and without proper cause. It's not the death part, it's that it was reckless. I'm better than that. I didn't have the proper information and acted carelessly. That's the part that upsets me, it's not his death, or that I even played a part. It's my failure to recognize the truth in the situation. My failure in deducing the overall construct that my nephew was trying to break down.

I guess one could say it was a breakdown in my ego, noticing a weakness for the first time in a long time. When I realized that I was acting carelessly with my nephew, I started to doubt myself, the processes I had in place. I realized I needed to remove the distraction of the FBI from my routine if I was going to continue to down this new path. I sat there, finding a way to clean up the mess, realizing if I had a clear mind, free of distractions, free from the bureau, I wouldn't be making careless mistakes.

I wasn't worried about being caught; as you can see, they didn't even realize that I had killed his best friend, Tony. It even took them months to realize I was the one who had killed my nephew. I had to spell that shit out for them, and I started to get annoyed at their carelessness. I was madder that his case went unsolved than I was about them trying to catch me. I think I also wanted to announce my presence to the world, to Neil, and to get the chase on.

After the murders in Ann Arbor, I went on leave from work and disappeared on a road trip. I sold my car for cash, bought a new car, never registered it, and went off the grid. This is how I evaded them for so long: I did the little things, kept it simple, used the credit cards of the victims I killed to buy supplies, load up on Visa gift cards and cash. Remember, I'm a fan of planning. There were four murders after my nephew that the bureau still doesn't know of, as I worked my way across the country running, enjoying the life I chose, found people that looked like easy marks, and enjoyed the time when I could find myself.

COLLOQUIUM

I know you're judging me, saying how can you be so flippant about the loss of life, how can you describe the taking of life in such a callous way? It's simple: I'm not wired like you. Never have been. If you had missed the events in my life that I had to, you might understand. That, mixed with the mental capacity and lack of empathy I already had growing up, you end up with Frank Cappelano. A famed FBI agent turned killer—*famous* killer, I might add. Before my time is done, when they realize the depths of my work they will see I'm the most prolific murderer of all time, killing all over the country.

Famously, the lead singer for Queen, Freddy Mercury, had a large sexual appetite, which ultimately led to his death. This was sad, not only for obvious reasons, but also because of his ability to bring a crowd to the edge of the heavens with his voice. That man could sing and entertain like no other. Why do I bring up Freddy? He was a rock star enjoying the fruits of his labor nightly with different people, and I was trying to accomplish the same type of numbers in my career. When you are done getting to know me and the FBI is done getting to see the depths of the work I have done over the years, they will see that the bit I gave them while I was on the outside was just a taste.

Back to the murders after my nephew, on my way out of Michigan I picked out a hitchhiker, a crazy-looking fellow. From what I could tell, he was messed up on something, or he was struggling mightily from a mental disorder. This was an easy one for me to rationalize, to work through. We barely made it a hundred miles; I couldn't stand the smell or his incessant talking. I pulled off the highway in the middle of the night. Then I acted like I needed to check a tire and beat his brains in with a tire iron. A little simplistic, but it got the job done. It helped me get him out of my car, work through some issues with my nephew, and realize that each time I killed, I could wipe a bit of guilt away from the weak moment I had.

Next up was the waitress in Fort Wayne, Indiana, who worked at the diner next to my motel. I stayed there for a week. Not sure why, but it was cheap, I liked the area, and she was nice. Yes, you would think it odd to kill someone you like, but I found out she was doing drugs instead of feeding her kid, and that pissed me off something awful. You might be sensing a pattern here: I have a tendency to judge people, then act on it through violence. That's only partially true; this was merely in the beginning. It was a way for me to keep a clear mind when I was killing and minimize the guilt until I could get past it all.

One thing I always appreciated about Neil was his talent to juggle so many things. Oftentimes he looks like he's unengaged, maybe not even trying, but he's working through many variables. He's always at a low simmer because he's never off and he doesn't need to get to a high boil to accomplish much. It also means he can get to a hot spot quickly if he needs to. I remember a case when we were on a stakeout and when we were rolled up on by a street gang, he got me out of the car quickly, jumped out, and got behind the car as they lit it up with bullets, saving our lives. With that same instinct, he hopped back in the car and chased after them in the same shot-up car, later totaling that car and a few others. He was and is nuts, but in the greatest of ways.

I disappeared and made my way farther west, killing as I continued outward. I realized this was something I was good at and enjoyed. Still, I had to ensure I used it for something positive. Nevertheless, I can't take all the credit for that idea, I got it from killing a professor from a small community college in the middle of nowhere, Iowa. I remember right before I killed him, he asked me if this is what I wanted my life to be about, simply killing. If so, what kind of purpose did that serve? It made me no better than a drug addict. He was right. I'll never forget his name, Dr. Michael Brown. His words really stuck with me. I mean, I still killed him, of course, but I made sure and learned from our conversation.

I see Neil is growing tiresome of my long pause. I should probably answer his questions.

8

I'm assuming closer to seventy-five, maybe even a hundred
murders during that time frame.

"Well, Neil, I think you can imagine what I was doing. You know I wasn't hiding, nor was I simply fishing and reading books somewhere. Knowing what you know now, that I was already killing, what do you think I was doing?"

"If you take the bodies into account in such a short period from Sarge to Tony to your nephew, I'd say you went on an impromptu traveling and killing spree across the country to find yourself. To find out who you were as a person, as a killer, and clear your mind of the issues that arose in Ann Arbor."

"Pretty close; the only thing is to what extent. In six months, a lot can happen. If you use the time frame in which I killed those three people that would put the death toll during those six months to well over fifty. If you think in more realistic numbers, maybe five to ten less or more. Don't forget you and the FBI never connected Tony's disappearance with my nephew's murder."

We always had a theory that he went on a huge killing spree after he disappeared once we realized who he was and what he was doing. The problem was trying to connect him to anything or any cases. We didn't have any data tagging to where he was or who he had been in contact with. He was essentially a ghost for six months.

"Judging by your smug answer, I'd guess the number is closer to something like this. Six months is one hundred and eighty days. You get bored easily and traveled a lot. I'm assuming closer to seventy-five, maybe even a hundred murders during that time frame." I'm playing to his ego.

"That is sound math, and yes, I do get bored easily, but even for a crazy ass like me, that's a lot of killing. Don't you think I'd get tired after a while?"

"Nah, you've always been in great shape, Frank. Why would this endeavor be any different?"

"Point taken. I guess we'll see over time where this journey takes us."

"How about your first kill after you left Ann Arbor? Let's start with something simple."

"Okay, that's an easy one. It was a woman in Fort Wayne. I don't remember her name, but she worked at a diner by a motel that I was staying at. When I found out she was doing drugs, wasting her money on herself, on her habit, instead of taking care of her kids, I lost it."

"So you took the mother away from her kids. Who was going to look after the kids?"

"I'm not heartless. I saw the grandmother was already doing most of the work and trying to take care of the drugged-out daughter. So I just removed the daughter variable for the betterment of the family unit."

"Ah, you were acting in good faith, trying to give the kids a better life?"

"Now you're getting it, Neil. I'm not just a psycho killing for no reason. Sometimes I try to do good with my lack of empathy."

"I guess that answers one of my questions. You feel that your lack of empathy is a good thing?"

"Yes. Because of it I can operate freely, without constraint, to do my work."

"You don't see anything wrong with the harm or damage you do to families, friends, and loved ones? Do you even care?"

"Let me tell you a story about the wildfires out west, which I learned about firsthand when I was out there. Did you know one of the worst things we could do to the forests is stop them from burning? We let them burn and simply work to contain them because of the circle of life. Being a predator, taking a life is natural. It's a part of life. People die every day from accidents, sickness, and no one arrests doctors or driving instructors for giving out licenses."

"I know for a fact that you don't think that shit's true at all, comparing what you did to a doctor not saving a life. You are just fucking with me. At this point I'm going to call it a day. I'll be back tomorrow if you're lucky, Frank. Have a great night."

"Neil, don't leave. We were just having fun."

"'Bye, Frank."

As I walked out, you could see he was dejected, a bit pissed, and starting to recalculate what he had done. He is used to being in complete control, not giving up power, and not getting stepped on so easily. According to all the text messages I have, Christian is out doing a stakeout on the head of security for Gaines Chemical Company. Once I get outside, I'll find out where and head that way.

Officer Colby tried catching up with me on the way out, but we couldn't meet up. By the time he started to notice me leaving, I was already two doors past, and he couldn't leave his post. I'll text him and have him hit me up when he's out of work. He had a look of concern; I wonder if he was surprised I left so quickly, or if something else is up. Making my way back through all the checkpoints, different doors, and locks is a reminder of how locked up even I am when I got in there. I'm free to leave, but only within reason. If there is a lockdown or the warden found cause to keep me there, it would be hard to get out. It's scary but true.

The air as I walked outside was cool, fresh, and had a bit of a bite to it. As the sun was setting, so was what little warmth was left in the Detroit winter air. The Midwest has a way of doing that to you. Especially Detroit, with the lake effect and all that moisture in the air. When it's sunny out, you can feel it, enjoy a bit of a nice day, but the moment that sun goes down, that chill fills the air as if someone dropped an ice cube down your shirt. As I entered the car, turned it on, and warmed it up, I shot a quick email to my contact at the bureau—yes, Maria—about Tony, then called Christian.

"Hey, Neil, what's up? Are you done for the day over there? Or just stepping out?"

"No, I'm done, and could use a change of scenery. Can you text me the address so I can swing by and hang with you for a while? I'd love to help in any way I can. I'll even bring some coffee."

"Always, man, as long as you promise not to drive anything into any police cars or buildings."

"You drive a truck into the front of a police station one time, and no one ever lets you live it down."

"Ha, I know, man, but it was epic. See you in a bit. I already texted you the address. Park on the block over and walk up."

"Sounds good. See you in forty-five."

Christian reminds me of a mix between Ken and me. He has Ken's pedigree, but my flair for the dramatic, for pushing the envelope. He came to us tight, wound up from years of service, but he's learning to live a bit in that gray area. That's what makes us work so well at BCI. Learning and teaching our investigators how to operate in the gray. It's not about breaking the rules, but learning to see the daily constructs that we can fall victim to, and working around them, next to them, not always within them.

Watching the team grow from Ken and me doing a few cases out of his bar into a full-service agency with a team working around the clock was something special. I must give Ken most of the credit for that part of it. I have received celebrity cases and brought us attention but he has organized and turned an idea into a functioning entity. Speaking of great influences in my life, I should check in on Sheila and see how she is doing.

"Hey, Shelia, how's the night going?"

"It's not bad. Just got done taking the girls for a walk with Carol Lynn. It was chilly, but we all needed to get some exercise."

"Thanks again, as usual. Today went about as good as could be expected. Six plus hours of talking to Cappelano about his favorite subject is always a blast."

"Yeah, I can imagine. Are you heading home now?"

"No, I'm meeting up with Christian for a bit to check up on the Monroe case."

"Hey, I've meant to ask you, why are you and the guys calling it that? The news is calling it either Gaines Chemical or Beddington. Why are you calling it the Monroe case?"

"When TJ was doing his dive on Erin, he came across a few pictures of her dressed up as Marilyn Monroe for a Halloween party. He and a few guys kept calling her that, 'cause she's a knockout and a socialite as it is. It stuck, and you know how the guys at the warehouse, they like calling cases by off-topic or different names."

"Those guys are always a little different. But they do a great job, so who's going to argue? How's your head after today?"

"It's okay, but I'm still a bit drained. I wanted to help out on the Monroe case to get my mind off Cappelano. Have a great night, Sheila. I'll talk to you tomorrow."

"Night, Neil. Be safe, as usual."

Carol Lynn is almost in high school now. She's only in seventh grade, but that's a hop, skip, and a jump from freshman year. She's already showing her mother's stunning looks and my brutal attitude. Needless to say, as a parent I know I'm screwed. I know she'll be okay because there's nothing like having a team of investigators, ex-cops, and ex-military keeping an eye out for you as you grow up, but that still doesn't mean you can't find a way to do dumb shit growing up. Plus, as much as I want to protect her from everything bad, I know the mistakes are the things that help define us as we grow up. I have to let her be herself.

COLLOQUIUM

That part of being a parent, a friend, and ex-spouse with Sheila was always hard with Cappelano on the outside. There was always the threat of knowing someone. Frank could come in to kill or kidnap them. It's hard to go through the day knowing it's a possibility. Having him behind bars has been great. As we've all learned from history, movies, and documentaries, there are always fans of crazy serial killers trying to win their affection. I'm more afraid of them than I ever was of Frank. We had a friendship, an understanding, but these other nut jobs are wild cards; the rules don't apply.

I parked a block away and made my way walking around the area, a part of the city called Dearborn. Detroit became a huge metro area known as Metro Detroit. Though it's not the city itself, its cultures spread out over time and built up communities all over the tricounty area. I could give you a history lesson but it's not needed for this story; maybe the next time around. For now I'm walking up Michigan Avenue to where I parked; the address is on a side street. It's a warehouse that Gaines Chemical rents; apparently the head of security and his goon squad operate out of here most days.

When I knocked on the window of the van I damn near made Christian poop; he was dialed in on something. I climbed in and grabbed a seat. It's a converted Econoline van. Though it's not like a government utility vehicle, it's just beat up enough on the outside that it blends in all over. It's a painting van, so we get away with it.

"Christian, how we doing? Here's your coffee, by the way; still hot. I grabbed it from the gas station up the street. Just like we like it, black, stale, and a bit of shit to it."

"You know me too well; that fancy stuff isn't for me. I like to taste like fuel. Pull up a seat, I'll give you the rundown on a few items. I caught their head of security outside a few times on the phone tonight smoking. From the looks of the number I could make out on his cell, it's the same number every time. It's written down over there if you want to get it to TJ."

"This one over here? There's no need, I know whose number it is. Well it's not a person exactly, it's a phone at the prison."

"Wait, you mean in Milan, where you were all day?"

"Yup, oh shit, this is what Colby was chasing me down for, I think."

9

Back in the van, you could see Christian was agitated as shit.

Gaines Chemical was started as a small family company by husband-and-wife chemists out of their house back in the eighties. Many people believe they were two-bit drug dealers to support and grow their legitimate business, but they have done a ton of great things for the community over the years, and also some messed-up shit. As they've grown over the years, they went from a simple chemical development and research company to one that specialized in cleaning up and disposal of harmful chemicals.

As they got older, the parents left their business to their son Jason Gaines and his sister Susie Gaines. There is another brother too, but he's in and out of prison for drugs and other dumb shit. Jason really took the company from a small family business doing good things for Detroit and the surrounding areas to an empire that pushed the limits of the law. Which is what Erin was protesting. She, with the help of a journalist friend, Jim Hammond from the *Ann Arbor Gazette*, found out that Gaines Chemical was disposing of only half the chemicals properly. For the other half, they were switching the labels, putting them into different containers, and disposing of with other items deemed corrosive and unsafe. They did this to save money, increase profits, and grow their company.

The icing on the cake they found was that two of the parks that Gaines Chemical built for the city were on chemical dump sites. They illegally dumped massive amounts of these chemicals, causing issues in the water table, which led to health issues for locals in the community. It's been a real cluster fuck all over, and this was the biggest protest Erin's ever done. Usually she goes after smaller fish or more general protests without legal ramifications. This one not only caused Gaines to get dragged into court, it also cost them a multimillion-dollar contract, and overall costs could be in the billions in lost revenue and fines. So yes, you could say there was a motive to silence or end Erin in this case.

"Christian, I'm going to call my buddy Colby at the prison, but I have to play it coy, 'cause I'm not sure why he was trying to talk to me earlier. I'm not sure it was even him, but you never know. I'll have TJ see if he can pull the phone and the footage inside the prison to see who had the phone and when the calls were made. That way we can see who was on the phone."

"Smart thinking, boss. What are the odds, though, that the prison where Cappelano is, where you're at all day, is tied to this case?"

"This is a white-collar case, and there are a lot of high-end criminals being housed there, so it's not too surprising."

"Let me know what you need from me. I'll be sitting here."

I stepped outside to call Colby but decided to text TJ all the info first that we had and get him started on the case if I got sidetracked on the call with Colby. The nice thing about TJ and his team is that they needed a very limited amount of direction to accomplish a goal.

"Hey Colby, you free to chat, or do you need to call me back? I hear people yelling in the background."

"It's okay, Neil. What's up?"

"I was finally following up from you trying to catch me earlier when I left. I thought you'd be out by now; that's why I waited so long."

"I just wanted to make sure you were okay. You headed out so quick, I wanted to make sure you were okay. I know Frank can rile you up." Colby seemed a bit shaky in his voice; that's not why he chased me down. I can tell.

"Yeah, I get it. Cappelano was getting all high and mighty. I figure if I leave abruptly when he does that shit, it will set a tone moving forward."

"Smart idea. You're good man, just checking up on you."

"Thanks, man, have a great night."

Back in the van, you could see Christian was agitated as shit; something just looked like it was pissing him off hard core. He was on the phone with someone from his team, but he wasn't happy. I've been there, probably asking someone to do something, and they didn't follow through all the way.

"Everything okay, Christian? You sounded a bit pissed."

"Yeah, just one of the new guys missed his check-in, I was trying to explain to him the reason why it's important in the beginning until you build trust. How'd it go with your buddy at the prison?"

"He's not telling me something, but it might be that the person he wanted to talk about was standing right next to him, or he's hiding something. I guess time will tell."

"We're both sitting here, agitated, and having to wait. Sounds like your normal stakeout."

"Good point, Christian, but I'm actually going to head out in about an hour. Do you have anyone coming to relieve or help you out?"

"No, I got this, I have a nice digital rig to help keep an eye on stuff if I doze off—that is, unless you think I should head in. I've done tons of these over the years, I'll be good until my handoff at about four a.m. comes."

"If you say you're good, I trust you."

Christian and I went back and forth for a while, breaking down the comings and goings of their head of security. Apparently he's been involved in some shady shit for years; the police just can't tie him to anything. The rumor is that they pay local cops too much money to do private security gigs, so the cops won't touch them, they need the money. It's not quite a bribe, but damn close. Hard to arrest the guy that helps pay your mortgage.

The bad press from hiding all those chemicals and needing to pay off and maneuver through the city means they had to be using other help. Their head of security has to be utilizing street gangs to move products around; that's the only thing I can think of. It makes the most logical sense. If I need to move stuff around the city and don't want to get caught, I go to the people who do it all day long for a living. Drug dealers and gangs have a tendency to take cash, just like the rest of us. The questions are how big is their operation, are they still dealing drugs, like the rumors of them back in the day?

I need to get ahold of Jim Hammond ASAP; I wonder what Christian has gotten out of him.

"Hey Christian, before I go, I noticed in the briefing earlier, no one really brought up Jim Hammond. It was more of a footnote. Any reason why?"

"We interviewed him, even tailed him for a few days just to make sure, to cover our bases, but we got nothing. He didn't say shit to us, not sure if it's out of fear or he's protecting something."

"Maybe you'd have a better shot. I'll send you his contact info, I'll even email him and cc you on it, to introduce you guys."

"Thanks, sounds great. I'll reach out to him tomorrow since it's so late."

"Night, Neil. Thanks for the coffee and the talk. I always appreciate the time you give us on the team. I know you have plenty going on."

"Never too busy for the team, man, it's the reason we get up in the morning. Thanks for being the next rock star we have coming up the ranks."

You could see Christian really take the compliment like a shot of adrenaline. He didn't look sluggish before, but he looks like he could sprint a marathon right now. I remember what it felt like when Frank praised me. Even though I wasn't looking for it, having someone of that stature look to you, tell you that you are doing a great job just carries weight with it. It sticks to you, gives you a boost, and it's probably why for so long I didn't see the signs he was a sociopath; I was too busy taking the compliments from him.

The drive home took twenty minutes from Dearborn. This late the roads were wide open, allowing me to turn the radio up and just cruise. Pulling into the driveway, the girls could hear me pull in and were already at the front door waiting for me. As I made my way in, they started jumping up, forcing me to get into a wrestling match with them. Dropping my keys, my bag, and everything all over, I gave in. I enjoyed the pure happiness my sister Dobermans were always there to give me. Jackie and Danielle—man's best friend, my best friends.

Now it's time to pour a drink, pass out in my chair, and call it a night. Yes, I'm still struggling to sleep in that empty bed. I know I should be over it by now, but some nights are just harder than other nights. Tonight it seems like a night where I'm going to start in my chair. I have recently upgraded my fireplace from wood-burning to gas since I leave it on for the girls; it's safer than wood-burning all day. Here's to falling asleep to some tunes and thinking through the different issues from the day.

10

I have changed a few habits, but I haven't given up on my showers.

The morning started off great since I fell asleep on the early side, before eleven, but woke up at about one in the morning. I then made my way to the bedroom. where the girls were already sleeping, keeping the bed warmed up. As I got up this morning, I noticed I beat my alarm by a solid five minutes. Which has become a regular occurrence more and more since Cappelano has been behind bars. The first month after he was caught, I slept so much it felt like I had mono or something; the only difference was I had no symptoms and wasn't sick. I just didn't have to deal with Cappelano. I've heard stories of Olympic athletes after their competitions sleeping for days because all the stress and training are finally over. That's what it felt like, along with the end of fear.

Making my way to the kitchen for my morning routine of coffee, I put the girls out and made my way into the basement.

I put on some music and put on my wraps for my new morning routine. Since coming back from Warsaw I've been cutting back on my drinking. I know I poured one last night, but it was two fingers, not six, like I used to, and it was one, not three drinks. I'm trying to focus more, be better for myself and my team. No longer with the excuses or crutches—I would use Cappelano for my vices—I have been focusing on improving myself.

After a good thirty minutes of mixed combos and loud rock music, I noticed my phone had a few messages on it, as well as some emails I had missed when I got up. It looks like TJ has some items for us to look at that are too big to email. He asked me and Christian to come in to look at them. Knowing Christian worked until four in the morning, I should be able to take my time and head in at about eight or nine. It's only six thirty now, so I have some time. I'm going to keep working out for a bit and then get a nice long shower in.

I have changed a few habits, but I haven't given up on my showers. One might think if I'm not hung over, there is no need to have the hot water running over me for a long period, but it still slows me down, allowing my mind to focus. For me, a shower is almost like a place of meditation, my mind is constantly racing, down multiple lanes of a highway at high speeds, even when sleeping. When that hot water hits me, slides down my back, and I get hit with the first wall of steam, my mind halts, allowing me to focus.

All cleaned up, ready to go, the girls were good, and I made my way out, coffee in hand, headed to the office. I can't help but think I should make today short with Frank, just to show control, at his first outbreak walk out, leave him, show him I'm not going to put up with his shit. I know there is countless intel in his head that we need to get out. I can only imagine the number of unsolved murders he committed that the bureau and myself never connected. I guess the best way to find out is to confront him, work him, and get him to talk.

Pulling into the warehouse is one of the joys I get during the day, seeing the coming and growing of the operation, my caseload, and what Ken's hard work has built. I say his hard work because the nuts and bolts are all Ken. I'm strictly the talent, I'm the front man for the band. The difference is I know there is a team of forty people behind me working their tails off, making it look easy.

"Hey Neil, you're here earlier than normal and you look refreshed. You trying to beat Christian in to talk to TJ?"

"No, Ken, but I am here to see TJ. I wasn't thinking about Christian." Yes, I was.

"Too late, Christian is already here and in with TJ. They just started, though. You can get in there and catch up quick."

"Thanks, Ken, we can catch up after."

As I made my way quickly to the conference room, I saw that TJ has some stuff up on the screen in the conference room. It looks like surveillance footage from the night Erin went missing. It also looks like he has footage up from the chemical plant and the warehouse where Christian was sitting last night. I hope he found a connection.

"Hey Neil, you got here just in time. I was telling Christian that I found some major issues in their security footage. Luckily, I found something useful, though, at their Dearborn warehouse, thanks to some nifty Internet snooping." TJ always finds something, even if it's nothing.

"Well, give us the rundown. This is Christian's case. I'm just overseeing, catching up, keeping tabs on everything, and lending a hand." And sticking my nose in for a few minutes before I go deal with the bullshit that will be Cappelano.

"Well, it's pretty obvious they edited the footage at the chemical plant; there are large chunks of time missing from the footage, gaps, and uneven cuts. As I went through the Dearborn footage, I found what looks like a car matching the tracks Christian found at the scene. A car pulling into the warehouse and we can see what looks like Erin in her favorite St. Patty's Day green Detroit Tigers hat. One she is seen posing in regularly on social media."

"A hat isn't a ton to go off of, you already know that, don't you TJ?"

"Yes, I do, Neil. If I've learned anything working here over the years, context is everything." Hell yeah, it is.

"Well said. What's the connection then?"

"When you use a timeline, match the car, make, and tires to the tread found at the scene, use the drive time from the chemical plant to the Dearborn warehouse at that time of day . . . there are way too many coincidences for it not to be her in that car. If it smells like it and looks like it—"

"It's probably a big-ass pile of shit! Right, boss."

"Yup, Christian, I agree. Let's get some eyes and ears in that warehouse, you guys work on some ideas. I'm going to talk to Ken before I go poke a hornets' nest."

I've decided to make today's meeting short and sweet. I'm going to hammer Cappelano on the details about the time following his nephew's murder, him leaving the bureau, and when he announced himself as a killer. As I turned the corner, I saw Ken was on the phone lighting someone up with some language. I wasn't sure what was going on, but he looked heated.

"Ken, everything okay? I haven't seen you that hopping mad in a long time."

"It was that book lady again; she is nonstop, man. We should hire her to track down the people that owe us money. She's vicious."

"Seriously, get her back on the line. Call her now and put her on speaker."

"Dude, don't tease me? I've been dealing with her shit for almost a year and you're telling me you might make the pain go away?"

"Just dial already."

As the phone was ringing, Ken was smiling like a kid on Christmas morning who knew he was getting a new video game console. It might not be the worst idea to work on a book with her, expand my talking tour, raise the profile of the company, and raise some more money.

"Ken, did you accidentally hit redial? You never called me back."

"Hey, this is Neil with Ken. I hear you've been trying to reach me for some time."

"You're not the easiest man to get ahold of, Mr. Baggio. Do you have time to talk about my offer?"

"No, but I have a counter to your offer. I'm interviewing Cappelano currently for the bureau. If we turn it into a book, maybe you triple the offer and you have a deal. Email Ken your decision, otherwise lose our number."

"I'll run it by our editors ASAP. Thank you, Mr. Baggio."

Click.

"Neil, are you serious about that offer, or are you just helping me out?"

"Ken, I'm not sure yet, maybe both. I guess we'll see what they say. What was her first offer?"

"They offered you seven hundred thousand for a book deal, and you just asked them for two million."

"She didn't tell me to eat shit, so there's that."

"Good point. Go give Frank shit. Let me know what I can help with."

"I just want to know who was on those calls to the warehouse yesterday from the prison."

"TJ is on it, lots of footage to go through, he said the phone disappears a lot and he thinks there are guards letting inmates use them to make calls. We are working on getting the call logs too. When we get more concrete evidence, we'll loop in the warden, assuming he's not in on it."

"Thanks, Ken. Talk to you later."

Heading out to Milan FCI is starting to become a form of relaxation. The drive takes me close to an hour one way. It's an open highway, lots of fresh air ripping by at ninety miles an hour give or take, just depends on the number of cops along the trip. Let's see how long Frank lasts before I have to walk out of there today. I'm still debating on how to work with Colby. Maybe I can ask in generalities, see what I can get out of him. Before I know it, I'll be there, so for now, I'm going to enjoy some classic Ozzy for a bit and cruise down the highway.

11

Son of a bitch, now I'm going to have the urge to draw pictures of logs.

Walking in, I noticed Colby was outside, waiting for me for a change. This is rare, but I guess he needed to talk to me without others in earshot. As I walked up, I noticed he was looking around like a major league pitcher checking runners on first and third. He was looking over each shoulder, then eyeing me down like I was the catcher calling the play.

"Hey, Colby, judging by your short tone yesterday and you meeting me outside today, there's something you need to talk to me about."

"You need to watch what you are saying, and who to, inside. I'm not sure who yet, but there are a few dirty guards; well, there're always some dirty guards, they pay us shit. Still, these are linked to Cappelano from what I can tell and a few other high-profile people inside."

"I figured. We're already looking into it quietly; don't worry. I'll see what we can come up with and see how far up it runs. You let me know what you hear and we'll go from there."

"Sounds good. Now let's go in before they think we're talking behind their backs out here. I told them I needed my smokes."

Going through the syndicated TV series *Federal Prison Lockdown* is getting more and more tiresome. Yet it's part of the gig. It's what needs to be done, like watching a sitcom you know is going to be corny, but sometimes it's what you need. You go through the same motions; you see it coming, but you still laugh. In the room, sitting there waiting for Cappelano, I couldn't help but think about what Colby said. I also wondered if he was sent out to gain trust, get info from me. I'll have to play it close. Here comes the man of the hour. The Abbott to my Costello, the Paul to my Simon, more like the Ren to my Stimpy. Son of a bitch, now I'm going to have the urge to draw pictures of logs.

"Morning, Frank, how are we today? Hopefully in a better mood."

"Me! You're the one that stormed out of here yesterday."

"I didn't storm. I was just done dealing with your shit; that's completely different. When you get in one of your controlling moods where you like to be satisfied, I'm not going to join you in that party. I have too much shit to do."

"Well, Mr. Busy Baggio, or BB for short, where would you like to start?"

"I'd like to start in the place where you kept beating around the bush yesterday. The gap of time after you murdered your nephew and his best friend, Tony, then disappeared and went on a private killing spree, starting with some waitress in Fort Wayne. My guess is that's bullshit, you probably killed someone else in between but you're saving that one for you, because some things aren't for sharing." As I said, I came to play today.

"Well, someone had their coffee today; I did enjoy my time after I left the bureau. As you mentioned, I went on a journey to find out who I was as a person, not defined by the constraints of my job with the FBI."

"You mean with the law? Being reminded about what you were doing was wrong since you were entrusted with protecting it, defending it, and not taking the life of others for pure enjoyment?"

"You will understand when we are done here."

"Enough bullshit, Frank. Let's get back on point. Do I need to bring doughnuts and coffee when I come to warm you up?"

"It wouldn't hurt to treat me as a guest and not a lab rat." Fair point.

"It's hard not to look at you in a poor light when you looked at all your victims with less than a humane intention. Now you want me to give you something you never gave them."

"Okay, that one was some harsh truth. Yes, Neil, I did go on some form of a killing spree, as you might call it. Looking back, it was pretty gruesome and sloppy. Still, no connections were made to me or anyone because all acts were done at random."

"If I gave you a week to write them out and try to remember them, do you think you could even do it? Were there too many to even notice, making them inconsequential? Do you think you forget some because they were just a necessity of the day?"

"More the latter. I could try, though. I think for my own growth I should, but it will take a request from you for the warden to allow me to have a pen and paper. They are worried I might stab myself, or someone else."

"Maybe we can give you paper and some crayons then. I'm not patronizing, I'm simply thinking outside the box." The crayon box, that is.

"Get me something to write with and write on and I will do my best, for both of our curiosity."

"Thank you, Frank. Let's focus on the first couple of months after you left. What was your mental state? Depression, excitement, maybe a mixture of both?"

"It was pure joy and excitement, being free, finally able to embrace the darker side of myself wholeheartedly. It felt invigorating."

Frank started to open up and for a good thirty minutes he was dialed in. It was like he tapped into that initial excitement he felt when he left the FBI, when he initially decided to leave it all behind and commit to this life of murder and eventually training me through his work as a serial killer. It was interesting to notice his body language change. When he would speak of the bureau or me reaching out, trying to track him down, he would get tense or angry. But when he spoke of the lives he took, he would get visibly excited.

You could see the joy in his posture. He would stand or sit up taller, stick out his chest, speak clearer and louder. He projected glee when we spoke of their deaths, of the experience each one gave him. In all, he covered five murders from the time he left until he came out of hiding, but we were aware of only two. With the way he is talking, the limited scouting he was doing back then, and the pure joy he was getting out of killing, I have to believe the number of lives he took during this time was much closer to seventy, or even higher.

"Frank, let me ask you two questions. What do you think about sharing your story? *Do* you feel this is part of what you wanted all along? Not merely to train me, but also to give knowledge to the FBI, to coach and train agents for decades to come?"

"Neil, the work I have done over the past ten years, mixed with my understanding of law enforcement, is priceless. The information you and I will cover will redefine the industry and show agents what it's really like to chase a killer."

"Are you claiming we didn't know what we were, or are, doing?"

"I'd say you do, you can be wrong sometimes, but you're one of the best. Most people think in one or two lanes; they struggle to think in multiple lanes, but it slows them down. That's what allows killers like me to keep going. They need to learn to assign multiple agents to a case, multiple leads to follow different instincts; that's how you will catch these pariahs in society much quicker."

"I can tell you think this isn't some bullshit to feed me. You truly believe this. You think that you have some untapped potential. Some context you can share that will better the law enforcement community in tracking down killers, especially serial ones."

"Yes, Neil. You don't understand how much I've learned."

"I'm not questioning that. I'm questioning your methods, Frank. I'm questioning the cost. I'm questioning myself for indulging in this bullshit of an exercise. You killed countless people, ruined lives, destroyed families, took children from mothers, parents from children, and didn't bat an eyelash. You don't care, didn't care, and continue to think you acted in a lab, that none of this shit really happened."

"Neil, why are you making this so much harder than it has to be? It's okay for politicians to send our sons and daughters on peacekeeping missions to countries we'll never go to and die so that our gas prices stay under two dollars. However, I kill some people, and I'm the asshole? At least I took the lives myself, I didn't send some eighteen-year-old with a machine gun to kill for me."

He has a good point, but I'm still not in the mood to agree with him today. This is insanity to the tenth degree. I just need to find a button to push, some way to get under his skin, so that as he gets riled up, I can leave, and show him he needs to stay measured.

"Frank, if you think your killing was justified, all of it, how do you explain killing your nephew? Especially when you did it for a bullshit reason, as well as killing his friend. That shit was passion and anger, the cardinal sins of killing. Don't give me your high and mighty routine."

"Neil, if you're going to sit here and provoke me when all I've done my whole career is work to serve you, serve the FBI, and make you better, then I guess this might not work after all. . . ."

Frank went on for a solid fifteen minutes and I started tuning him out. I had the camera on and my recorder on. I'll review it later. For now, I need to think through this other case. I understand Cappelano is my priority, but I hate jackass douche bags that think they can get away with doing anything they want. Gaines Chemical and its fearless leader, Jason, are starting to appear in that light. I know he is just ranting and trying to work me up, barely giving me any real information. It's all about control, and that's why I'm using my time to save a girl's life.

Erin is a socialite in that she has the looks and is continuously on social media and at all the big events in town. With her relationship with Jim Hammond . . . fuck, I forgot to call Jim this morning. I need to call him as soon as I get out of here and find out what he thinks happened, see if anyone has reached out to him. For obvious reasons in cases like these, often the local police get less info out of witnesses than we can, especially with our current local reputation. With the state of things involving Gaines Chemical and the local authorities, many believe they have the police bought and paid for. Even if they don't, it's a hard perception to shake.

"Frank! Are you done wasting my time? If this is how it's going to be, I'm going to leave. You know as well as I do if I were to teach in a classroom with the shit you just gave me, students would leave with less info than they would've from a lecture from Bob Hendrickson."

"Neil, why can't you allow me to build up to it? There is some form of artistry, some nuance to what I have accomplished. As for Bob, don't ever compare me to that bloviated bastard."

"I won't compare you if you don't act like him; it's as simple as that. That two-cent speech was about as much Bob as I can handle. Pull that shit one more time, and I'm out of here for the day, maybe the week. I'm not going to keep coming out here and wasting my time so you can feel important."

"Fine, Neil. What do you want to hear? The gruesome details about how I killed each person, like an autopsy report, would it be easier if I simply wrote or typed it out for you?"

"Yes, maybe I can just get you approved computer time with no Internet so you can type it out, that's a great idea, that way I don't need to even bother coming out here anymore. I can even have some newbies read it for me so I don't have to deal with your Bob Hendrickson bloviating bullshit like I am right now."

"Message received: tone down the artistic approach. I will stick to the facts and less colorful additions. You are right about my nephew and his best friend, Tony; those killings were done out of traditional sin, as you put it. They were emotional, they were part of what pushed me away. Also, their deaths pushed me to kill randomly, to ensure I didn't go down that emotional road again unless I had a grasp on what I was doing."

"Is that why it took so long before you came back around to the bureau? Simply because you were busy in Mexico building up funds and having fun doing the cartel's work?"

"Probably a bit of both; living like a king and being paid handsomely for my talents were nice. Not being treated like a drain on society was nice for a change. I was in no hurry to get back to my work, but then I realized I was doing a disservice to myself and the FBI and that is why I went down this path in the first place."

"You really believe this shit, don't you? You believe you are killing for the betterment of all law enforcement, especially the bureau? On that note, and since we still haven't gotten anywhere, I'm heading out for the day. I know it's only been two hours, but I have a lot to do on a case. Since you ended strong, I'll be back tomorrow."

"Good luck on the Monroe case, Neil."

"'Bye, Frank."

Wait, what the fuck did he just say? How did he even know that's what we call it? Here we go again, now I'm going to have to look into every guard in this place; there goes my week.

12

I interviewed my victims as I was killing them.

Welcome back to the dark side. I told you I would keep coming back. I do only get to talk to you when Neil brings you to me. He may have left abruptly, but it gives me another chance to tell you my side of the story. I can see why he is getting so frustrated, but I don't want to be looked at like a simple case file. I know what I did is looked at brutally and cold. Nevertheless, there is some beauty to it, design to it. I was trying to gather information, I wasn't simply doing it for pure enjoyment.

Leonardo DaVinci was looked at like a monster by many for what he did to the human cadaver, even if he wasn't killing people outright. However, he did design weapons of war and befriended many people who did the same. History has a way of looking the other way on great people of science and intellect if they helped civilization achieve great things. Could you imagine if the great Sherlock Holmes were real, and decided to go on a killing spree for five years simply to understand the mind of a killer? Though I'm no Mr. Holmes, I do have a high intellect for solving crime, understanding for what it takes, and have dedicated my life to the pursuit of that knowledge.

I do understand the time I spent in Mexico cannot be explained away in the same manner. That was a straight ego trip, a time I enjoyed, embraced, and when I pushed myself to the limits, learning to embrace who I was and not shying away from it. Though I knew what I was doing was needed, there were difficult times. I felt people would never appreciate all that I was doing, especially Neil. That was right around the time I kidnapped his family, trying to send him a message to leave me alone, get back to his life, and calm his mind. He would never be open to learning the knowledge I had gained if he were snarling like a dog trying to hunt me.

You can understand that I'm not completely disconnected from the damage I have done; the only difference is that I have weighed both sides of the equation. I feel my cause is just; you and Neil feel it is not. I guess history will be the judge, but I'm a firm believer that I will come out vindicated for the knowledge of the human psyche and what victims go through in the moments before death.

I not only took notes on my view of killing, but also I interviewed my victims as I was killing them. There are tapes out there, interviews of me after my killings, that a therapist has. They are dealing with life under duress, wondering if my associates or I will come after them if they release it to the authorities. You may ask yourself how I could keep someone under that kind of pressure even after I am locked up. Well, I devised a little plan.

I hired a private investigator to collect on a debt, but in a very specific way. He tracks her movements, takes pictures once a month, and sends them to her with a letter that says, "We know where you are; it's time you hold up your end of the bargain." He does that once a month, and he gets paid. I set up a bank account with enough money to keep autopaying his fees for the next ten years, cross your fingers. I can keep her going nuts without any real work. I truly do love the way our world is set up. We can automate anything, even veiled threats.

It looks like one of the guards has a call for me.

"You have a call from outside; they asked for you specifically."

"You know my cost. It's information I can use. Do you have any, Colby?"

"I'll get you what you need. You help me, I'll help you. My kid needs braces, this job pays shit, and someone needs your help bad. I'm assuming the info I gave you recently was big enough to carry us over."

"Fair enough. Neil's face was quite lost when I dropped that nugget on him. I'll take the call. Please give me some privacy."

As he walked away, I spent twenty minutes talking to a very interesting man called Mr. T. He was asking how to deal with Neil and the company and if there was any way to make them go away. I tried explaining to him multiple times that it was not something I was interested in. If he required consulting on crime, perhaps, but working with insider detail to undermine a friend, I will not do it. I know I surprised you with that one. I do have some honor, but just with Neil; he is off-limits and so is his team. They do great work, and he's teaching the next great group that will make a difference.

"Mr. Cappelano, it's time to go. I need the phone back, and you need to go to your cell."

"You don't need to be pushy, simply asking is enough. Don't forget, without me, your cash cow is gone."

13

So TJ was involved?

Walking out the front door, I noticed I had a crap ton of missed calls and messages from TJ, Ken, and Sheila. Sheila was just texting me, double-checking if I was going to be gone all day, but TJ said he found what we were looking for and told me to call him immediately. My guess is it's Colby; they wouldn't have gone nuts if it were some random guard, but they know I have a bit of a relationship with him. Let's start with TJ; it'll probably answer the most questions.

"Hey, TJ, I see you were trying to get ahold of me. You know when I'm in there my phone barely works."

"It was worth a shot. I'll get you the Wi-Fi info so you can hop on their signal and get better service at least for text and emails. That's not why I called; it looks like your inside guy is—"

"Colby. I figured that out today from two different events."

"You always take my thunder. How'd you figure it out?"

"Well, he met me outside today, to talk to me, trying to gain my trust. That was number one. The second one was a few moments ago when Cappelano dropped the nugget about the Monroe case. We only call it that internally and just a few people know that, Colby being one of them. Frank knew I would figure it out; he's probably letting me know that people are conspiring against us on this case."

"Frank, help you? I'm confused. Really?"

"Frank has no problem messing with me, but only he gets to. It's like a big brother relationship with him. Only he can pick on me, no one else. It's messed up a bit, but it's one of the few things I truly understand with him."

"The other reason we're blowing your phone up is that I was able to get into some old footage and get eyes on Erin at the warehouse. Whoever their security team is figured it out though and cut the external feed so we can't see it anymore, but even now I have confirmation she's alive and she's there. We have a team out there now, keeping eyes on the building in case they try to move her. Should we call the feds? That was part of the reason I called."

"I'll call Maria and see how she wants to play it. Without probable cause they can't go in, and we found out illegally. It's a tough spot for them."

"Ken said you'd say something similar to that. Let me know if you need me to send the information we have anywhere, or make it look like an anonymous tip."

"That's not a bad idea; work something up. If we need it, I want it ready to go."

"No problem. I'll talk to you later, Neil."

"Thanks, TJ."

That's interesting. They have her held up in their warehouse. What do they think they are going to do with her long term? My guess is they're using local street thugs to handle her so they can keep their hands clean of the situation. It still doesn't make the most sense to bring her back there; she's smart enough to be able to witness people and point out where she was. They must know the endgame has them killing her. Maybe they plan on doing some sort of ransom eventually? Only time will tell. I'll work with Maria, see what she says.

"Agent Garcia, FBI Detroit office. How can I be of service today?"

"Maria, it's Neil. I've got some intel on the Gaines Chemical case."

"Good news, I hope."

"Good news, but might be useless to you because of how we obtained it."

"So the usual Baggio news on a case. Give me what you got."

"They have her held up at a warehouse. I won't tell you which one unless you really want to know. She's alive and we have someone sitting on it now, in case they move her."

"Jesus, how do you have confirmation? Or is this where the it's useless to us part comes in?"

"Bingo! It was obtained in a less than admissible in court way. Is that enough information for ya?"

"So TJ was involved?"

"You're getting used to working with us."

"Neil, we call you guys in for a reason, because you can do and are willing to do things we can't. Let me run it up the flagpole. Off-topic, how are you doing with all these Cappelano visits to the prison?"

"It's not great, but it's not horrible. We are working through the rough intro part, figuring out the ground rules. Once Frank realizes I'm not going to get pushed around and I am the voice to the outside world for him, the better it'll be for both of us."

"Just worried. I know what he does to you—your personality changes after you talk to him. I know it's different now, but I still worry."

"Thanks, Maria. How are you doing these days? We should grab a coffee and meet up soon."

"I'm doing good, working a ton, especially since I became single again."

"It didn't work out with you, and . . . I'm not going to lie; I don't remember his name."

"It's okay, I wouldn't expect my ex-boyfriend to remember my new boyfriend's name. The fact that you talk to me about him is amazing enough. Are you dating anyone these days?"

"No. Between you and Sheila, I'm not sure serious will ever happen again, casual date here and there maybe, but I'm over it otherwise. I've got an amazing group of people around me, and I'm happy with that."

"We are a pretty great group of women around you, especially when you throw in your awesome daughter. How's she doing? Before you know it, she's going to be dating, if she isn't already. I was about her age when—"

"Stop it, stop right there. That's the last thing a dad wants to hear. Why do you think dads come up with speeches to intimidate dates the daughters bring home? We don't want to hear that shit, but yes, I am lucky. Back to the case, let me know if you want me to do anything. Maybe we can grab that cup of coffee and not talk about how to proceed."

"I'm pretty sure that's the next step. I'll text you when I get the word."

Like that, I hung up. I know what you're thinking, you didn't say good-bye. It's a thing I've been doing lately. It's an old habit I used to have bad in my twenties and early thirties, but the bureau broke me off it. I used to get ripped by my bosses all the time. I noticed it started to creep back in. The conversation is over, so I hang up. It's not about being rude, just efficient, if confusing to the person on the other end. The time they spend wondering if the call was disconnected on their end makes it inefficient to them until they figure out it's my thing.

Next call is Jim Hammond. I'm going to make my way toward Ann Arbor now, it's not a far drive from FCI Milan, plus this way I can put a bit of pressure on him. I'm sure there is plenty he is aware of and just doesn't want to talk about. A better idea: I'm going to have Ken and the boys help me play a bit of a con on Mr. Hammond.

"Ken, can you do me a favor? Can you and the guys look up Jim Hammond's office info? Get them on the horn and tell them I'm coming in to give a comment on the case to add to their follow- up story. Tell them I'm looking for some media presence on the case, and maybe he won't be as worried about me coming."

"I'll have one of the girls up front make the call; it'll seem more genuine for them to try to set up an appointment. Tell them I'm in the area and I'll swing by. If I have to wait, it's fine. I understand I'm dropping in."

"Sounds good."

Driving down US 23 can be tricky because some cops like to sit at the bottom of the bends and curves. There are plenty of hiding spots for them to sit there and catch you. Though I'd love to speed, I'm just enjoying my quick ride over to the small office building where Jim's office is. Though they are a smaller paper, they have a big impact. Some of their stories have been picked up nationally this year. The *Ann Arbor Gazette* has been around for almost a decade, at least from what my memory serves. The building looks similar to what you'd expect from an average CPA firm—nothing flashy, just substance and economical service to the writers inside. As I made my way inside, I noticed it was a quiet day; let's see if he's even around.

"Good afternoon. Is Jim Hammond around by any chance? I had my staff call ahead."

"Neil Baggio, I presume?"

"Yes."

"He is; let me call him for you."

After a few short minutes, a young man in his late twenties walked up. He was a bit under six feet with brown hair, a little on the shaggy side, and he had a decent scruff going. Not uncommon in Detroit during hockey season, especially following no -shave November. He was wearing some worn-out jeans, newer tennis shoes, a button-down white dress shirt, and a sport coat. It was your perfect Ann Arbor dressy casual look.

"Neil Baggio? Hello, my name is Jim Hammond. I heard you wanted to talk to me. However, I don't think I got the message correctly."

"You did, I just think you're too smart for it, that's all."

"I appreciate the compliment and your awareness of the situation. Now that we're on the same page, why don't we go for a walk toward downtown for a cup of coffee and talk?"

As we walked out the front door, he didn't say anything, not even small talk. Not surprising, with everything going on. Having a good friend of his missing put a lot of pressure on his shoulders. You know you're doing good, think you're doing good, and then you end up having someone's disappearance on your shoulders. It's not easy, even if you're trained for it or expect it.

"Neil, I'm not dumb. You're here to talk to me about Erin, and I don't have a ton to say. It sucks, I can't sleep, and I don't know what to do."

"Calm down, for starters. We're on it, we're good at this shit, and we can do things the fed and local law enforcement can't. Also, we're not dealing with the same political influences others are dealing with."

"You say political, but I know you mean financial. The amount of money Gaines Chemical spends in the community means that the local law enforcement officers won't touch them. I partially don't even blame them. If your bills are due, are you going to arrest the person cutting your paycheck?"

"I'm here because I'm trying to build a case against them, not just what you guys wrote about. I know a whopper when I see one. You're sitting on a crap ton more evidence, but I can tell you're waiting to drag this out, or you were scared to after Erin went missing. Has anyone reached out to you, trying to get what you have on them?"

"We have way more than what we wrote about and I'm sure they're aware because we asked for a comment on the piece and one of our researchers let it slip by accident, that we had more when they were rude to on the phone."

"What's the reason for holding it back? Holding it from the FBI?"

"My only concern right now is Erin's safety and my only bargaining chip for her safety is that intel. If I hand it over, there's no telling what they'll do."

"That's a fair point. Is there anything you are willing to share with us that you think can help us figure out what is driving them to make decisions?"

"I can tell you the story we wrote is fluff compared to what we have, and that's what Gaines Chemical is worried about. They know what's out there, they know what can come out, and they grabbed her to find out what we know. Erin isn't going to give them anything because she knows as long as they're in the dark she's got a chance."

"We have confirmation she's alive but working with the bureau on making it more legal to act on. That's why I'm here, trying to figure out if you have any actionable intel."

"You guys walk in that gray area that we sometimes approach but rarely cross. That's what makes you BCI and not the FBI. You and I need to find a way to build trust because this is too big a risk for me to take on my closest friend."

I can appreciate someone's concern with their friend's well-being. I need to convince him that I am here for him. I guess I can share the intel with him of where she is, or I can share that we know someone at the prison is in contact with Gaines Chemical. Maybe I can limp in with the prison info without playing my big trump card.

"Tell ya what: I will give you a hypothetical and you tell me if it sounds familiar and if you have matches. Maybe we can build trust through sharing and comparing together."

"I'm willing to listen to you, which is more than I can say for anyone else. Your reputation carries great weight across the board."

I spent the next fifteen minutes walking Jim through the details we found from sitting on the warehouse, leaving out the proof that she is in there. I did explain to him we had circumstantial evidence pointing that she might be at a warehouse but can't confirm it yet. I walked him through the connection to the prison as well as the local street gangs. We are pretty sure they are using a local gang to try to intimidate Erin and move drugs throughout the city.

Jim followed suit by confirming that we are on the right path, especially with the drugs and the local gangs. Apparently this is something Gaines Chemical has been doing for years. He also said this is one of the big things they have on the company. They have concrete proof tying them to the drug trade. He said the connection to the prison is probably a gang tie to some of the guards; there have been connections for years that they have investigated. The picture is starting to get a bit clearer. Yet I still don't have all the details. I don't think it'll be as easy as driving a truck through the front door, like in Warsaw.

"I think I can continue to communicate with you, but I'd like to do it in person. That way I know nothing we say is compromised. Is that okay with you?"

"That's fine, Jim. I'll keep you in the loop. Plus I'm out at FCI Milan almost daily, so I can swing by after, and we can follow up."

"Sounds great. Thank you for your time, Neil."

"Thank you for the info and the coffee."

As I made my way out of Ann Arbor, I couldn't help but think of all the loose ends now that Jim pointed out that could be driving Gaines Chemical to be frantic. They have fingers in so many pies that we can't be certain of what is driving their paranoia right now. The best bet is to try and get someone on the inside or get Gaines himself cornered. Guys like him are frequently so cocky we can at least get the map to what they're working on, to narrow the field. I'll be home shortly, and I'm going to use these final fifteen to twenty minutes to clear my mind. Maybe I can get the office to set up a meeting with me and Maria at Gaines's office tomorrow; it's still early enough that they might be able to get through.

"Hey Ken, can you see if our secretary can get a meeting with Gaines Chemical's CEO tomorrow? Ask if he'll meet with

Agent Garcia and me from the FBI. Tell them it's to help find Erin as well as look into all the destruction of their properties, their case against her."

"Got it. I'll text you the details as soon as we have them."

As soon as I hung up, I shot Maria a text, making sure she had time to meet up tomorrow for coffee and a meeting at Gaines Chemical. It looks like she can make time, not surprising for a case like this. It'll be nice to see her since I haven't seen her in a while. Ken hit me back after a few minutes saying eight forty-five in the morning is all they have available. I passed the info on to Maria. I made sure we'd be set up to meet for coffee up the street from Gaines Chemical in Troy, Michigan, at seven thirty.

14

I was wondering if I was going to hear from you tonight, Neil.

The night is going to be a long one, I can already tell. I've been home for a bit now; dinner was a waste. I heated up some leftover pasta, not in a microwave like a savage, I did it in a pan with a little water and some olive oil to make sure the noodles have some moisture. Dinner isn't why my night is going to be rough. Dealing with Cappelano and the number of open-ended cases are. These compounded with the fact that he and Colby have some form of working relationship mean Frank has a connection to the outside world. This minimizes my power over him, though he can't leave. He can communicate and find ways to get items he needs or wants to be brought inside the prison walls. You laugh, but I once saw a prison down South where an inmate had a desk and flat-screen TV. The warden said if they can pay for it, they can have it.

Dinner is done, kitchen cleaned, girls out, and I even wrestled with them a bit, so I know they're good now. I can take some time and head to the basement. If I want to work out distraction-free, I should probably call Sheila really quick and check in.

"Hey cutie, how are you tonight?"

"I was wondering if I was going to hear from you tonight, Neil."

"Yeah, it's just been a lot of different shit today. Between the Monroe case and Frank's crap, I'm a bit spread thin mentally."

"It's understandable. You have Christian taking the lead you said?"

"Yeah, but this covers such a big company with a large revenue. I have to help out, do some interviews, and use the Baggio name to carry some weight."

"You've always been good at that. Do I need to let you go so you can get back to it?"

"I'm getting ready to hit the heavy bag and work out, need a good sweat to clear my head."

"You always do your best work doing one of three things: showering, working out, or . . . well, you know the third," she said, chuckling.

"Sheila, always a flirt. Get some rest and kiss Carol Lynn for me. I'll text you in the morning."

"Night, Neil."

With that done, I could focus on the case at hand. I grabbed my notebook and file I had compiled with Cappelano as well as the items from the Monroe case. Since they are overlapping,

I couldn't help but think there is a bigger connection here somewhere. I don't think Frank is pulling strings. This doesn't have his feel to it—way too sloppy, for starters. I made my way down the stairs and laid everything out on a small table I have next to the heavy bag. Then I cranked up the local radio station 101 WRIF, one of the best local rock radio stations around. I needed to listen to some rock and just whale on this bag.

As I went through my ritual of putting on my wraps and reviewing case material, I could feel the stress of the day start to fade. The distractions slowly dissipate; they knew they were about to get smashed into submission. They know my routine. Though they try to cloud me all day, they know when the radio comes on and the wraps come out, they better run for cover. I mean business, and it's time to focus.

Each passing combination turned into another case review; I went through different subsets. I matched them with different case issues I was working through.

One-two as I worked through why Frank would be working with anyone outside.

One-one-two as I worked through who Frank would be working with.

One-two-three as I reviewed the items Jim and I went over and how to use them for probable cause.

Two-three-two as I reviewed what it was going to be like seeing Maria again and all that entails.

A good hour into sweating, reviewing, and thinking through everything, and the only thing that's clear to me is that Frank is a loner. Chances are he isn't reaching out, he believes no one is on his level, so it has to be someone reaching to him, which means they need his help right now. The second thing I am starting to see is why he would be doing it. He gave the lead away by giving me that comment about the Monroe case. He led me right to who and what is going on. It just took me a day to put all the pieces together.

Someone at Gaines Chemical is reaching out to him. The question is who. Someone has to be arrogant enough to think they can call one of the most prolific serial killers and ask them for advice. It takes a special kind of psyche to think that is a good idea, to work past all the red flags and go straight to the best option you have. As for Maria, the feelings I know we both have for each other are complicated. When isn't my life with women? Between my situations with Sheila and Maria, I am in a state of being single and partially attached. I'm forever happily miserable. I'm just not fulfilled. My childhood friend Father Roberts will tell you I need to work through my own internal shit, and he's right.

I bet he's still up; this is when he usually does his normal late-night routine. It's a little after ten at night. I think I might give him a call, it has been a few weeks since we spoke, and I still need to plan a mission trip with him overseas that I promised him.

"Neil, it's late, but you know I'm up. That being said, you better be calling me to give me some dates for us to do our mission trip. You know you need it for your soul as well as our friendship."

"That's a good point. How about we shoot for July? What better thing to do than plan on a trip to somewhere hot and muggy in the middle of July?"

"I'm going to hold you to that."

"I'm planning on it. Just set it up with Ken and let him and Sheila know to clear my calendar so that even if I flake, I have no excuses."

"Sounds good to me, but I know this isn't why you called. What can I do for you?"

"Just the usual, seeking love advice from my best friend who has been single his entire adult life, choosing God over women."

"Smart man. Is this about Sheila, Maria, or someone new?"

"The first two, but mainly Maria. I'm meeting up with her tomorrow, and every time I see her, all those feelings come rushing back, they hit me hard. It's hard not to; she's an amazing woman."

"That she is. She is your intellectual rival and beautiful. I'd say you need to commit to her a bit, but she's also scared of what might be, which is understanding. Maybe invite her as a friend on the mission trip. Building a strong friendship is key to any relationship."

"I'm not sure how to bring that up to her, but I think you're right, that's a great idea. It'll give us a chance to work through some stuff. Thanks, Father."

"Neil, it's getting late; unless you have a killer on the loose, can we catch up tomorrow?"

"Yeah, I'll talk to you later. Thank you."

I know you're thinking you call your best friend, Father Roberts. We've gone over this in the past; it took some time to get there. Now it just seems natural; to call him Bob or Bobby just seems odd. If your friend becomes the president of the United States, you will eventually call him Mr. President. It's a part of reverence for the position. It's not weird, it's just how it is.

Tomorrow will be a fun morning dealing with Maria, trying to keep that together, and a meeting with a megalomaniac control freak. No, I'm not talking about Cappelano. I'm talking about the head of Gaines Chemical, the son of the founding family—one Mr. Jason Gaines. For now, though, I'm going to clean up and review Jason Gaines's background and the expanse of his company, especially since he took over leadership.

If you've known me long enough, that means you know what's coming next. It's the part where I hop in the shower, and I finally get a moment to slow down. I know it seems like a cliché, but we all have our mechanisms in life. I was drinking for a while—okay, like ten years—and some people smoke cigarettes or weed. I have found something that works. For me, getting a good workout in, followed by a hot shower, really gives me time to work through a ton of things. I can't sit in front of a screen or a case file; I need to read all the information, do my investigating, then let it rest. Think of it like a baker allowing the dough to rise. You have to trust the recipe has been done correctly and that with the right approach and time, you'll get the dough to just where you need it.

As the steam hit me, opening the door to the shower, I could already feel a sense of relaxation come over me. It was time to review the man behind the company, causing so many issues in the community, a driving force on both sides of the line in Metro Detroit. His name is J. Gaines—Jason—but most people call him Mr. Gaines. You rarely hear his first name unless you're at a country club or bar. You will often find him at a bar, or a place such as the Whitney downtown, drinking in the Ghost Bar. He is a man who likes his libations. He isn't a scholar, but he isn't dumb. He has a degree from the University of Michigan, where he studied medicine and focused on pharmaceutical science. There he became enamored with the design of new drugs, and specializing in new street drugs, when his parents needed to use their influence to keep him out of trouble.

He is forty-four years old, married to a lobbyist in the medical field who also works for one of the largest insurance companies based in the Metro Detroit area. I'm not sure how they met, but it's not surprising with so many crossovers. They are a power couple that appear in the papers, on the news, and all over the social scene. They are active in charities, showing up in the front row of basketball and baseball games, and always seem to find the cameras. They know how to put on a show for the community. Though they are damaging it behind closed doors to earn a buck, they put on a great show.

If I didn't know any better, I would think he's going to be running for office soon. Which might be the case, but with all this bad publicity, they are scrambling. Then again, it's more like felonies than simple publicity issues. Gaines is a street man, though he went to college. He craved to be the big man on campus more than most. Trying to get noticed, get in with the "it" crowd. To his dismay, his money wasn't enough. There were plenty of families and friend groups with money. I'm merely guessing, doing a breakdown of what I see, what I can read into the file TJ has composed for me, mixed with the info Maria sent over from the bureau. Everyone has a file on Gaines Chemical, especially after all the publicity.

The exit from the shower to bed is going to be a quick one. It's about to end with me asleep on the bed with a towel on. Hopefully, the dogs keep me warm. I'm mentally drained, a little tired from the workout, and just need to sleep.

15

I've noticed you're no longer drinking your coffee like a sixteen-year-old girl.

The morning went quicker than normal, and today I had a crap ton to do. I woke up at about five, took the girls on a two-mile run, getting them good and tired in that cold Detroit air, and followed that with a quick shower. As I made my way out the front door, I said good-bye to the girls like a TV husband from a fifties sitcom to his wife, though they are Dobermans and not a well-dressed Stepford wife. I shot Maria a text, letting her know I was on my way and on time for a change, then started on my call list.

Working my way through the usual morning check-ins, I called in and spoke to Sheila, caught her and Carol Lynn on their way to school, which made my day. Hearing my daughter telling me to have a great day is always a treat. Then it was on to my morning call with Ken, getting a rundown of what TJ and the crew had figured out, dug up, and been able to tag together.

Jim gave us a few leads that TJ was able to use as starting points to gather more intel on Gaines Chemical, as well as some other dirt I'm pretty sure no one else has. He found wire transactions to accounts all over the country, spreading out money to different funds, some tied to some not so nice people.

The final call was to Christian to check on the teams keeping an eye on the warehouse and Erin. So far we didn't have any movement, just a status quo. They did have a few trucks coming into and going out of the bay. Christian foresaw this problem already and had teams sitting on trucks to ensure she wasn't on them. It may be a lot of manpower, but he wanted to be safe. This isn't a truck depot, so keeping two extra teams on ready alert wasn't out of the question. Especially with all the guys we have and active cops who can drop in and tag a truck until we can get one of our guys on the tail.

Pulling into the coffee shop where we were meeting, just a few blocks from Gaines Chemical, I could see that Maria had arrived before me. This is not surprising; she's early to everything. As I walked in, I noticed a lot of Gaines Chemical badges, also not surprising, but this did mean our conversation would have to be on the quieter side.

"Hey Maria, I made it on time, even early for a change."

"Wow, is this the new and improved Neil Baggio? I might just like him."

"I'll come early more often if that's what you like."

"You know a woman doesn't like a man coming too early too often."

"I walked into that one." She jokes like a frat boy.

"Did you order yet? I'm just going to get the—"

"Usual black coffee? I know I've noticed you're no longer drinking your coffee like a sixteen-year-old girl. I'm so proud of you."

"I realized I was eating dessert, not drinking coffee."

"It's about time. You're early, drinking coffee like an adult; so much as changed. Did all of this happen while you were in Poland?"

"A lot of good things changed over there. I came to some realizations. Staying in a small hotel outside my routine made me realize what was really important and what wasn't."

"You're still taking long-ass showers though and hitting your heavy bag, I assume."

"Yes, I just cut back on drinking and all the sugar in my coffee. You know the things that are brutal for me."

After a good thirty minutes of banter, we finally got into the case and the issues they saw with acting on our intel and what they would need. I informed them of the other information out there on Gaines Chemical, mainly their CEO, the connections they have to street gangs, drug trafficking, and what look like large arms and drug purchases. I'm working with TJ to help pinpoint details so the government can find it on their own. She was appreciative and agreed that might be the best way to get him off the streets.

Oftentimes the best way to get the crime bosses off the streets is with the Al Capone tax evasion tactics. They hide money, the cash-heavy drug industry can't make deposits daily, they launder it, then they don't pay taxes. Busting drug dealers on tax evasion is not glamorous, it doesn't always make the front page of the news, but it gets the bad guy off the streets, and at the end of the day that is what we're in this for.

"Okay, Neil, so we have the game plan. You really think this might work?"

"I have a feeling that Mr. Gaines is the one calling Cappelano, trying to get dirt on me. If I play it straight, come at him like an ally, and you come at him harder, I might be able to throw him off. Cappelano gave me a heads up for a reason. I want to use it, not waste it."

"If you say so, your instincts are usually right. They're some of the best in the business. That's why you're so sought after."

"Thanks, Maria, that's high praise from you. I know you of all people don't need to give it to me; I expect you to drop the hammer on me more times than not. I guess I'm saying thank you, I appreciate it."

"No problem, Neil. I still care about you and still think you're the best agent I've ever worked with. Hell, you caught one of the greatest, if not the greatest, serial killers of all time."

"I guess I did. As much as I love talking about how awesome I am, let's head over. We can take one car from here; let's hop in your car. I miss that Corvette. Not getting out of it, but driving in it, hearing that engine, it just sounds so right."

As we pulled into the parking lot of Gaines Chemical, we were met with security and hold-ups all over. It was a pain but also expected. The thing that drove me crazy was that we have a confirmed appointment but not a place to park. I guess they thought we would be walking over from twenty-plus miles away. Finally we parked and walked up to the front door of the gorgeous seven-story building built by his father a few years ago. We were met by Mr. Gaines's assistant.

"Hello, you must be Agent Garcia and Neil Baggio. I'm the assistant. I thought I would meet you downstairs and walk you up."

"Do you always walk up to Mr. Gaines's guests or just the ones you don't want talking to anyone else?" Maria was starting early.

"That's not it at all, Agent Garcia. I was just trying to be a gracious host to law enforcement per Mr. Gaines's directives. He is thankful for the attention being given to this case and the tragedy of the missing girl." The assistant is playing her role nicely.

"Though I appreciate the gesture, you must understand the optics may not be what you intended. As my colleague Neil might say differently, that's just my two cents." I have to play the nice guy, which will be hard, but that's the curveball we're throwing.

"I'll wait and hold judgment until after we get done sitting down with Mr. Gaines, and I'm assuming his lawyers and team?"

"Actually, there will be no lawyer present, but I can see why one would assume so. We are almost there, just need to take the elevator up to the top floor. Would either of you like something to drink?"

"I'm fine, I still have my coffee from down the street. Agent Garcia, how about you?"

"I don't need anything other than some truth and answers." She's hitting it hard.

"That is what Mr. Gaines and I are here for. If you need anything, don't hesitate to ask. Here he is."

Walking into the office, it was what one would expect from the evil villain of a bad guy in a DC Comics movie. It was large, a ton of windows and expensive art all over the walls. All that was missing was an East European woman who looked like a supermodel and serial killer all rolled into one. He had a combined office and apartment. I was surprised that the building was only seven floors; with his ego I would have assumed it would have been seventy. But his father built the building. There are a ton of offices on the top floor, but none like this, I can assure you.

COLLOQUIUM

"Hello, Agent Garcia and the infamous Neil Baggio. I am honored to have two of the greats from the Veritas case looking into this. I'm a bit surprised; I didn't think our case was big enough for such talent at the FBI. Maybe it's a slow week?" Maria is snarling at this point.

"You're assuming we're here to help you, Mr. Gaines. There is always the possibility we are here to look into you. Maybe the FBI has put this talent together to look into everything you've been accused of previously. You can only ignore the smoke for so long until people realize there is a fire burning." I'm going to sit back and let them rile each other up for a bit.

"Agent Garcia, I expected this kind of aggression from Neil. From what I've heard over the years, he's the pit bull, the one doing the crazy things to get the bad guy. You, the measured veteran agent, coming in and picking a fight with a pillar of the community. This surprises me a bit. You know what my wife and I have done and continue to do in the Metro Detroit area."

"If you donate a million dollars and build a drug rehab facility, that's amazing. It's not amazing if you're making twenty million selling the drugs that are putting people there in the first place." Damn, Gina! Nineties TV reference.

"Neil, are you just going to sit idly by while Agent Garcia badgers me and tries to take me out to the woodshed with accusations that are unfounded and unproven? Both of you should know, when you become as successful as my family, you become a target. Everything we do leads to coverage, which then in turn becomes fodder for some asshole to judge me and my parent's legacy."

What he's leaving out is that he is a drunk and drug-pushing prick who is known all over for being almost psychotic. Seriously, for years people have talked about him being damn near an evil villain. This dude really pushes it to the edge and takes it to the max. He will shoot your mother, then ask you out to dinner.

"Agent Garcia, Mr. Gaines is right. All of these are simply allegations. We should give him the benefit of the doubt and simply let the facts do the talking here. I know we can take things such as drugs personally, but we can't let our judgment be clouded by media conjecture in this case." Right now he is looking at me like a confused dog, with his head tilted. It's working.

"Neil, I don't agree with you, and I'm not going to. I'll go out and grab a cup of coffee from his assistant to give you two some privacy to bro out." Well played, Maria.

"I think that's a good idea, Agent Garcia. Thank you for respecting the situation. Neil, thank you for understanding everything as a whole and seeing the big picture."

This is why you do your homework before a big interview, whether it's for a job or a big case; use every means necessary to find out who you are going to talk to. The more information you have, the better you can plan. In the case of Mr. Gaines, we played into his ego, into his feelings of self-righteousness, and mixed that with the belief that I'm the one being nice. We have a newfound friendship and trust we can build on.

"I've seen a lot of cases and don't like risking information to preconceived bias of any kind. If I learned one thing from dealing with Cappelano, it's that you can't judge anyone from the outside. I'm just here trying to find the truth, trying to help you guys stop these attacks and find this missing girl."

"Thank you, Neil. I'll have our head of security email you the footage from all the attacks so your team can go through it. As for interviews, our teams are busy, but I can get a list together. Along with the interviews we already did, we'll get that over to you, and anyone you want to re-interview, we can schedule it out." Damn, he's a control freak.

"That'll be just fine. I'm not sure we are going to find anything extra from interviews, but I'd love the information to build the file just the same. Thank you for your help in all of this. How are things going with your company since all of this started? I've been reading some pretty nasty shit about you and it must be stressful."

"It has been. Then again, every day is pretty stressful when you run a billion-dollar industry-leading company." And you're a drug lord and a street thug and kidnapping people. Go on.

"I can imagine, but how is your company doing with all of this? It'll really help us on where to look. Who might have the motivation to create this chaos? And not just a fringe girl or group looking to disturb what they don't like. Remember, frequently it has to do with money."

"I see what you mean. Well, there are the rumors that we are looking to sell, there are the rumors that we are looking to acquire. As a publicly traded company, all this negativity drives down our stock, which in turn minimizes our positions and cash to make moves. It also minimizes the prices that others might offer us or use to try and do a takeover."

"Are there any internal issues, Mr. Gaines? Is your board giving you pressure? Could someone be trying to create a mess to push you out?"

"The way we are set up, the only person who can even make that kind of move is my sister. However, she is off in the Amazon doing research on new animals and plants, trying to find the next big thing."

He seems to have an answer for everything, which isn't surprising. Still, I'll have TJ do some digging on the financial side and have the bureau do an accounting review of their stock options and who might be making a play on them. When you add it all up, there are many options on the table that can lead to the stress in this man's life as well as in his company. Add that we and others have connected him to street gangs, pushing drugs from his factories, and continued illicit activities that come with them.

"Mr. Gaines, I won't take up any more of your time. I will look for that information today and get it compiled immediately."

"While we were talking, I emailed my head of security, told him to call your office and start coordinating now. He said you'll have it all within the hour."

"Thank you. That is very gracious of you, Mr. Gaines."

"Have a great day, Neil. It means a lot knowing the great Neil Baggio is looking into this for us. We really need help getting our hands around this."

"I'm just doing my part. I know Agent Garcia got on you, but she will follow the facts, don't worry."

"Thank you, Neil. Have a great day."

We were escorted out, again by his assistant. I couldn't help but notice the two or three different people that kept eyeballing us like we were behind enemy lines. It was just such a weird feeling. When you work for a company that is as big as Gaines Chemical, and you continue to be a driving force, you know that there are some illicit things you are doing. Still, you rationalize them because of the good you are doing. It's not uncommon; we as humans can damn near rationalize anything. Think of all the times you've made horrible decisions and the dumb- ass reasons you convinced yourself they were okay. Before you or any of us judge others on who they work for, remember that part of our psyche that convinces us ice cream is a good idea when we need to lose ten pounds for our heart health.

Outside, the assistant went in and we put the building finally in the distance. We got in the car and began our drive back to the coffee shop where my car was waiting for me. Maria looked over at me and gave me a shot.

"So that went well. Did you get as much good stuff as I did?" Maria smiled.

"What do you mean? Was the assistant forthcoming the second time around without her boss's prying eyes?"

"How about them apples?" Maria replied, making a *Good Will Hunting* reference.

"I see she gave you her number. I didn't know you were into girls. I mean, she was stunning. Way to go, Maria."

"Shut the fuck up, Neil. We are meeting for coffee later today to talk outside of work. She's going to try and bring some files too. She hates her boss and is pretty sure he knows what's going on with Erin. She just doesn't know how much."

"That's huge. Mr. Gaines was what we expected. An arrogant prick didn't get much out of him if anything at all. His security team is sending everything to our office, I'll have Ken and the team send it over to the bureau to sift through it as well."

"Sounds good. What do you have going on next?"

"Back out to FCI Milan to keep chipping away at Cappelano."

"That should be fun."

As we pulled into the parking lot and began our good-byes, I leaned in to give Maria a hug, but she decided to give me a kiss, which caught me off guard. I wasn't about to not kiss her back; shit I still have feelings for her. Oh well, I'm used to having my life in shambles and mirroring a daytime soap opera.

"Good-bye, Neil. Good luck with Frank."

"'Bye, Maria. I'll call you later."

"You better."

What was that?

16

*The last thing you want to do is be unbalanced on the scorecard
with Frank.*

Maria is on her way back to the FBI field office downtown. I'm
on my way to the prison, shifting around in my seat, all riled
up from Maria laying one on me. As if that wasn't enough, she
just texted me, asking if she can swing by later tonight to hang
out. Of course she can. Who am I to stop a brilliant and
gorgeous woman from coming over to my house tonight?
Especially one I'm still head over heels for. Maybe I'll have the
courage to talk to her about coming on that trip with me and
Father Roberts this summer. I need to get my head out of the
clouds and down into the mud since I'll be dealing with
Cappelano and his shit. Also, I need to touch bases with Ken
and ensure we are good on all fronts before I end up in the
Bermuda Triangle of communication known as a federal
prison.

"Hey Ken, did Gaines Chemical's security head send some information over?"

"Yeah, there's a crap ton of it. I have the team sifting through it now. They even set up a share of it all with the bureau. I'm sure they're trying to bury us in crap and hope we miss the details; little do they know we have people that specialize in finding the absurd." Ken is spot on.

"Do we have any updates from Christian and the team sitting on the warehouse?"

"It doesn't seem that Erin has been moved. From the warehouse now, they have pictures of Gaines Chemical employees and their head of security working shoulder to shoulder with gang members, handling drugs and cash. The problem is the pictures are indistinct."

"I know they're constantly working on getting more intel and more info, keep me updated as anything breaks. I noticed TJ emailed me the Wi-Fi info for the prison so I can get better service. It won't be perfect, but text and emails will come through."

"Yeah, TJ said he was able to track that down for you. That'll help us all while you're pulling double duty, Neil."

"Thanks, Ken, I'll talk to you guys later. I might have to put some time in today. I left early to make up some time and get information out of him. Especially after he helped me with Gaines and after tipping me off with the guards, it doesn't take much between the two of us to communicate. Now I need to make it right."

"Smart man. The last thing you want to do is be unbalanced on the scorecard with Frank. Do you have any ideas?"

"I'm going for something trivial to start."

"Oh shit, you bring him a PayDay. You said he used to love those things."

"I have a few in my bag, figured it might be an easy way to buy his affection," I said, laughing.

"Hey, sometimes a little sugar to someone who can't get it goes a long way. That's how I parented for almost a decade." Ken has a point; I think many of us fall into that scenario.

"I need to get in and get going, I'm already behind my normal start time. Keep me updated if anything changes."

"Will do, Neil. Talk to you later."

As I walked in, greeted the usual guards, faked a smile, and judged them knowing many were on the take, I realized that this is the system we have designed. We have created this counterculture separate from ours and allowed it to happen. I don't judge the guard who takes the extra money to support their family; it's the system that's set up. Imagine if 20 percent of the students in every classroom could pay teachers for better grades and more help. There would be an abundance of bribing going on, especially with the way we pay teachers in a lot of our communities.

Finally, through the black Friday maze of obstacles and locked doors to my room of paradise known as Room 107-C, I sat down, set my stuff up, and prepared for Frank's grand entrance. I say it because he likes to hang out in the hallway, I can see him through a mirror and few other doors, but he just sits there, making the guard wait. He watches me, gauging me, and my response to his waiting. I'm seeing if he waits for a certain level of impatience. As he finally entered, I wasn't going to be the first to talk. I just sat there quietly, patiently waiting.

"Neil, how is your day going? A little bit of a later start than normal today. Did you have a date before me?"

"Judging by the clue you gave me yesterday as I left, you know more than you're letting on. I'm not going to play a game of cat and mouse; you can simply tell me how much you know or keep it to yourself. Either way, you know that I know that you know some stuff, and that's fine by me." Frank was smiling.

"I had hoped you caught on to the real reason why I spoke yesterday before I left. You have learned a lot over the years of our interactions. I had hoped you wouldn't think I was merely trying to get under your skin. How did the meeting go with Mr. Gaines?"

Okay, now it's getting a little old. I didn't tell anyone at the prison about my meeting with Gaines Chemical. He could be fishing for information, or he could be communicating with someone on the outside. Do I have an informant on the inside of my team? I doubt it's us, but the thought has crossed my mind that he had someone inside the bureau still. The more logical idea is that the phone calls into the prison from outside somehow involve this crazy jackass.

"I have bigger things to worry about than why you're fishing for information on a case outside of these walls. Let's focus on turning your research into the culminating event you so wish it to be." Maybe some flattery will get Cappelano back on track.

"I see you're trying to placate my finer side. It will work for now, especially since the last couple of days I feel we have not put in the work I had hoped we would." Frank looked put off.

"That's on you, old buddy. You're the one who doesn't seem to want to stay on topic. When I try to get you to explain to me in detail what you were doing from the starting point of when you left the FBI, you go off on some tangent about the concept of what you were doing. I understand it's not just killing, you were finding your voice, finding your tone in what you were doing, but that's not why we're here." Is he lost, or just stubborn on this subject?

"I know, Neil, but you have to understand, you make it sound so dirty sometimes, and I don't want to respond in kind. I would like it to be spoken about in the proper tone." Frank is starting to lose it, seriously.

"Frank, let me walk you through this as simply as I can. You killed a shit ton of people, you told everyone your reason for doing it was to explain to and teach others the motivation that someone goes through. Now we are at the teaching part, and you aren't saying shit. Essentially I'm calling bullshit on you, and I feel you're struggling with it yourself. You're starting to realize maybe the world you created to make yourself feel better on your killing spree isn't as airtight as you thought."

He stood up, leaned into me and damn near yelled,

"Guard, I'm done here! Fuck you, Neil, I don't need this shit."

"See, this is what I'm talking about, you can't even face me, the one guy who was there all these years, but you somehow want to be looked at as some great teacher. Quit on me now, and I'm never coming back." Right then, I pulled out a PayDay, set it on the table, leaned back, and stared him down.

"Bribery, sugar bribery. What do you think, I'm seven years old or something?"

But he took the candy bar and started eating it. Right then, the guard at the door stuck his head in and asked if Frank still wanted to leave. Cappelano changed his mind. Apparently I saved this whole thing with some peanuts, caramel, and nougat.

"As you sit there quietly, please tell me how we make this work. If you want to tell your story, but by certain rules, inform me so we can be on the same page. Don't get upset when I break some unwritten rule."

"You're right. I haven't been playing nice, and I have been getting worked up. This has been much harder than I had anticipated. As I walk through it with you, I just get emotional. There is no good reason why, it just happens."

"Frank, it's called guilt. You're dealing with the emotion of everything you did. You've never dealt with it. You were driven by some internal force. At the time, you were operating on instinct, more than likely, and minimized your emotional response. Now that you're locked up, the fight- or-flight response isn't blocking your emotional receptors, and this allows you to feel more. You are going to have to deal with this shit one way or another."

"You really think I'm dealing with some form of guilt for what I've done, in some capacity?"

"Think of it like this. You felt something when you killed. If that weren't the case, you wouldn't have done it. So there was some emotional response, which means somewhere you had to register that negative with the positive, but it was outweighed by the positive. Now that there is no positive to outweigh the negative, you are left only with the shit feelings. A massive pile of shit feelings. Me asking you to be forthright forces you to deal with them. That is why you get short, cut me off, and drone on about shit that isn't what we are really supposed to talk about."

"I guess I never thought of it like that before." He just sat back and took a deep breath.

"Why don't I take a quick call, give you a few minutes, and when I come back, we can start over again. Let's start by simply listing off who, when, and where. We won't deal with the how until you're ready. Let's work through a list, then we can have something to work off of, like a to-do list of what needs to be covered."

"Okay, I've got nothing but time. It's your show."

I stepped outside to check some imaginary messages that didn't exist, give Frank some time to collect himself, and hopefully get somewhere today. Dealing with someone such as Cappelano isn't like the movies make it out to be. It's not instant. Even with the relationship we have, it takes time to build trust to work through the emotions that come from working on either side of a case. Especially covering so many deaths, so many miles, and so much damage. It's rough, it's hard, and it's emotional on both sides. I understand it's going to take time; there is nothing easy about it.

17

There was a moment I almost didn't go through with it because he would slide into and out of lucidity.

I'll be honest: I didn't expect Neil to drop some knowledge on me. I didn't expect to really feel these emotions about all the deaths that came at my hands. At the time, everything felt right. I felt vindicated in what I was doing. Now that all I have is time on my hands to sit, contemplate, and review all the things I've done, I'm starting to work through all the lives I've taken. Even if I invest only 10 percent of the emotion that an average person would, it still adds up to a ton because of the sheer volume of lives I've taken over the years. Not to brag, but it has been a ton of lives. Just that small window of time when I left the bureau, I'm pretty sure I came close to taking a hundred.

"Guard, is there any way I can get a cup of coffee while I wait for Neil to come back?"

"I'm sure we can get you a cup of black coffee, Frank. Is that it?"

"Thanks, man, I appreciate it. I need some caffeine to settle my nerves."

"I could hear you and Neil talking. It sounds like you two got into it a couple of times this week. None of my business, but are you two getting anywhere? Just sounds like a lot of bickering."

"We're working on it; there is a lot to overcome before we can get into the meat of it all. It's going to be a slow-moving process in the beginning, like setting up a Crock-Pot or a roast. It'll take some time, but the payoff will be way worth it."

"I can see that, especially with the history the two of you guys have. It's not going to be easy. I can see how it would take some work to get through all of that history and emotion."

"Exactly."

While talking to the guard was a nice break, I wanted to spend some time thinking about all the souls I had taken during that first break from the FBI. I say first break because no one knew I was a killer yet. They still thought I was just stressed out from the loss of my nephew, but I was out there on a killing spree. Murdering teachers, waitresses, bus drivers, I even took the life of a nice old man who begged me to do it. He was dying of cancer, a war veteran, and didn't want to go out that way. Looking back, I feel bad, have remorse, not for his life, but for what his family went through. I see what Neil was talking about, it's the culmination of the murders that is starting to take its toll on me. I remember it like it was yesterday, his name was Captain Mike Adams, he was from Michigan, but when I caught up to him, he was in Columbus, Ohio. You may be asking yourself, *Why does he know so much about a guy he killed, one of many?*

Believe it or not, the two of us spoke for days. We talked about his life, what he saw, how he grew up, the choices he made, the things he regretted, and the things he was proud of. For example, he was from Michigan but went to school at Ohio State. This drove his family nuts, unsurprisingly, but made his uncle, who was living in Ohio at the time, extremely happy. Mike even played football before he joined the military; he was a linebacker for the Buckeyes, wearing number forty-two. Not hard to remember, he had it tattooed on him, and he brought it up multiple times during our talks. As his mind was slipping, that was one story he would bring up continually.

There was a moment I almost didn't go through with it because he would slide into and out of lucidity. When he wasn't lucid, he would forget that he had asked me to kill him. This made it difficult for me to act on the request; it was like dealing with two different people with completely different needs and desires within the same man. After two days of talking, getting to know him, and even staying at his house one night after a long night of drinking, we decided it was time to end the charade.

He asked that I please make it quick so that he wouldn't have to deal with the long-term pain of his illness or death at my hands. I honored his request and when he lay in bed I slit his throat, watching him fade into an eternal slumber, the doubt and stress leave with his soul. It was quite freeing to watch a man fighting so many demons and dealing with the burden of his cancer get instant relief. I could feel it leave him, all of it, the good, the bad, the indifferent. I had killed before, I had slaughtered before, but this was mercy, I hadn't done that and it was a different feeling.

I don't think I'll ever forget. We sat there talking all night. I spoke to him about things I told no one. He gave his life to his country, devoted twenty years of his life to the army, and when he was in need no one was there. This was a sad case that falls on so many veterans, but that night he served me, he gave me an ear, listened to the confessions of a killer. I spoke to him in detail, poured out my heart about the depths of the loss I felt when I took the life of my nephew, how it felt when I realized he didn't know about Tony, not to the extent I believed.

He told me he had seen things that were much worse than what I had described, and men had rationalized their behavior in the name of freedom and the pursuit of a greater good. What I was doing was not in the name of freedom or the greater good; I had yet to find a purpose. I was merely killing, finding my voice, finding my stride in what was a thirst for taking life. Michael had an odd way of calming me, though; he would reassure me like a soldier who was getting worked up during battle. He would put his arm over my shoulder. He was large, standing at 6 foot 4 and weighing nearly 250 pounds. Having Michael draped all over me weighed me down, slowed me down, almost made me feel safe. It gave you that nostalgic feeling you get when your mother would hug you, curl you up in a blanket, and tell you everything was going to be okay.

I knew it wasn't going to be okay, I knew he had to die. I knew I had to take his life, but those couple of days were great. I was able to bare my soul to someone without judgment and know it would go to the grave with him. That is an amazing feeling. I will never forget Michael. I wonder if thinking of that time is what's bringing up these feelings. He is one of the few murders in my life that carried weight to it. More than a notch in a post, he carried weight.

Forever etched in my mind and in my life, Michael Adams. I could see by this point that Neil was making his way back in. It's about time to get back on the interview train and put some work in.

18

Wait a minute. Did you just admit to having some form of guilt?

This back and forth is getting old, but it's not surprising. We have had a long relationship of cat and mouse. Even when we were partners, I was chasing his shadow. In a way, I have been chasing Frank since day one, whether it was his records at the FBI, his status, or him as a killer. Now I'm chasing down his story, going after all the lives he took. Though we have him behind bars, we have only a small understanding of what he did as a killer. We don't even have the border to this puzzle; it's frustrating and intriguing. It's mainly a pain in the ass. Like that level in a video game you just can't beat, it's brutal.

"Frank, where were we? That's right; we needed to find a way to deal with you realizing that you are finally dealing with all of the lives you took. Have any ideas yet?"

"I think we should start by listing off the lives, names, and places and minimize the details of who and what was done. That way, we will have a framework. I am not going to list every life I took, but perhaps we can do six months at a time, then work through them."

"That sounds good. Why don't we start with Tony, then your nephew, and so on? We'll work from there and compile a six-month list that we can go over."

"It's a place to start."

For the next two hours, Frank and I went back and forth, covering a large number of murders. Consistently he would remember murders out of order, and I would have to put them back into a timeline. I just started noting the dates, realizing I would have to organize them later. I could always put them on an excel sheet, put the dates in, then organize from there; it's going to be the easiest way to simplify this pile of murders he racked up. From my quick count, we're already at thirty-plus murders in six months. I'm guessing he's missing some since he rarely went five days without a kill, from what I can see in these dates. It's crazy to look at this list and see teachers, doctors, lawyers, homeless men and women, military veterans, even somewhere he said, occupation unknown. We listed out the information by victim's name, age, location, and occupation to have a starting point, a way to remind him of who we were talking about as the list grew.

Frank also realized that the point of these interviews was to compile data on him, the murders, and his approach. If he gives us data to cross-reference from a law enforcement standpoint mixed with the detail and psychological notes, we can use the combination in a new manner. It took some time for him to come to grips and for me to help find a rhythm. We eventually found a way to hit our stride, just as we have in all aspects of our unorthodox relationship. Even when I was chasing him, we hit a stride—a harmony, if you will. I did things in a way to counter his actions that no one else did.

The list kept getting more disturbing, and you could see after five hours of talking about death, and the occasional change of subject, it was starting to weigh on him.

"Frank, I think there is a ton for me to work on the rest of the week and weekend. Why don't we stop here? At least as it pertains to these case files and your work, I think we can stop here."

"Are you sure? There's not that much more. I'm okay with stopping and changing the subject for a while."

"Thank you for the heads up yesterday. Do I need to press on you more about who or what is going on, why you knew what you knew? Or can I trust you at this point?"

"If it were serious or worth your attention, I would tell you. You know my rule when it comes to you and your team. Only I can mess with you guys."

"I do remember that, even to the point of you killing a few people at the bureau, such as one Bob Hendrickson."

"I know we said we were going to focus on a list first, but Bob was one I truly enjoyed. He was a prick on so many levels: didn't give anything back to the community, treated his staff and basic people like shit all around. Even as I'm talking to you, I don't have the slightest guilt."

"Wait a minute. Did you just admit to having some form of guilt?"

"I may be a monster who killed more than a hundred, maybe hundreds of people, but I'm not a sociopath." What the hell did he just say? But he does make a point.

"Frank, you and I get along to a point because we operate at a different frequency than most. That means we understand the stress, the anxiety that come with it. We can almost be described as autistic children who are overstimulated. The difference is we absorb the stimuli, work through them, then need a drink."

"Exactly. That is why I have always been drawn to you, Neil. It wasn't about manipulating you; it was about noticing someone who had the same burden as me. Though I learned quickly, I have to work harder to get things past you. It may seem like I'm smarter, but often it's just experience and the fact that I'm a little crazier than you. It's not about intelligence."

Did this guy just give me a compliment? More importantly, did I take it and appreciate it? I think all this time with Cappelano behind bars is starting to change the dynamic between us. I mean, why wouldn't I expect it to? He isn't out on the run anymore, and I'm not chasing him down. When all that stress is removed, we almost naturally go back to our friendship in an odd way. I know, he did all the killing in these cases. It's as if Veritas was doing all the killing, but now Cappelano and I are reviewing the case files.

If I look at it like dealing with two different people, maybe I can minimize the damage to my mood. As Sheila and Maria were alluding to earlier, I have a tendency to become a shit show of myself when dealing with Cappelano. Maybe I can find a way to trick myself into handling it differently.

"I can appreciate the way you described that and I take the compliment Frank, thank you. Also, thank you for your approach to me, my team, and my family over the years. For a killer, you've always had a code, something that could be measured and counted on; at least it felt that way."

"Thank you, Neil. Are we going from jumping down each other's throats to finding common ground? I think we can get through this. I know we aren't going to star in a TV cop drama with a twist anytime soon, but I still think we might make it through this thing alive. As for my ability to gather information, I'll let you know if I think it harbors attention. Otherwise, stick to the case you're working on; don't worry about me. I'm not going to interfere with anything."

"You've not been known to be a liar since you left the bureau and didn't have to hide anymore." Frank smiled.

"You're starting to see a driving force behind me leaving in the first place. I wanted to stop the lying and all the hiding, to be myself in the open. It was liberating once I walked away and announced to you and the world that I was a killer, no longer hiding in the dark."

"I can imagine the burden that comes with hiding that kind of truth from the people around you, not to mention yourself. I think you're lying to yourself a bit when that was happening until you jumped in full force."

"It took me a bit of time to realize it. I would say it was about the third month into my spree, following the deaths of Tony and my nephew." Notice that neither he nor I use his nephew's name.

"It takes time to create a new habit, though we are talking about killing. Anything in life takes twelve to twenty-eight days just to learn, regroup, then start anew. To change and make such a large difference in your life takes time. Regardless of how any of us look at it, time is needed."

"You're looking at this more abstractly than I ever thought you would, at least up front. I knew you would get there eventually but didn't think it would be this quick. If you're up for it, I'm game to continue tomorrow."

"We'll see how the case is looking. Even though my guys aren't relying on me, I still want to make sure I'm there for them and can be effective when needed. There is also a lot of work to be done in these cases."

"On that note, after a long day, I think I'm going to head back to my cell. Have a great night, Neil."

"You too, Frank."

COLLOQUIUM

You could see Frank looked tired, spent mentally and emotionally as he walked away with the guard. When he got to the second door where I catch him looking at me and making me wait, I caught him looking back and smile a bit as he turned away. It wasn't a smile meant for me, but one for himself, one where he had found a moment he had been looking for. Since he has been in here, I'm sure he had felt at a loss, nothing was getting done, no information shared, and he was merely a rat in a cage. If he was just another inmate, what was all the death and pain for? That smile showed he was in a place where he could share freely, be open to me, as open as even he can be. Spending a decade on the run, hiding, and being secretive have ways of changing you.

Outside, in my car and making my way toward the warehouse, I heard a jam on the radio. One of those songs that makes your foot heavier than an anchor for a freighter. Crushing the gas pedal, I caught myself cruising down US 23 upward of ninety to a hundred miles an hour. This should make the trip to the office quick. I'll wait and make calls when I get there. For now, I'm going to cruise and just enjoy the music.

19

I guess I'll just have to think of all my favorite Hall of Fame baseball players and every statistic I remember from my youth to survive the night.

At the warehouse, I noticed it was getting late and the staff there was minimal. Ken had headed home for the night, but TJ and a few of his key guys were still there. We built a small dorm in the warehouse with a set of bunks with a locker room. The locker room has twenty lockers in it, a set of six showers, then a separate small area for our female employees. They have a private locker room. We didn't have it when we started building, but halfway through we realized it was a good idea. Actually, Sheila made a comment, and Ken made it happen.

"Hey TJ, how's your night going? Any breaks in the case today? Anything new on the docket?"

"Nothing major, but Ken did tell me to have you call him and Christian if I heard from you before you spoke to them." TJ looked strung out on Red Bull and coffee.

"TJ, how much caffeine have you had today? You look like you're already about to tweak, and it's not even that late."

"You know it's how I function, I go days on end, then sleep for a day or two. That's how most of us operate. It's just our routine. It works for us, especially since some days can be brutally slow. With those bunks here, we can always crash, and they're comfortable anyway."

"That's true. I've slept there a few times after late-night poker games with Ken and the guys. Not why we built them, but handy just the same. Okay, let me know as usual if anything pops up. I'll call Ken and Christian."

"Talk to you later, Neil."

As I was walking around a half-empty warehouse, I started to ask myself why the hell I drove here in the first place, forgetting that Maria wanted to hang out tonight. Walking around and digging through Ken's office, I was reminded of why Ken has a large office with an extra desk in the corner. It's for me if I'm ever around long enough to need one. We built a nice office and wing for me, but I never used it. Then we decided to turn it into TJ's office and a space for his guys. My office is a heavy bag and a small table next to it; those are all I need.

Finally out of the office and making my way back to my house, I got on the phone to Maria. Feeling like an idiot since I could have called her an hour ago, and not to mention the kiss we had earlier today, I'm playing this cool like a high-school senior boy, so dumb as shit.

"Maria, I'm sorry today has been stressful and hectic. I didn't get out of the prison until late, just now leaving the warehouse and heading home. What are you up to?"

"Just got done taking your dogs for a run; they needed it. I was about to hop in the shower. How long before you get here?"

"That's right. You still have a key for the pups and dropping in. Are we going to talk about the kiss earlier, or are you just going to play it cool?"

"You know you liked it."

"That's not the question. What are your intentions, especially with just having broken up with someone you cared for? You know how I feel about you, Maria, but I care enough to make sure your head's in the right spot."

"I don't care what all those Internet blogs say about you, you're a sweetheart."

"Really! Now you're going to have me scouring the Internet trying to find what you're talking about. You're an ass sometimes, Maria."

"I know. How long before you get here? Momma doesn't like waiting, even if she knows it's worth it."

"I'm here now. I'm actually walking in."

Maria greeted me at the door in a towel and a smile, every man's dream. The last time I had a beautiful woman over here under these circumstances, I turned her down; it was my ex-wife, Sheila. Maria, though, is so hard to say no to. I don't know how long she's going to hold it against me for doing what's right, though she may not agree with it at the time. Sheila and I, on the other hand, have such a history together we don't move the needle in either direction as much. We sit in the middle way more; that's what makes it work.

I know what's going through your mind right now: *Neil, you're standing in front of your ex-girlfriend, she's only in a towel in your house, late, and you are talking about your ex-wife. Dude, you have issues!* I know this—hell, everyone knows this—and that is why I work so hard in my life.

"Neil Baggio, come here, you sexy man. You don't mind that I came over, do you?"

"Let me see, a gorgeous woman, matched only by her intellect, is standing in my house wearing only a towel. Hmm, ya, I'm okay with it," I said, laughing.

She leaned in and laid another kiss on me that I felt in my toes. The hair on my neck stood up and made me feel like a kid in high school kissing the popular girl in school. It felt like a movie scene that I didn't deserve to be in. Especially after a long day with Cappelano, staring into Maria's eyes has me lost. We ended up in my room, where I laid her down and began kissing her all over, rolled her over, and gave her a massage, leaving her beyond relaxed. After a good twenty minutes I got up and turned on the shower for her as she looked at me perplexedly.

"Neil, what gives? I came over here to throw myself at you, and you're not going to jump me?"

"I'm using every ounce of willpower I have not to right now. I hope that it might salvage our relationship and a chance at a real relationship moving forward. I know right now you're vulnerable and hurting. It just wouldn't be right. But I'll kiss you, curl up with you, and hold you all night, no problem."

"I'm cool with that. Why did we break up again?"

"You mean besides me almost getting you fired from the FBI and lying to you about Cappelano and breaking your trust? Other than that part, not sure."

Maria smiled at me.

"At least you know it was all you, but there was also the part of me thinking Sheila was too much for me. I think I just used her as a way not to deal with the shit you just mentioned. Tell ya what, I'll hop in the shower. Can you grab me a hoodie when I get out?"

"Yeah, I still have that soft Red Wings hoodie you loved to curl up in. I'll grab it for you."

Maria got in the shower as I walked into the front room and grabbed my notes, turned on my computer, and prepped my work area to input all of the data Frank gave me. I realized I have TJ and his team just sitting there all night. Shit, I was there, had all that, and forgot about it. Oh well, I guess I'll just scan it over to him and have them input it all for me. The perks of being the boss with a team at your disposal, it's got its great moments. Sadly, it took me almost fifteen minutes to scan everything and get it over to TJ, but while I was doing that, I had time to reach out to Ken and Christian.

Christian informed me that his team had gotten confirmation of where the drugs from Gaines Chemical were coming from. What they were selling on the street, and how they were distributing it. He also said they might have an in on how Gaines Chemical's head of security is pulling all of this off without getting any exposure from the police or the community. It turns out one of our cop buddies has an informant working with the street gang they are using to distribute. Trying to get them to flip is the hard part, and they are hoping if they get me in the room with them, it might help them feel safe.

It may seem odd—hey, I still don't get it sometimes—but we carry a lot of weight around here. It's not simply because of the Cappelano case, but of all the people we employ. The part-time police officers we give overtime to, the military vets that come on and stay with us, and how active we are in the community. Ken this past year brought his wife, Grace, in full-time to run the D-Strong Campaign, a fund we created for projects we feel inspired to give to and support in the area.

"Hey Neil, what are you doing? Did your team find any new leads on the Gaines Chemical case?" Maria walked in, wearing only the hoodie and wet hair.

"Damn, you're sexy. Hard to focus when you're standing there like that. As for the case, TJ and the midnight crew are working through the footage and files they sent over."

"Well then, let's go to bed, then we can find out in the morning what they were able to pull together, if anything at all. Is Erin still sitting there, from what we know?"

"Yeah, I'm a bit concerned because we haven't had eyes on her in a while. I'm really wanting to get a set of eyes on her ASAP, at least some confirmation. One of our cop associates might have a CI that can help us with that."

"Ken and your team have more connections in this city than the Detroit PD and FBI combined."

"Yeah, I can see that."

As we curled up in bed, Maria slid right into my shoulder, that space right below my arm. As she looked up at me, she gave me a kiss on the cheek and thanked me for being me. I began to melt. Inside I was a mess, wanting to tell her I love her still, can't stop thinking about her, but it's not the time or place. Her heart is broken and on the mend. Now is not the time to drop my emotions on her. I guess I'll just have to think of all my favorite Hall of Fame baseball players and every statistic I remember from my youth to survive the night.

COLLOQUIUM

"Good night, Neil. Thank you for being so sweet. I needed this tonight."

"No problem, Maria. I still care about you. I'm always here for you. Good night."

20

I didn't get into this business to chase down comic book villain wannabe dudes.

For a change, I woke up before Maria. The perks of not drinking like a fish and being stressed out beyond belief trying to chase a crazy-ass killer. I rolled out of bed, no alarm at four in the morning. Now, most days, just the smell of coffee from my auto coffeepot starting is enough to get me going. Obviously it depends on the night and what I'm doing in the morning. Since the end of the Cappelano chase and the time I spent in Poland, I've spent more time working on getting into a healthier routine.

The girls woke up slowly, eased their way out of bed, and made their way to the back door, where they shot out like cannons into the yard. As I sat there sipping my coffee, I took out my phone and started scrolling through emails, seeing what TJ and the crew had come up with sifting through footage. TJs memos on everything seem to show lots of discrepancies, which we already knew from the footage. He put a list of witnesses together, along with synopses of their statements.

As I started reading and making mental notes of each person involved in the case, I couldn't help but hear Maria getting up in the room. I poured her a cup of coffee, made it just how she liked it, and walked into the room.

"Here you go, cutie. Just the way you like it."

"You mean with a handsome gentleman early in the morning handing it to me."

"Flattery will get you everywhere, Agent Garcia." She blushed a bit and smiled.

"You know I love it when you call me that, especially when we're playing around."

"I know. I think this is the first time I've ever woken up before you, I think I could get used to this."

"You mean me staying over, seeing you more often, curling up?"

"You know I miss it, I think we both do. We were a great couple; life just got in the way. Cappelano got in the way."

"Fair enough. I'm open to trying it again if you are. I really am, it's not just the heartache talking. It's why my ex and I broke up, same with the last two guys. They said they can tell I'm not over you."

"Really, you never said anything to me about it." Nor would she.

"I wasn't ready to deal with it myself, but I finally realized it's time to give it a shot all the way, not let the petty things stop me. I really care about you, Neil. I miss you."

I leaned in and gave her a passionate kiss, one for the ages. You have to understand this woman drives me nuts, in all the right ways. We rolled around for a few minutes in bed, eventually ending up both leaving with smiles on our face for the morning.

I'm sensing a pattern I have with the women in my life, but I really don't want to get into that right now. For now, I'm going to enjoy the time I'm spending with Maria and just go from there. Keeping it simple for a change.

"That's what I came over for, the old Neil full service," Maria said with a grin.

"I'm glad I could leave you with a smile. Why don't you head out, get cleaned up, and into work? I've got to meet up with Christian and his team at seven this morning. I'll let you know if anything comes up."

"Can I shower here first before I head out?"

"You know the answer, and it's because that shower is awesome with extra steam jets, isn't it?"

"Maybe. Are you going to be here when I get out?" Maria said, hinting at me to join her.

"No, I think I'm going to swing by the office, hit the shit out of the heavy bag for a bit, review this info, and then head out to FCI Milan, depending on the briefing with Ken this morning."

"Suit yourself. I know you have a lot on your case. I'm finally meeting up with Gaines's assistant today. We tried the other night but couldn't connect. I hope I can get some information out of her; we're meeting up at Bar Louie around six if you're free."

"Send me a calendar reminder with a two-hour lead time to make sure I can get there. I'll do my best."

"Sounds good. Have a great day and good luck."

I gave Maria a quick kiss, grabbed my stuff, and headed out to the warehouse to get a workout in before the team got in. Usually Ken and Christian come in at about eight or nine in the morning. I should be able to pull in around seven. This will give me enough time to get a good sweat in, followed by a quick shower in the locker room. There are two private showers built in the warehouse for Ken and me, but I've essentially given one of them to TJ, since he pretty much lives in the warehouse two thirds of the week.

I used the locker room showers; they're always spotless. We used to have a self-cleaning policy, but that quickly got nasty. We decided to hire a cleaning crew to come in regularly to ensure we are not living in filth. As I made my way in through the empty building to the back, where the gym is, I laid out my notes and opened my laptop to review the work TJ had done. As I was putting on my wraps, I decided to make my morning a bit more efficient and sent a text to Ken and Christian, letting them know I was back in the gym. I may have told them to head back and bring a cup of coffee with them.

Thirty minutes in, I noticed a pattern in the data that TJ had put together from my interviews with Cappelano. He never went longer than four days without killing, and he rotated between sexes. I wonder if he did that knowingly or subconsciously. He would kill a woman, then a man, and so forth. This went on for almost forty murders over six months, never repeating genders in a row.

Hitting the heavy bag clears my mind, allows me to reset from the day, from a shit week. I can let out that aggression, the stress that has been pent up all week. With each punch, hit of the bag, I turn into releasing the frustrations that have built up. I was dripping wet with sweat, working on the files, hitting the bag in intervals of three to five minutes when I heard Christian and Ken make their way in.

"I'm not sure I'm going to get used to seeing Neil in here early. It just seems odd, doesn't it, Christian?"

"This shit is odd. I miss when you would come in after eleven," Christian said with a smile as he handed me a coffee.

"Very funny, guys. I'm trying to better myself, be healthier, and be better for the company. Here you guys are giving me shit for improving."

"Neil, we're not quite sure if it's going to be better or not just yet. Case closure is more important than your health. Sorry, just the way it is." Ken was partially true.

"I guess we'll see how the next couple of weeks work out. If I'm not hung over, I might not get the bright idea to drive through any buildings, though."

"You did some of your best work tired and cross-eyed." Ken knows me best.

"Hey, I was there for that last one, that's why we're worried. We need that, Neil."

"Christian, when the time arises, I'm sure I'll be there. Don't you worry, crazy doesn't go away because it drinks more coffee." In unison, they laughed and said, "Good point."

After a few minutes of shit talking, I informed them of where I was with Cappelano. I then asked Ken to get a few people assigned to tracking down as much info on these murders across the country as we can. Since it isn't time-sensitive, it's a great job for some of our newest team members, maybe have someone on TJ's team to oversee it. Christian said that he's getting frustrated sitting at that warehouse; he's going to do some recon tonight.

"Neil, as I was telling Ken earlier, I'll see if I can get a camera or two inside to get some eyes and ears in there. TJ said if I can get into the server room, we can sync to their system even if they have it shut off."

"Do you have a plan B if you can't find it or get to it? You know that's going to be mine and Ken's next question."

"I was going to attach a camera to a security light or two, especially if I can find where they're keeping Erin. I know we can't move her just yet because it'll blow up the case."

"Exactly! This case is hard because we need to keep Erin safe, but we also have to ensure we tie as many crimes to Gaines Chemical and their CEO, Jason."

"Do you ever get the feeling we replaced one evil villain, Cappelano, with another?" Christian has a point.

"Well, Christian, just as you said about my closure rate, only time will tell."

As we sat there talking about the similarities of Jason Gaines and those of Kingpin, we wondered if he was using him as a road map. Don't laugh, it lines up if you think about it. He is using a legitimate company to run drugs throughout the city, controlling multiple facets of the city. Still, he's doing it from the confines of his CEO chair. He does a fairly good job of allowing his team's hands to get dirty while keeping his squeaky clean. Today is going to be one of those days. I can already tell that I'm going to merely be along for the ride, merely spectating.

Ken and Christian dipped out quickly after we got caught up on our directions for the day. Ken and TJ are leading a team tracking down the data from Cappelano and looking into more concrete connections between Gaines Chemical and all the drug running from the street gangs Christian has spotted them with in their warehouses. The short version is, we are trying to track down the money. It has to exchange hands somewhere; that's how the bureau and we are going to eventually get the operation to stop. We also have to figure out how to get Erin out of there.

All showered up and halfway to FCI Milan, I realized this was going to be a quick trip; my head wasn't in it. Part of me felt like I needed to give him some attention, keep up the routine to ensure we can work through this, and build on it. I was going to go over the list with him, see if anything is missing, point out the holes that I feel are missing, and see if he agrees. Then I might pick his brain on Gaines Chemical and the CEO who wants to be a supervillain. Someone needs to have a conversation, probably me, to explain to this egotistical jerkoff that I didn't get into this business to chase down comic book villain wannabe dudes.

As I mentioned earlier, my brain is covering so many topics right now, I can barely focus on what is in front of me. For example, the cars that I nearly ran off the road on my way to the prison. I made it here in record time. Breezed through the security checks, barely talked to any guards, mainly burying my head into my phone like a teenage girl the week before prom. Now I find myself sitting down in the room that will eat up so much of my life.

"Neil, you look a bit off your game today. Do you need some coffee? Should I ask one of the guards to get some for you?"

"Frank, though I appreciate the kindness I'll be okay, just working in all highway lanes of my brain right now, starting to get backed up. Once I work through some things, I should be okay, like some of these holes I think I found in your timeline, it might help free up some mental capacity if you help clear the air."

"Well, let's see what you have," he said as he grabbed the sheet from me and started to look over it.

"Let me grab a pen for you, so you can fill in any spots you see that might be missing info."

"I see the pattern you're speaking of; let me think about a few of these for a few minutes."

Frank sat there writing diligently, then stopping, thinking for a moment, then he would be writing again. This went on for a few minutes with no speaking. It was starting to get eerie in here, but I didn't want to step in and throw him off his rhythm.

"Frank, hey, you've been going at this for a good twenty minutes. What gives?"

"The first ten minutes I was filling in the gaps, the last ten minutes I was just messing with you. The more you squirmed, the more fun I was having."

"Jesus Christ, Frank, good to see you in better spirits today. So what do you have for me?"

"There are a few missing murders, but I just remember the cities, not the people. Maybe you can pull some files from the dates and cities and we can figure it out together, like a puzzle. The other two months were times I was sick; I just couldn't do anything. Even I have my limits. I need to be at my best if I'm going to perform. I don't want to go into something and risk getting hurt or caught."

"Okay, that makes sense, even though you were going through these fast you still wanted to be efficient and careful."

"Exactly. The volume doesn't imply carelessness, it just implies that I wasn't as selective." Fair point.

"You were many things, Frank, but careless isn't one of them. I can see how life has a way of affecting even killers with an agenda or plan. The flu doesn't care who you are."

Part of me knows that Frank knows precisely what he is doing. I'm certain that he is aware of the cases that are missing, but he is stuck inside, he needs some form of a chase, a case, or a riddle to make me solve. I'll play along; at least I know these are cases in the past and he is not out there killing anymore. I miss chasing him a bit, not the stress, but just having it there, it's almost like smoking a cigarette with Frank. You know it's horrible for your health, but you still miss it.

"Neil, you are correct, life has a way of getting in the way. Remember, I still had to shop for groceries, do laundry, and I would even get sick. Just like the rest of us, life would get in the way."

"Frank, hold up! There is no way you just told me that laundry would get in the way of your killing schedule. This isn't taking the kids to soccer practice. You were taking lives, I feel like laundry would come in second or third on that list." This argument is insane right now.

"Everyone assumes that killers are heartless robots; we're not. We have lives just like the rest of you. I had bad days just like everyone else, there were days I didn't feel myself, days I was stressed out about you and the bureau. I mean, you were never close to me until the very end, but you know what I mean." Nice burn, Frank.

"I understand we're all human, I also understand that is what we are here for. It's to have these conversations to gather this information and compile a bigger psych profile than ever before. One might say that it was a daunting task to balance everyday life and your extracurricular activities." I mean killing a shit ton of people, but you get it.

"Yes, Neil, it's not that easy, it never was. There were easier days than others, but regularly it was a struggle to get through the day. In those first six months, I fought to find direction until I realized I wanted to push you. Use my newfound freedom and thirst for knowledge of killing. That's when I came alive and gained a second wind that carried me through until you found me in Mexico."

"That's one hell of a long wind, Frank. That covers a lot of years, these conversations, these days are going to take a long time, but I think we will get there. I actually have to get going. I have a few meetings I need to get into, but I wanted to stop in, go over these with you, and see what we could find."

"I guess there is no other way you can get ahold of me. It's not like you can email or call me. Unless you find a way to let, the warden allows it."

"That's not going to happen. He's not a fan of mine, but I'll work on buttering him up."

"Thanks, Neil, be safe out there. I'll let you know if the situation I'm aware of requires your attention. For now, I still don't think it does."

I made a quick exit. Frank and I have gone so many rounds we simply know there will be another day, and we leave it at that. I noticed that lately Colby can't look me in the eyes. Probably because he's figured out that I'm aware of the shit he's gotten into and knows that he lost his chance at long-term money. He chose his side; he must stick with it. He just chose the wrong side, but hey, we all must live with our choices.

For now I need to get out of here, head over to Gaines Chemical to mess with Jason and his staff a bit, rile some feathers, and see what turns up. I know Maria and Mr. Gaines's assistant are supposed to meet up for drinks soon; I should be able to get him at the tail end of the day.

21

I'll take my martini without everything except the gin, and a few
ice cubes.

As I cruised down US 23 enjoying the curves, dips, and tight turns at high speed, I remembered joking how I felt today would be one of those days when I would be along for the ride. Barely there half the day, enjoying it, but just cruising. I didn't even turn on the radio, I just drove. Before I left the prison, I sent Sheila a message checking in on her and Carol Lynn. Asking her to call, we needed to talk about Maria and me trying it again. I know Sheila will support it; I just like to be up front. I also don't want Sheila coming over for a late-night surprise if Maria is already over. Wait, maybe I shouldn't tell her, and I can just see where this goes. I'm kidding, but come on, you know any guy would have that thought for at least thirty seconds, minutes, days, maybe days.

As I pulled in and parked, I saw Sheila had texted me back. She noticed that Maria had spent the night last night. She figured that's why I needed to talk. She's busy most of the day, but she said we can talk tomorrow. This is why we get along and make it work, we're both nuts. Distracted and thinking through twenty different things, realizing it's already four thirty in the afternoon, I needed to let Maria know what was going on, so I shot her a message. I then walked into the lobby with my laptop and notes and sat down in one of the chairs and began to work, just sitting there, minding my own business. Let's see how long it takes for someone to notice the FBI/BCI investigator Neil Baggio sitting in the lobby. Anyone want to get in on the wager? I'm taking three-to-one odds for fifteen minutes.

I was sitting there working away, emailing TJ the updated notes from Cappelano, having him and his team continue the search. Calling Christian and going over the case, his plan for the night. Yes, I was talking to Christian about him breaking into a Gaines Chemical warehouse while I was sitting in the lobby of Gaines Chemical's headquarters. I may have taken Ken and Christian's banter this morning as a challenge like the inner fifteen-year-old in me would have.

"Hang on, Christian, some lady is being rude." This is going to be fun.

"Sir, I've noticed you sitting here for a while. Are you waiting on an appointment?"

"I was going to try and speak to Mr. Gaines. My name is Neil Baggio from BCI and the FBI. I was trying to get some work caught up before I came to see if he was free. My apologies."

"We all know who you are, Mr. Baggio. I will ring up to Mr. Gaines's office and see if he can make time for you."

After a quick three or four minutes, I noticed Mr. Gaines's assistant damn near sprinting down the stairs and toward me. Walking as fast as she could without running, it was funny to watch, since she was dressed to kill in tall heels and a tight skirt. My assumption is she needs to keep up that appearance to ensure her employment as Mr. Gaines's assistant.

"Mr. Baggio, what are you doing here? I mean, we weren't expecting you. Is everything okay?"

"Everything is fine. I just had some follow-up questions for Mr. Gaines, figured I would stop by since I was in the area." As we made our way into the corridor toward the elevators, she pulled me aside.

"Mr. Baggio, you know I'm heading out soon. What are you doing?"

"Don't worry, I'll get you out of there ASAP, I'll make sure of it. After a few minutes, ask your boss if you can leave and I'll make sure to encourage it gently if he doesn't oblige."

"Okay, I hope you know what you're doing." Me too.

COLLOQUIUM

In the elevator, there was an awkward silence—not surprisingly, she was nervous. I'm used to this environment. She's a twentysomething girl doing her best to do what she feels is right and keep her shit together at the same time. Maria will handle her with care and look out for her; if she feels she's not up for it, she'll give her an out so she doesn't feel bad. That's just how Maria is; she isn't going to put someone in harm's way—other than me, perhaps.

Here we go again, the office of all offices, the one that is designed to make you feel like you fell into a comic book. I'm telling you this guy has visions of being an evil villain. I hope he doesn't see me as the hero or protagonist in his story. Judging by that shit-eating grin he is wearing right now, this is going to be one of those evil villains backstory meetings. Why the hell did I think coming here was a good idea?

"Mr. Gaines, I don't think I can ever get over how amazing this office is. How are you doing today?"

"Neil, my man. I'm doing great, as always. What brings you by the office today, besides the free Wi-Fi in the lobby?"

"Oh, you saw that. I was just trying to play catch up on a few things and wasn't about to waste your time."

"Well, you're here. What can we do for you? Was there any issue with the information my team sent over?"

"There were some discrepancies in the data, but our team, the FBI, and your team are working through it. I don't think it's anything that concerns you and me."

"I like the way you think; let the small things go to the small people." Not what I said, but okay douche bag.

"Some people don't understand the stress of running a big company. I can't compare to what Gaines Chemical is, but I can relate to stress."

At this moment his assistant stuck her head in, and you could tell he was a bit irritated. I think he was about to go off on a spiel.

"Sir, it's a little after five, and I'm meeting a friend for dinner. Can I get out of here, or do you need anything else?" She is playing it cool.

"Mr. Gaines, don't keep her here on my accord. I know the way out, I can leave if you need me to."

"No, Neil, you stay. As for you, honey, you can head out, we'll be fine. Neil, would you care for a drink?" Did he just call her "honey"? Yuck.

"Sure, what are you pouring?" Anything to rinse this taste from my mouth, he called her "honey."

"I'm going to pour myself a martini. Care to partake?"

"I'll take my martini without everything except the gin, and a few ice cubes."

"Sounds good, then. A gin on the rocks for Mr. Baggio."

"I don't like anything coming between me and my liquor. Other than some ice and the occasional peel of citrus."

Twenty minutes into bullshitting and small talking, the conversational tone changed drastically. I noticed he had checked his phone a few times throughout the conversation. Maria messaged me a few times, noting that his assistant hadn't made it to their meeting yet. She wasn't answering her cell phone. I told her to call the warehouse and ask TJ for help, he could try to track her cell phone.

"I've heard a lot of things about you. I even tried to dig information out of your greatest adversary, but he wouldn't budge. He told me you're off-limits, though I tried. I guess we will see how his night ends up, such a shame. Back to the great Neil Baggio, the man that brought down Veritas and countless others." Told ya, this SOB thinks he's Kingpin.

"Mr. Gaines, you're the one that was talking to Cappelano in prison, getting to the guards. I can only assume you know more than you're letting on about my team and me then, and our understanding of your involvement with the local gangs."

"I'm just an upstanding citizen, Mr. Baggio. Whether or not some of my associates make poor decisions with whom they associate with, there is nothing I can do for them. If my head of security, Bryan, goes about associating with gangsters, I won't claim accountability for him. I am not responsible for his actions, publicly."

"Let me guess, privately you'll tell me otherwise."

"I knew you were a quick study; I also was pleased when I heard you were on this case. It meant I was going to get a chance to interact with you much sooner than I had anticipated. It made me have to alter some plans, but that's the best part, adapting to such a great man such as yourself." This dude is talking in circles; maybe he started drinking at noon.

"Let me save you some oxygen then, or maybe I will burst your bubble. You are more than a simple CEO; you are a drug-peddling street gangster, dressed to kill, willing to kill, and ruthless for success."

"I'm no mere gangster, Mr. Baggio, I'm a pariah in society. The only problem is that no one knows it, and no one will know it. You may get me on some trumped-up charges, tax fraud, et cetera. Yet I will still operate in the shadows. I will grow my company, my reach in the underground, and continue to wreak havoc on this city. Detroit is mine; you and everyone else in it are merely my guests."

He grabbed his phone as he noticed it blinking, looks as though he turned off his ringer as not to be disturbed but still paying attention. I could barely hear him, but it sounded like he said, "Did you get both? Oh, shit." I texted Ken right away, to call Maria, track her down, track down Gaines's assistant from the cell phone number Maria last called right after we spoke at five forty-five.

"I'm going to assume you are aware of what is going on, Neil. Welcome to the game, welcome to the hunt, or as I like to call it, welcome to the chessboard. May the better man win, and remember to protect your queen, even if you have to sacrifice a few pawns."

COLLOQUIUM

I didn't even say good-bye. I just rushed out the building, went sprinting down the stairs, skipping the elevator. Skipping whole flights of steps, leaping down, sprinting, feeling my heart rise in my throat. Running out of the door to the street, I looked back to the seventh floor to see Mr. Gaines staring at me, smiling, making a toasting gesture. I hopped in my car, peeled out, and called Ken.

"Ken, get in the crown Vic now. Is it still fully loaded?"

"You know it always is, for just an occasion. We going to war?"

"Meet me at the warehouse, call Christian and Terrance, tell them to get ready to roll. Also, call any cops we can trust; this is going to get ugly."

"I'm on it, Neil. I'll meet you there ASAP."

Why do these crazy fucking guys love challenging me? What is it with them? I get it, I'm good at what I do, but that doesn't mean you have to go and kill or set up some amazing scheme to challenge me. I'll tell you what, if Gaines touches Maria, I might let Cappelano out to help me murder his ass and hide his body. You don't fuck with my people, not like this, not on my watch.

22

I saw Ken reaching in for me. He came back; he always comes back.

It's seven at night, the sun is starting to go down, you can feel the cool air drop to freezing temps. As we talk to each other you can see the words fill the air and crystallize. Ken was only a few minutes behind me. The Dearborn warehouse isn't too far from where we are, and I was already speeding down Metro Parkway, ripping through red lights. I figured if I got pulled over, we could use the help with any cops.

"Ken, did we get ahold of any of our friends?"

"We have a few on patrol today that will keep an eye out, but this city is his; no one will come here without their permission. We are flying solo. I tried calling Maria a bunch to see what's going on, still no answer. TJ is trying to ping her phone for a location; he said he'd call or text us ASAP."

"Christian, do you have any plan for how we can get in there, or how many guys you think might be in there?" My heart is thudding, and my adrenaline has me on a psycho level.

"Well, I saw a van pull in about fifteen minutes ago; it was there for only a short while before it pulled out. I'm not sure if they dropped off or picked up. Terrance is on the other side of the building with one of the newer team members but an old member of his squad, so he's ready to enter."

"Enter? You guys think the only move we have is to go in, don't you?"

"Neil, we've waited long enough, it's time to go in, take on the fire. If it's a street gang, it won't be hard for guys like us. It's still a risk, but it's the right move."

"Okay, let's stack up. Christian, grab your rifle and find a perch, communicate to the rest of the team, and keep a lookout. Ken and I have done plenty of these cowboy runs, we got another in us."

"Speak for yourself, Neil. I've been behind a desk, but it feels good to get out, that's for damn sure."

We waited ten more minutes for the sun to go down, then went to the doors and stacked up. Terrance and his partner on one door, myself and Ken on the other. It felt like all our heartbeats began to sync as we lined up, even the guys on the other side of the building. We were ready, focused on the task at hand. Christian started the count, and when he got to one, we entered.

Stacked up with Ken, we turned the corner. Ken noticed there were a small group of guys heading our way.

"Get ready, Neil."

We started taking fire, quickly returned it, and two went down quickly. The others started to find shelter, shooting blindly around walls. Ken and I began working our way around the room, trying to get a better angle. Christian told the two of us to duck, and as we crouched deep you could hear a slam in the wall. A large hole where the large bullet pierced the wall appeared, and the shooting stopped. We approached slowly to find a man down, and we kicked the gun away. Ken pulled out some zip ties and secured his hands quickly.

As Ken stated, this isn't our first rodeo; we've been doing this dumb shit for some time. Entering the next room, I couldn't make out what Terrance was saying, then it all made sense quickly. Bomb.

We started booking it back the way we came in. Barely to the door, you could hear the explosion erupt, the combustion creating a loud smack that felt like someone popped your eardrum while you were sleeping. Let me be the first, or fifth, to explain to you. That movie shit where they walk away from an explosion is bullshit. Ken and I got tossed around like rag dolls. Ken made it out the door, but his arm got scraped up badly from some metal. I, on the other hand, was tossed into a garage door. "Slammed" is a better description. As I stumbled toward the door with debris and fire behind me, I saw Ken reaching in for me. He came back; he always comes back. As our two old asses limped away from the building on fire, and starting to come down, I looked to Christian on the rooftop. Our comms were shot; neither Ken nor I knew if Terrance or his partner made it out.

"Ken, are you okay? I'm pretty banged up, but I'll survive. I didn't see anyone in there, at least not any of our people, or Erin."

"I didn't see anything. I'm trying to see if Terrance made it out; maybe I can call him since our comms are shot. Nope, my phone is smashed to shit. What about your phone?"

"Nope. Mine is smashed too."

"Christian is almost down here. Let's see what he says."

"Hey guys, I haven't heard from Terrance yet; let's double back and head around. One of you stay here, see if they come through."

"I'll stay. Neil, you and Christian go look for them."

"Christian, give me your phone. I'm going to call TJ and have him start setting up new phones for Ken and me; ours are FUBAR."

"I see Terrance, but I don't see his partner. I didn't even get the guy's name, he just started with us recently."

"Guys, he didn't make it out. He was the one that saw the bomb, he told me to go, grabbed it, and ran with it inward. It had only ten seconds on it. Had he not done that I don't think I would have made it, not sure any of us would have. It was next to a bunch of chemicals that probably would have blown this place sky high fast as shit."

"Terrance, you going to be okay?"

"Yeah, but we need to get out of here. This place is going to be crawling with cops, and not the friendly kind, either. I didn't see Maria or Erin in there, no signs of anyone but a few lowlifes and that big-ass bomb."

"My guess is that the van that came by earlier picked up Erin and moved her to a new location. I'll have TJ start tracking it, we'll have the FBI, and have the locals put out an APB."

"We'll have to do it from the office, since our phones are smashed to shit. Terrance, Christian, let's get out of here, clean up, meet back at the warehouse."

Heading back to the office was brutal, with no phone, no way to call anyone, just driving pissed and angry. I wanted to ring that asshole's neck. I kept hearing him call his assistant "honey" in that douche bag voice. I just know he's sitting there with the three of them saying creepy shit like that. I was running red lights, rolling stop signs, swerving all over. I was driving like an old lady late for a bingo knowing it's her lucky night—hey, that shit's real. We all pulled in within a few minutes of each other except Christian, he was nowhere to be found. Then again, he didn't get his ass blown up, and his phone is working. Where did he go?

"TJ, where the hell is Christian? Can you pull up his location?"

"It looks like he's at Gaines Chemical headquarters, or at least close to it. My guess is that he's looking for that van; he has a hunch that they are there or heading back there."

"Not a bad idea. Mr. Gaines is arrogant enough to bring them back there. He feels untouchable."

"Here's your phone and Ken's. It has the essential apps, your phone contacts, email, et cetera, all backed up already."

"You rock, man. How many of these do we keep in stock?" I break a lot of phones.

"I got tired of you getting mad, so I bought a few refurbished phones of the models you guys use, just in case. I ordered new ones, too; they'll be here in two days."

"Full service from TJ, as usual. Back to what the fuck just happened. Ken, call Mike over at the bureau, fill him in with what's going on, especially with Maria. TJ, start an active trace on Mr. Gaines's cell at all times; I want it up on one of the screens. I also want you tracking his head of security, but for him just hack his security system at home, so we know when he comes and goes."

"On it, boss man."

"I'm going to call Christian and see what he's working on. Terrance, are you going to be okay?"

"Yes, I'm going to talk with Ken and your friend Mike at the FBI to ensure my buddy, or what's left, is taken care of properly."

I gave Terrance the biggest hug—we held it for a good minute and just took a deep breath. It was a moment when we knew we wouldn't let this shit go without a cost to Gaines. I had TJ get a list together of all the known associates, street gangs, etc., and all the addresses that might be stash houses. I was going to send the team on some hunts. They would be looking for drug houses, lighting them ablaze and burning some cash and drugs to dent the operations of one Gaines Chemical.

"Christian, TJ said it looks like you headed toward the Gaines Chemical headquarters. Is that true? What are you seeing over there?"

"Right now I can't get a clear shot from my vantage because of how dark it is, but I verified that the van from earlier is here. And the lights are on in Mr. Gaines's office. Do we know anyone that can get me into any of these buildings? I need to get to the seventh floor or above to look into that office."

"I'll put TJ's guys on it. We might have someone who works security in one of the buildings. Give us a few minutes."

"Don't take too long; I don't want to waste any more time."

It took TJ and the crew ten minutes to find out we had a freelance part-timer work with us who happens to work in a building over there. Since drastic times call for drastic measures, I grabbed his number and texted him.

Hey, bro, this is Neil! From BCI. I need your help ASAP on an urgent case. Call me.

Within a minute my phone was ringing, and he was beyond helpful. Though he wasn't there, he called up, got Christian in, and access to the eighth floor. This gave him the best view possible to look directly into Mr. Gaines's office.

"Hey Neil, we have a bit of a problem." Ken and TJ don't look good.

"What is it?"

"You have to go back to prison. Apparently Frank stabbed a guard and killed him. He won't talk to anyone other than you. It's not looking good."

"You know what this is. It's Gaines, what the fuck, they are going to lock me down in there, I know it."

"I need to find a way to be protected there. I need a trump card. I need to make a phone call."

Right then I looked down to see a text from Christian.

All three ladies are in his office! Erin, his assistant, and Maria. The assistant isn't tied up!

23

It should be fun; maybe TNT or TBS will make a shitty movie
out of this experience.

I really don't want to call them, but I have no choice. There is
only one other person I can bring into this situation that might
be able to help me get through this shit. I need to call Mike at
the FBI and see if he can help me pull rank with the warden,
but I can't let too many people know. It's the only way I'm
going to survive this thing, get in, deal with Frank, and get out.
I know you're thinking, *Don't go, you dumb ass*. Well, this is the
game, these are the rules, this is the chessboard that Mr. Gaines
has set up.

"Mike, it's Neil. Did Ken explain to you what's going on?"

"Yes, and we already have a team on site at the warehouse.
With the explosion and us investigating him already we were
on site quickly. We'll take care of your guy. What's this about?
We're also looking for Maria, I have a team on it."

"Well, I can save you time on that one, just not sure you can
do anything with it."

"You know where they are, don't you? What's the
problem?"

"He has them at his headquarters, but something isn't right. He would know you can walk in there to grab your agent; he blew up his own building. There's a bigger game here. He's got to be prepping for a fight."

"Without real cause, there's not much we can do. Without a threat to her or demand for her, our hands are tied. You already know that; you also know the local police won't help you for shit. Again, what can I do for you?"

"To play this guy's game, I need to go to the prison and see Cappelano. He apparently killed a guard. I'm fairly sure the guard was trying to kill Cappelano and lost. I think they're going to try to kill me or lock me in there. What I need from you is a trump card. Any way you can get in there with some agents to the warden's office and ensure my safe and quick exit?"

"Under normal circumstances I might say no, but this is Maria, and you have an impeccable track record for being correct when dealing with sociopaths. I guess I'll just take your lead on this. I'll meet you at FCI Milan. I'll call a judge to be safe and make sure they're ready for a court order if we need something. Making Cappelano a protected inmate, for instance, as well as you have safe passage in and out."

"All right, see you there."

I can't believe it has come down to me dealing with dirty guards, dirty wardens, and a handful of people on the take. I guess it is unfair of me to call them all dirty. When the mortgage is due and your check isn't enough to cover all expenses, you take the money that's being handed out, simple as that. If you go in with this mentality and you're not growing the friction, but instead trying to grease by, you have a chance. It's a different world.

Almost to the prison, it's getting late. I called Christian to calm my nerves, though not the best idea, because I'm getting information on a crazy man holding Maria at gunpoint. At the same time, I'm about to walk into a prison where they are more than likely trying to hold me captive for some weird bullshit. In my current state, the more information I have, the better it will keep me moving, keep me grounded.

"Christian, what do you see? What's going on over there?"

"It looks like Mr. Gaines and his head of security, Bryan, have Erin and Maria just sitting on a couch. They have a few people around them with guns; one looks like a guy who used to work for us on a few jobs, which is crazy. It also looks like he's gearing up for war; men are starting to line up all over the neighborhoods out here. Different streets, not in front of the building and obvious, but I can see them. He's got a good twenty or so inside and another forty to fifty in the surrounding houses."

"If at any point you see them make a move on Maria, especially a violent one, Mike at the bureau said to call him and they'll move. Just make an anonymous tip to their call-in line. Without it, though, not much they can do."

"I know red tape bullshit sucks, I get protecting freedoms, but fuck, I'm here and keeping an eye on them. If needed, I can always blow his brains out and go from there. Maria can think quickly, right?" Christian has a point.

"Just wait for the guys and me. Ken should have some guys out there soon; we just don't want to spook either, so we're trying to do it right."

"Got it. Be safe, see you soon, Neil."

Walking into FCI Milan, it felt different and not because all the guards were different, it being a night shift. You could tell by the way people were looking at me, they knew something was up. The warden was still there, which would help my angle with Mike a few minutes out with a few agents to put pressure on the warden. By the time I made it to the third security door, the warden was waiting to escort me to where they were holding Cappelano.

"Neil Baggio, nice to see you tonight. I wish it were under different circumstances. I would have to say that it's not surprising. People like Cappelano are killers, they only know one way. We have him over in a holding area, but first I need you to take a call from a mutual friend."

"Let me guess, Mr. Gaines. This smells of him; this whole day does."

"He said you're a great chess player; he also said that you aren't a big fan of losing." And he handed me the phone.

"Well, Mr. Baggio, it seems as though I have your queen. What's your next move? You have something I want."

"What is it that I have that you want? What is it that you could possibly need from me other than a good ass kicking?"

"Neil, I told you. I want to know more about you and I want to get the information firsthand from the man that knows you best. However, he won't talk. I want Frank Cappelano. Until he talks, gives me everything I want, I won't release your friend Agent Garcia over here. I'll even throw in Erin for fun, just to be a good sport."

"Let me get this straight. You want a best friend who happens to be a sociopathic killer that knows me from back in the day. And you kidnapped an FBI agent thinking that's the best way to do it." Maybe he and Frank should be buddies.

"It's not for me to explain my plans to you. You need to do what I ask, or we can see how my patience wears thin and what happens next." He's trying to act like a comic book villain.

"Well, I guess I can give it the old college try." I need to buy time until Mike gets here.

"That's the spirit, Neil. Thank you for your cooperation."

Just like that, the phone went dead. Then the warden grabbed it and started to walk me down to the closed-off portion of the prison where they were keeping Frank. It kept getting darker with fewer security cameras and guards; more and more this felt like me getting stabbed. It should be fun; maybe TNT or TBS will make a shitty movie out of this experience. Steven Segal can play me, and Frank Stallone can play Cappelano. He doesn't get Sly; he gets the brother Frank. Yes, I'm cracking jokes; it's how I cope with this shit.

"Well, here we are, Neil; Frank is in there. Here is the phone, you have ten minutes to get Frank talking before Mr. Gaines will call you back."

I entered a small, dark room, no chairs, just Frank in the corner beaten pretty badly and a guard standing in the shadows. Frank whispered something to me. I couldn't make it out, and he whispered again. I made my way over to him and knelt down.

"Frank, what the hell is going on? Are you okay? What happened here, other than the obvious? I'm assuming someone tried to kill you, and you did your best to stop them from doing that."

"The guard behind you is going to kill you, Neil. Turn around now." Oh, fuck.

Right as I turned around, Frank shoved me out of the way, and the guard lunged with a shiv intended for me. As they struggled, I came up behind him, got him in a chokehold, and pulled him off Cappelano. For someone in charge of killing Frank and me, he gave up quickly. He sank to the floor in the corner and began to sob, saying "They're going to kill me, they're going to kill my family."

"I knew it was wrong, Neil, I knew it was wrong to take his money, but I needed it. I'm sorry, man, Frank is innocent, he was just defending himself earlier. The guards roughed him up pretty bad." Is that Officer Colby?

"Colby, is that you? Man, what is going on? Does Gaines have your family, or is he threatening them?"

"Yes, and I have no way of stopping it from happening other than killing you and framing Cappelano here."

"I have a better idea." Or I'm about to as soon as I come up with it.

I took a few minutes and remembered that TJ gave me the Wi-Fi info. Knowing him he preloaded that shit into this phone; he did, sweet! I was able to get a text to TJ and Ken to track down Colby's family and get them to safety. The next step was to send a text to Mike to let him know what's going on. The final step is to come up with a master plan that doesn't involve me driving a car through the front of a police station.

"Colby, Frank, are you two guys going to be okay? We are probably going to have to work together to make this shit work. I have a plan and I brought it back up just in case I needed to run some interference."

"What about my family? No offense, man, but I'm concerned about them and only them. I couldn't give two shits about you or Cappelano right now." Colby was shaking.

"I don't take offense. Neil, you good?" Frank was starting to gather himself a bit and lean up on the wall.

"Yes, I'll be fine. As for your family, Colby, some of my guys are on it as we speak. They are going to get them and make sure they are safe." I was doing my best to reassure him.

"You know Neil is a man of his word; now let's figure out how to get you two guys out of here alive. I'm stuck in this hellhole, I'm not worried about me as much, but if your plan includes me helping you escape, I'll do what I can." Nice try.

"Frank, thank you for your generosity. I think you're going to have to stay here. If the top prisoner in FCI Milan goes missing, they might shut this place down with us in it. I thought I was supposed to be getting a phone call from Mr. Gaines to check up on me and my ability to get Frank to talk. Then again, it's probably to see if I'm dead and to check in with you, Colby."

"Yes, sir, more than likely." Colby was still shaking.

"Then let me get on the phone to ensure we can sell this shit."

I got on the phone and was able to get a weak enough signal to call Mike, and explain to him what was going on. He was in the warden's office. They already had him in handcuffs. Apparently, they found plenty of reasons to arrest him in the short time they got there, along with some phone records and search warrants. Evidently the hunch to get a judge on the horn paid off for Mike. He said if Mr. Gaines calls the warden, he'll ensure he plays along, he wants his sentence to be as lenient as possible—the warden, that is.

"All right, guys, we are good, we should be able to get out of here. My FBI counterpart got the warden tied up and will make sure that he plays along by claiming I'm dead. Frank, I think Mr. Gaines is going to want to talk to you, that's what a lot of this is about. He is playing some weird twisted game to get to you to talk about me. Maybe he thinks that if I'm dead, you'll tell him about me."

"I can't make fun of or judge crazy, especially in my position. Originally I wasn't going to play along. You know my rule when it comes to you."

"No one gets to fuck with Baggio except Cappelano." Colby looked at us weirdly.

"Damn straight. I'll play along with his game as long as needed. Just let me know."

After a few minutes of planning and organizing what we would do once we sell the ruse to Mr. Gaines, I started texting the team. Letting Ken, Christian, and Mike know what is going on. How we're going to play it, and even what my overall plan would look like. How I'm going to get into the front door of the building without anyone the wiser.

I told Mike to have one of the agents meet us outside shortly with a jumpsuit that matches Cappelano's with his name on it and a prison guard's uniform for Ken. We're going to pay Mr. Gaines a visit and end this shit once and for all. Right then, the phone in Colby's hand started ringing, his hands started shaking, and he started waning.

COLLOQUIUM

I could only hear what Colby was saying in the conversation, but it wasn't too hard to figure out that he was telling Mr. Gaines that he had finished the job. I was dead and Cappelano had taken the fall for it. He said that the warden could confirm it, and he would wait for his confirmation. Once off the phone, you could see the fear in his eyes. He slumped back down to the floor and sat there, breathing heavily for a few minutes, then shallowly as he realized what was going on.

"Neil, are you sure this shit is going to work?"

"No idea, Colby, but I do know a few things. My team has your family. Didn't they send you a text with a picture so you can calm down? I know Gaines is nuts and the only way to stop him in his tracks. There is no running or hiding from guys like him."

"I should have turned to you in the first place. I'll trust you now, Neil. Even though I just tried to kill you, that didn't stop you from doing what's right for my family. Thank you, man."

"Let's focus on getting out of here, Mike just texted me saying the coast is clear. We can get out of here as soon as you think it's clear. What did Gaines tell you to do?"

"He told me to leave a burner phone here for Cappelano to use, then head over to his headquarters for my thank you. He wants to talk to Cappelano, but the way he sounded on the phone and the way you were talking, it makes me sound if I walk in there, he's going to shoot me dead on sight." Colby was starting to get it together but was still worried as shit.

"You're going to have to trust my team and me. We will get you in there, be with you, and make this work. Frank, I'm going to need you to hang up on his crazy ass when I tell you to I'll text you when we pull into the parking lot out there. Got it?"

"Neil, this is going to be the most fun I get to have for the foreseeable future. You can count on me."

Colby handed the burner phone to Cappelano. I looked at him, checked on him one more time, and Frank reassured me he was good. We walked out, made our way through the checkpoints as quickly as we could, flying through since Colby had his badge. Once outside, I quickly changed. To my surprise, Ken was waiting for us and already changed in the guard uniform, waiting with an FBI agent.

"Hey, guys. Mike sends his regards; he's dealing with a pile of shit in there. They found a room full of drugs; it looks like Gaines was using the bays here to store and ship drugs out of state, according to the warden."

"Without some concrete proof to connect it to Gaines, it's all circumstantial at best. He'll probably throw his head of security, Bryan, under the bus."

"That's what he gets paid for." Ken makes a good point.

"He wants to be Cappelano's buddy, maybe he can make a deal to be his cellmate."

"Hey guys, call me perplexed, but did I miss something?" Colby looked lost.

"Colby, we are going to have Frank hang up on Gaines if they're still talking by the time we get there. You can walk in and play the hero who brought Cappelano to the boss man. The only problem is you, Ken, and I will be heavily armed with a sniper in our back pocket covering our asses."

"Neil, please don't get insulted when I say this. You've seen one too many action movies to think this shit is going to work." He's got a good point, but I don't watch much TV.

"Colby, the crazier the idea Neil has, the better it seems to work, so let's hope at some point he asks you to shoot a hole in a fish tank or some shit, 'cause that means we're golden." I chuckled.

"Ken's a funny guy, but he has history on his side. Let's get going. Ken, since I don't see my car or yours, I'm assuming you had some guys grab them for us."

"You know it. Let's roll out in Colby's ride. We have to sell it all the way."

24

Do you know what a colloquium is, Mr. Gaines?

Welcome back to the Cappelano party. Did you guys miss me? I know I missed you. Then again, it took me getting my ass kicked by a bunch of dirty guards and almost getting shanked to get an audience with you, but it's worth it. When you're stuck in here, you'll take any chance to talk to the outside world. I guess I'm just supposed to sit here and wait for this man to call me, I wonder what it's like talking to a sociopath. I mean, I know what it's like inside my own head, but talking to someone else, that is entirely different.

I'm looking forward to seeing what he has to say; I do wonder what his endgame will be, what he wants to talk about. If Neil is correct in his assumption, I'd have to assume Mr. Gaines is going to hammer me on details about Neil. This point still lacks depth. Why kill Neil, why try to kill him, if you are intrigued by him? Unless there's the chance that he didn't die, and it's all about the charade. I noticed the phone ringing as I sat there on the floor.

"Château la Cappelano, we're taking reservations for our summer getaway. How may I direct your call?" The other line was dead air.

"Mr. Cappelano, my name is Jason Gaines, but you can call me Mr. Gaines. I am calling to become acquainted."

"Hello Mr. Gaines, the guard Mr. Colby said you would be calling. What can I do for you?"

"I would just like to talk to Mr. Cappelano. I would like to get to know you, learn from you. Find out what made you so successful at evading the great Neil Baggio."

"Well, I guess I should be talking to you. I'm in prison, and you're out there. Not to mention you killed him and found a way to pin it on me. I'm not sure how you thought this was going to get me to talk to you."

"I can pin that murder on anyone in there, make it go away, look like an accident. Just keep talking and we can make this all go away."

"Do you know what a colloquium is, Mr. Gaines?"

"A what? No, I do not."

"It's Latin for a seminar—a talk, if you will. It's a way to describe the kind of dialogue we are going to have. I guess that's what I was making Neil go through before you killed him."

"You were making Neil interview you? I was unaware of the nature of his visits. I knew he was talking to you, but I wasn't privy to the nature of what you were talking about. I had hoped to find out, though."

"We spoke of my days shortly after leaving the bureau, before I made my announcement to the world that I was a killer. The process I went through, the steps I needed to break down before I could accept it myself, then come up with a way to deal with it day in and day out. A purpose for the killing, not simply for the mere joy of it."

"I can see that. It's not like I woke up one morning and decided to become evil. It was a series of poor choices that led me down this path. One thing led to another. I enjoyed each bad decision and then found I also had a knack for it."

"I can relate to that a bit. It started off with a few justified shootings that became a bit more aggressive each time out of curiosity. Before I knew it, I was pushing the envelope way past anything I should; those decisions added up and brought me to a precipice. Is that where you feel you are now, one of those no-look-back decisions?"

I'll be honest. I really couldn't give two shits about this guy. As I'm talking to him, I'm actually fantasizing about killing him. The way he has tried to ruin my friend, attacking him, going after him in the way he did. Only I can mess with Neil because I do it out of love. But this man is doing it out of spite, fear, and anger. There is no place for a criminal like this; maybe he needs to get arrested and thrown in here with me so I can work on him a bit.

For a solid fifteen minutes I kept him talking. I noticed Neil had been texting me along the way, letting me know where they were so I could string him along and let him know I would have to let him go soon. I was getting tired of playing this game with him, he was on my last nerve, it was taking everything in me not to jump down his throat and tell him what a whiny little bitch he was being. He reminded me of a kid who is spoiled rotten his whole life only to grow up thinking the world owes him some shit. When he doesn't get it, he starts to lash out.

"I guess you could say that. Killing a person as prominent as Neil, taking on as many people as I have, and coming out on top have put me in a position to take this city over. I am looking forward to laying my plans out accordingly and fulfilling what is rightfully mine."

"If you don't mind me asking, since I am a little bit aware of what is going on, what is your plan, your endgame? From one mastermind to another, I would love to compare notes, if you will."

"I would have to say that it's the overall process of building something from scratch. Taking the drugs from our lab, selling them to consumers legally, then using that same cash to sell them on the street for double. It's amazing. I love being in the drug business, legal and otherwise."

"I guess you're saying it's mainly ego. I'd be lying if I said that for a long time ego wasn't the main driver in what I was doing."

No, it wasn't, but Neil needs me to keep this guy on. Not to mention, it is quite fun seeing where he's going to take this conversation. I miss this part of the hunt, the psychological breakdown of my victims, working through their fears, the acceptance of their fates. Though it won't be the same, I can toy with him, play with him, and get him to go down certain alleys he might not otherwise want to go down.

"I believe anyone that is as successful in what they do, especially as you and I have done, they must be driven by a healthy ego. You don't drive to perfection without it. A desire to be the best has to be coupled with an ego that is strong and dominant."

"At least in the case study of myself, you, and the former Mr. Baggio, one could say that. It's a shame you went and did that to Neil. He was formidable, and that was the best part."

"I was hoping he would overcome the obstacle; I guess he was caught off guard."

Did this guy just make a shit pun about killing my one and only friend in the world? Who makes a "guard" pun? I mean, not only is it in bad taste, it's also shit work, and he's laughing at his own joke; I haven't said a word in almost three minutes, and he's just giggling. This crazy shit show of a human being thinks he's Jerry Seinfeld.

"Yeah, I guess he didn't see it coming. Mr. Gaines, I'm going to have to let you go soon, I have to use the bathroom, then head to lights out. Though you have pull, the federal system still has its rules."

"Until next time, Mr. Cappelano. It was a pleasure making your acquaintance. I just wish it were under different circumstances."

"Likewise, Mr. Gaines. Who knows? Maybe you'll be lucky enough to see me sooner than you might expect. I'll do my best to get out of here."

I know what you're thinking, *Are you getting him off the phone already?* Well, you judgmental pricks—yes, you—I'm getting off the phone because Neil texted me saying they were about to pull into the parking lot of Gaines Chemical. That means my part is about to be over.

"If you find yourself on the outside in need of a safe place, look me up."

"Sounds great. Thanks, Mr. Gaines."

"No problem; the pleasure is all mine. Call me Jason."

Like that, we ended the conversation. I threw the phone against the wall, smashing the phone into pieces. I was so pissed dealing with that guy I couldn't take it anymore, I had to let my anger out. From being set up, almost killed, and then watching someone try to kill my friend, it was just too much. I wish I could see his face when he gets excited to see me, only to find out it's Neil and a few guys with guns. Then again, after talking to him, he's going to enjoy it.

My take on Jason Gaines is that he is a boy trapped in a man's body. He's still fighting to get the attention of his friends, doing dumb and cocky shit to impress people, and he thinks it's a good idea. Even the way he talked was immature and ill-advised. I understand that I'm a sociopathic killer. Still, at least I know how to carry on an adult conversation with proper tone and prose.

I hope Neil doesn't shoot him. I hope he kicks his ass old school. Maybe a few pistol whips, but just an old-fashioned ass kicking. He deserves to get a fat lip, black eye, and some bruised ribs. Just for that weak-ass guard pun, that is going to drive me nuts all night. If you haven't guessed, I can become fixated on things.

25

We need to get fired up, get our game face on, not lighten the
mood for a proctology visit.

Arriving at the parking lot, we had to stop before we got there
for a quick stop. Get gas, some caffeine, and do the one thing
no one seems to want to talk about. We went to the bathroom.
Even in the most famous of Christmas movies, my favorite
action movie of all time, didn't it surprise you that never once
did he ever have to go to the bathroom? Hell, sometimes I can't
go shopping without the urge hitting me because I get worked
up over spending money. You bet your ass that if I'm going
into a shoot-out, my intestines are going to be growling.

"Neil? What gives, man? You look like you're lost." Ken
flicked me between the eyes.

"I needed that, Ken. I'm not lost, just my mind wandered a
bit."

"Oh great, our fearless leader is off in dreamland moments
before we walk into a gunfight."

"Colby, calm down. As I said before, Neil does his best work in these situations. You just need to trust us. Do I look rattled? Just follow my lead and we'll be okay." Ken had a point.

"Just remember, don't question me. If I ask you to do something, just do it, and think later. Understood?"

"At this point I'm assuming the only way to survive this is to give in to the crazy. I'll get there once we walk in those doors and that adrenaline kicks in. I did undercover work for a few years. I transferred for less dangerous work."

"How'd that work out for you?" Not the best time to lighten the mood.

"Neil, really, this isn't the best time to be joking around. We need to get fired up, get our game face on, not lighten the mood for a proctology visit."

"Okay, my apologies. Let's get this over with. Where's the hood you brought, Ken? You said there is a spot where I can see out of it if I position it just right."

"Yes, also these cuffs are the broken ones. They'll be on, but you can simply flip them off and grab for either of our spare guns, whoever is closer."

"This seems like a great plan, guys. Ken, can you call Christian to check in on everything one last time?"

While Ken was checking in with Christian, I took a few moments to calm Colby down. He was worked up still about trying to kill me earlier. If you ask me, it was a pretty lame-ass attempt at killing someone. He was making an attempt. I'll give him that, but I hope he tries much harder on the seventh floor when our lives depend on it.

"All set, guys. According to Christian, there are only about seven or so guys in the building that he can count. Most of them are in the neighborhoods setting up shop, waiting on Gaines's call to arms, if or when that might come. If we surprise them, we'll have the upper hand."

"I guess this is the part of the movie where the music gets loud, the action sequence starts to build, and the audience gets to the edge of their seat. Right, guys?"

"Fuck it. Let's do this and put this asshole in his place." Colby was finally ready.

"Thataboy, here we go. Here's your hood Neil. Let's start to walk, time to shut the fuck up."

As we walked our way into the building, all I could think about was Maria, Sheila, and Carol Lynn. Getting Maria out of there alive. Making sure I made it out alive so I could spend time with the amazing women in my life. Going through the parking lot with a hood on my head, I couldn't hear and see everything, and it was an odd feeling. I had been in this building a few times, I knew where we were going, what we were doing, and what we would have to do. The moment was a bit surreal, walking through the doors watching Ken and Colby talk small talk and explain to the guards what they were doing there.

COLLOQUIUM

The guy radioed upstairs to let Gaines know what was going on; you could hear the excitement in his voice about everything. As we walked to the elevator bay, past the bathrooms, I was reminded about the moment we all took before we got here. You laugh, but it's smart thinking. Do you want to be in a gunfight about to shit yourself? I don't think so, and I bet you one of these dumb-ass guards will be fighting the urge to piss or shit when the bullets start to fly. You need every advantage you can get, even if it's an empty bladder.

The ride up the elevator felt like twenty minutes. I could feel my heart rate starting to slow, my breathing getting shallow, and everything starting to slow to a halt. Before I knew it, time was standing still. I could stop and have a meal between each breath; time ceased to exist in that elevator. I took the time to take inventory of everything we had packed, the items I had hidden. The blade on my ankle, the AR-15s on their backs, and the extra pistols on their hips. Under normal circumstances they might look out of place, but Gaines was going to war, he was ready to fight, and they were just two more soldiers.

I took a moment and nodded at Ken, and he made a gesture back. We walked out of the elevator to see a room with only three goons; Gaines. his assistant; our two ladies in distress, and the one guard that escorted us here. I didn't realize at the time, but I was wearing my blue Chuck Taylor shoes that Maria bought me last year. It was when she looked at the shoes, then smiled at me, that I realized she knew what was up.

"Mr. Colby and associate, it looks like the two of you have brought me a present. Oh, how I love presents. Here I was thinking I was talking to Cappelano while he was in prison and you guys were bringing him here the whole time. This makes me excited, very excited; I can't wait to finally get to meet the amazing Cappelano in the flesh."

Gaines stepped back and gestured to Colby and Ken to remove my hood. As they started to, he realized quickly I wasn't Frank Cappelano. The look on his face was priceless for only a mere moment; then it quickly turned to joy.

"Here you go, Mr. Gaines, your surprise."

"Neil Baggio is alive. . . . Hell, yeah!" Gaines was happy.

"I wouldn't let the game end that quickly, Mr. Gaines. As you said, it's just beginning."

"You're in handcuffs, Frank is in prison charged with murder, and I have all the leverage. What is your move? Let me see if I can figure this out."

Gaines went on a rant and I could see Ken and Colby waiting for me to do something, make the first move. I was having too much fun letting Gaines ramble on about what he thought my endgame was, how I thought I could get out of this. Sacrificing myself to let Maria go, which he thought was a great idea. He spent a good ten minutes on that one. He even had his assistant grab Maria and walk her toward the elevators, teasing good faith, which none of us believed for a minute.

I just kept letting him go; then I remembered there was a fish tank in the back corner. I could see it and had this brilliant idea. Maybe not so brilliant, but it felt so good. I leaned over to Colby and whispered to him to shoot the fish tank on my signal. His face was priceless. Ken tried so hard not to laugh, but he couldn't do it.

"What is so funny over there? Am I amusing to you three?"

"Mr. Gaines, I just made a comment about how beautiful your fish tank was. If this speech went on any longer, though, the fish might keel over and die."

As he turned around to admire his fish tank, which measured nearly six by ten feet, I leaned over to Colby and told him to light that shit up. At first, he still didn't get it, so I flipped off the handcuffs, grabbed a piece from Ken, told him to free Maria so she can help, and took off toward Gaines.

"Colby—now, bro, light it up!" Finally he grabbed the AR from his back and started.

Bullets started piercing the fish tank. The water began leaking, then eventually opened up, completely filling the room. Gaines screamed,

"Get those mother—"

Before he had even finished his sentence, I was up on him and coldcocked him. He turned to look and met my fist in unison like a perfectly thrown pass or a jab-cross combination from Rocky Marciano. He staggered for a moment and fell back, giving me a moment to survey the room. I grabbed a gun lying on the floor, probably from one of the guys Ken had knocked out, and saw Maria fighting with Gaines's assistant. Colby was stuck behind Gaines's desk, taking fire with Ken from a few guys who had just come up from the elevator.

"Hey assholes, I just knocked your boss out, might want to shoot at me." Yup, I get caught up in the moment.

"Neil, get down, you crazy ass." Ken is always worried.

I began firing at them, getting them into the elevator. It gave Ken just enough time to move to a better vantage point to flank the elevators and take out the remaining guys in the elevator. Maria was dealing with Gaines's assistant quite handily, but she was still putting up a fight. I can't wait to give her shit over it later. If I were telling this story at a bar, I might tell you Gaines's assistant had the fighting skills of a Russian KGB agent, but this is real life and she was fighting like some girl that had taken some kickboxing cardio classes.

"Neil, Gaines is back up, turn around." Oh shit, Gaines just coldcocked me back; that's fair.

"Fuck that hurt! Luckily you hit like you talk, long and slow."

"Oh, I see Mr. Baggio has jokes. Come on, asshole." Gaines hadn't realized his team was gone at this point.

"Remember to protect your queen, Gaines. I've got mine."

Just then, he glanced around the room and realized what was going on. He doubled down but didn't have it in him to give up. A lot of guys like him don't and they go down swinging. He didn't give much of a fight, but then again I hit a heavy bag almost daily and have been for years. It took only a good minute or two for it to be over. He eventually stayed down with his nose bleeding and his jaw messed up.

"Hey Ken, have we called Mike at all? Find out where the FBI is, let them know we have their agent." Maria looked at me, smiling as she made her way over.

"I used Ken's phone and called Mike; they are already rounding people up outside. Hey, Colby, can you tie up Mr. Gaines over there for us?"

"Yes, it would be my pleasure. Nice right hook, by the way," Colby said, laughing.

"Agent Garcia, are you doing okay?" I wanted to kiss her so badly, but it wasn't the place.

"Neil, just kiss the girl, for crying out loud, we can all tell you want to, even the dead guy in the corner." Ken has a point.

"I agree with Ken, I think you should kiss the girl. You did do a brave thing and saved her life, after all." Maria leaned in and kissed me.

"That's what I'm talking about. Now, that's how you end a shootout action, movie-style. Maria, I'm going to need you to change into a smaller dress and some heels, and we're going to reshoot the whole scene."

"Ha ha Ken, very funny," Maria said with a smile.

"Really, Ken, you had to go with the reshoot pun." It was funny, though.

The next two hours were a procedural nightmare involving paperwork; agents; statements; and luckily for me, a change of clothes. One of the hard parts about walking the fine line of agent and private investigator is when it comes moments like this, watching people do the paperwork. They are trying to figure out the best legal protection for my actions. I enjoyed watching the symphony of crime scene investigators, agents taking statements and arresting people. It was a sight to witness. I think my favorite part was watching Mike show up with my favorite Channel 4 News lady she was out front waiting for the perp walk with one Mr. Gaines.

"Mike, you guys are finally getting Mr. Gaines out of here? I noticed the Channel 4 News van down there. It isn't Christina Moore, is it? I don't know why, but I would love for her to be all over this story."

"I thought it would be a nice touch. She already got some footage over at FCI Milan. Normally we aren't huge on the press, but this case needs to be blown up. Let people know we're coming for them." Mike also knows the FBI needs a win in the press after years of bad PR with Cappelano.

"Enjoy the perp walk, it's well deserved. Thanks for the backup at the prison and the trust here." Without him, not sure I'd get to do this shit.

"Neil, we need each other. Because of you, we get to close cases that might otherwise still be open. Do you want to walk down with me?" He knows I'm going to say no.

"Thanks for the offer, but I'm good."

"Suit yourself. I'll talk to you tomorrow. Come by the office and we'll continue to debrief everything."

"Sounds good. Talk to you tomorrow."

Like that, Mike and the rest of the agents finished cleaning up the scene, walking Mr. Gaines out of the front of his building. Something his family built, an empire, could come crashing down because of one arrogant prick; then again, this is life. When you look at some of the greatest empires, they fall from one weak link in the chain. It's time to take Maria home, clean up, and get some rest. I'm hoping Ken has some of our guys here, or we can bum a ride from Colby to the warehouse.

"Hey Ken, do we have a ride waiting for us downstairs?"

"Neil, you know I did one better. Your car is already at home, and yes, some of our guys downstairs are waiting to drive you home. I wasn't sure how this was going to end, so I was planning ahead."

"Thank you, Ken, there isn't any chance you had them order Buddy's pizza and leave it there for us at Neil's place with a six-pack?" Maria said jokingly.

"Maria, I'm good, but I'm not that good. I can text one of the guys to order one for you; I think one of the locations by you is still open. You can grab it on your way."

"That sounds like a plan, plus I have the stuff to drink at the house. Let's get out of here, Maria."

Like that, we slid out the back, were picked up by one of the team members, and made our way home, grabbing our Buddy's pizza for Maria, who hadn't eaten in more than a day thanks to Gaines's crazy ass. As we walked into the house, the girls ran right by me and jumped on Maria. Their treachery was duly noted. I grabbed the TV remote and put the news on, hoping to catch some of Channel 4 News coverage. To my surprise, I caught something different.

"Coming to you live from the front of Gaines Chemical, we have an interview with the lawyer for Mr. Gaines and Gaines Chemical. He claims the CEO was kidnapped by his head of security, forced into a hostage situation, and coerced. They were then attacked by Neil Baggio and his team, only to be unjustly arrested by the FBI."

"Neil, did I just hear that shit right? That's the story she's running with?" I told you I hate her.

"This is why I can't stand the news and some of their reporters. This is going to be a mess. Call Mike and give him a heads up."

"I'm on with him now. He's already aware, but there's something worse."

"What could be worse than this shit?"

"Gaines escaped."

26

*How about Glass Jaw McGraw? Might even start a rumor
among other crime syndicates to mess with his ego.*

I guess we are going to be working all night; so much for a
relaxing night stuffing our faces with pizza and beer and trying
to decompress. I know you could be set up for a cliff-hanger,
but I can't do that to you again. I've already done that to you
once. Plus, Cappelano and this guy aren't in the same class, so
he doesn't get that kind of treatment.

"Maria, why don't you hop in the shower, get cleaned up,
and scarf down some pizza. I'll get on the phone with Ken and
TJ and see what we can gather. Mike is already on it, so I'll
follow up with him in a little bit."

"Thanks, Neil. I need a nap too, but I know I'm not going to
get one now. I'm fairly sure my car is still at Bar Louie; I'll have
you drop me off after we get ready so I can head home to
change, then the office."

"Works for me, except I wouldn't go directly to sleep," I said with a smile.

"I know, right."

Once Maria left the room to head into the shower, I found myself sitting on the edge of the bed watching the TV again, just sitting there in disbelief. The brass balls on this guy and his lawyer. They are setting up a story of plausible deniability to get him off, or with a massively reduced sentence. Part of me, a very small part, is a little impressed with the audacity and the smarts to pull it off. I can't talk, especially with some of the crazy shit I've done over the years; part of me wonders if this is what it's like to watch me from outside.

Whether it's the time I crashed multiple FBI cars on one stakeout with Cappelano, to creating a crash site to distract a cardinal, or driving a truck through a police station in Warsaw. Those are just a few of the crazy things I've done in recent memory. Going back to the early years with Cappelano and me, there have been plenty of calls that led to me having more confidence and making brazen decisions. Perhaps Gaines is falling into a similar category; he's just doing it from the other side of the law.

Sitting there, watching the news had me working through possible places where Gaines might end up. I know who can help: TJ and his team.

"TJ, it's Neil. I'm assuming by now Ken has filled you in, and you're aware of the craziness that has ensued?"

"Yeah, you guys had a crazy-ass night. I'm glad everyone made it out safely. What are you calling me for? Shouldn't you be relaxing and getting some sleep by now?" Apparently Ken and the office aren't aware.

"Well, Mr. Gaines seems to have escaped capture during transport, and his lawyer went on TV to make it sound like he's being kidnapped by his head of security."

"Shit, what do you need from me? I'm assuming a possibility of places where they could be hiding."

"As usual, TJ, you're a step ahead. I'd start with subsidiary companies, maybe see where the offshore money is hiding, then track it back. That's most likely how we'll find him."

"You know that shit's not going to be easy. I'm about to call Ken, find out where the money is hiding. Then, if needed, we'll send someone out to the bank in person."

"You got it, boss."

Off the phone, I was getting ready to dial Ken when Maria came out of the shower, wet hair and all, leaned in, and gave me a quick kiss. She was looking for comfort after a long ordeal, and I was just the guy willing to give it. As we stood there, Maria damn near knocked me off my feet.

"Hey Neil, I was thinking, through all this since we got in the car, dealing with all those agents, did you take the time to let Sheila and Carol Lynn know you're okay?"

"No, I haven't. Then again, I didn't let her know I was in any trouble, and we have an understanding that sometimes no news is good news. If I'm in a bad place and can't communicate, Ken will take care of it. I can always talk to her in the morning. I appreciate you thinking of them, though."

"I know the first go-around I was worried about your relationship with them. I'm pretty sure I'm past that. I have to realize you are a parent and always will be. It's who you are, and I can't get in the way of that."

"Thanks, Maria. Why don't you get dressed. I'll call Ken, and we can go find your car."

"Thanks, Neil, for everything. Especially the part where you risked your life to come back and save mine."

"I wasn't about to let you sit there I was coming for you even if I had to fly a small plane into the building." Referencing the truck in Warsaw.

"This isn't Poland, Neil, but I appreciate the sentiment."

Once we got done playing around, I got around to calling Ken. By now, though, TJ would have spoken to Ken and given him a heads up, making my job easier. This wasn't my plan in delaying between calls, but it's not too bad a strategy.

"Hey Ken, has TJ given you a heads up about everything going on with Gaines and his bullshit escape? And the shit with his lawyer?"

"Yeah, we're all over it. He also said that you wanted him to follow the offshore money. Are you thinking he's got money somewhere like Grand Cayman? You know it's always a pain to get information out of those guys."

"That's why I want to find out where. Worst case, we can send Nicolette down there with Terrance, not to mention he could use the sun, he needs a minivacation after that shit the other day."

"Good call. As soon as we figure out what's going on, I'll let you know. Hit me up if you need anything/ I'm going to catch a nap in the bunks."

"Will do. I'm going to get Maria back to her car, then I'll figure it out from there."

When they make this amazing story into a movie, even if it's just some shit on TNT on a Thursday night stuck in a motel somewhere starring a fat action star, it will rock. You know this scene will change to Maria not having wet hair in my car soggying up the headrest of my car. It also won't have me inner dialoguing this and worrying about her making the headrest soaking wet, especially with a crazy-ass like Gaines out on the street.

Nope. In the movie version, the cable version you're watching in a motel, remember this scene. Maria will be dressed to kill, full makeup, and ready to rock. Even though she hadn't eaten in almost thirty-six hours and just took a shower, scarfed half a pizza, and slammed a cup of coffee and a Red Bull. She's all mine, this crazy lady ready to take on the world with a stomach fighting over pizza and caffeine is mine and no one else's. Enough sidetracking; we were almost to her car when she started panicking because she couldn't find her keys. We all know that feeling—they just disappear.

"Neil, I swear I grabbed them and put them in my purse. Shit, where are they?"

"We can get out of the car and look under the seat and stuff. It's okay. Calm down, we're both tired, you more than me from how long you dealt with Gaines. Calm down. Worst case, I'll drive you home, then to the office, and you can get a car from the FBI office."

"Okay, I just don't want to leave my car here all night again."

"If we can't find your keys . . . oops, Maria, get up a second. I think I see them under your ass."

"Here they are; they must have fallen out when I got in, and I sat on them."

"This should be fun; we are losing our shit, and we have to think straight enough to catch an asshole. I think I'm going to head to the warehouse, get a nap in there in the bunks so I can be close if anything happens or any intel pops up."

"I'm going home to change. Mike said to get rest after everything; they won't let me back to the office for forty-eight hours minimum anyway. I can help you guys out; I'll call you in a few hours. Message me when you're up."

"Sounds good, Maria."

"Night, Neil."

I made my way to the warehouse, where I found Ken passed out in the bunks. TJ and two of his best guys were working like crazy, with one of them on the phone. The rest of the warehouse at one in the morning was dead as expected, and I can see why TJ and his team enjoy working in the middle of the night.

"Hey Neil, how's it going? Don't take this the wrong way, but you look like shit. I suggest you get some rest in the bunks with Ken. I'll get you if anything major pops up."

"Who's your guy on the phone with over there? And thanks for pointing out what I already know."

"He's on with the forensic accounting department at the bureau. Mike called and woke up their guy over there; he has him working with us around the clock to find the money. He agreed with you that he thinks it's one of the best shots at finding Gaines."

"Since we are just grasping at straws right now with no real, actionable intel, why don't you just wake me up with anything that seems important? You know I can fall back asleep quickly. If you think it's important but not wake-up worthy, just message me."

"Got it; we'll find this crazy bastard. Ken was saying you kept referring to him as a comic book villain wannabe. Should we come up with a nickname for him? Since he wants one so badly?"

"How about Glass Jaw McGraw? Might even start a rumor among other crime syndicates to mess with his ego."

"Neil, you're always pushing these guys to their brink. Get some rest; I'll get you if anything is needed."

As I made my way to the bunks, I saw Maria messaged me that she was finally home and in bed. She will probably sleep the day away. Even if she does not want to, her body will shut down for her. Protecting itself. The limbic system, which is believed to be the oldest developed part of the human brain, is about the survival instinct. When something horrible happens to you, even if you are prepared for it, used to it, or desensitized to it, your brain will do the work for you to protect itself. The easiest way to do this is rest. Getting you to sleep allows you to shut down and allow your body and brain to regroup.

Sometimes people look at me like I'm crazy for the habits I keep. Disappearing midcase to hit a heavy bag or even get some rest, it's about performing at peak capacity as often as possible. Remember, it's about the output in life; what good is operating at 50 percent for eighty hours when you can operate at max capacity for fifty hours?

Laying down in the bunk, I'm glad we built these things; we went all out, too. They are not twin beds. We put full-size custom-built bunks in; in total there are six beds. We have two sets of traditional top and bottom bunks and two sets with a top bunk and a recliner below with room for an IV next to it along with some medical hookups such as oxygen lines. I know what you're thinking, *Why not just go to the doctor?* We have a lot of ex-military and we do a few off-the-book jobs that require us to keep a low profile if someone gets shot, that's why.

Don't get me wrong, we're not some black-ops security company, we just keep growing more and more and doing bigger and bigger jobs for friends. The bureau has been leaning on us, almost using us as a makeshift spook agency. That way they don't have to deal with their friends at the CIA. Historically the CIA and the FBI have never played well together, so Mike and his team love having us in their back pocket. I'm lying here, thinking about everything fading away. I couldn't help but think about how I got to this point with everything, especially that six-month window when Frank was gone. We thought he was on a leave of absence and he was out killing.

Looking at that list, seeing all those names and thinking if all the murder that's on my hands. I know you will think *Neil, that shit isn't on you,* but my conscience will tell me it is. I'm better than the rest, I'm not supposed to miss that shit. I know I'm better now than I was on my best day back then, but that's no excuse for missing so many egregious red flags.

COLLOQUIUM

27

That was harsh. Okay, I just self-checked; maybe he was just spot on.

Back in the early 2000s, before Frank left the bureau, he went on a string of aggressive shootings during cases. We had been knee-deep in some federal drug cases, where shootouts kept occurring. This isn't always the case at the bureau; it's actually rare for many cases, which is why people flock there. It's long investigations sifting through paperwork, it's not drug kingpins and shoot-outs. It's more going through accounting paperwork, tracking down leads, and looking into the mundane than the exciting worlds you see on TV. There are some exciting cases, but the truth is that it's a long game, it's a marathon, it's not a quarter-mile sprint. It's a hundred-mile marathon in the dark with glimpses of light. You don't get to see much; it is a lot of faith, hope, and trusting the process.

As you can see, it's hard for me to sleep even when I'm tired. Then again, I did slam a ton of coffee a while ago, thinking I was going to work all night. But rest is rest and I'm going to close my eyes and do my best to get some sleep.

Seven in the morning rolls around and after several forty-five-minute naps, I am throwing in the towel. It's just going to be one of those days. I see Ken is still sleeping soundly. Then again, Ken is as routine a human as you can imagine; he wakes up at eight in the morning every day. Not before, not after, always at the same time. I get it, he lived the military life for so long he craves routine; it keeps him sane. We all have things we need for our routine to keep us sane. For me, it's showers and coffee, which is why there is a coffeepot next to the community showers. I know I have issues, and the worst part is I'm spreading them to others. I'd say that close to 50 percent of the showers now that go on in here have a coffee accompanying them.

I yelled down the hall, "TJ, you still here?"

"Yeah, check your phone! Or just walk your lazy ass down here!"

I rolled out, made my way down the hall, and took the fifty-yard stroll to TJ's office. I'm sure I've mentioned it before, but TJ's wing of the office was intended for me. We built one side for Ken, the other side for me. When we realized I was never using it, and TJ was around all the time and really bringing in the business, we gave it to him. It was one of the best decisions we ever made. The success of BCI is Ken as the backbone, TJ running as the brains, and me as the legs propelling us forward. That means without them, I'm running aimlessly, and they know that without me, we wouldn't grow in the fashion we do. I would say understanding our roles, growing in them, and working together are what make us successful. Don't get me wrong, I can be an arrogant prick sometimes, but it comes with the territory of carrying the weight of the world on your shoulders.

"Okay, what do you have to show me, TJ? I scanned the emails and text you sent. It looks like you and the bureau found where he is hiding the money but can't find too many details about how it connects back?"

"That's where the hang-up is, as you and Ken already suspected it would. They are waiting to see if the bank in Grand Cayman will help, but we both know they aren't going to do anything over the phone. It's going to take someone in person with cash to make this transaction happen."

"TJ, look at you, learning that not everything can be solved from a computer. A lot of things can be, but some things just need good, old-fashioned cloak-and-dagger shit."

"Exactly. Ken is waiting in his office. He said Maria also is aware of what's going on. She messaged you and Ken earlier trying to find out what was going on when she didn't hear back from you."

"Thanks, TJ. Keep pounding the keys."

I love how my closest friends have learned how to manage me, like a dog in a way. Make sure not to wake him or he'll be cranky. It's kind of funny, but also caring. If this were a few years ago, Maria would have been blowing up my phone, but she's learned that's not going to get her anywhere. Walking into Ken's office, I noticed he was on the phone. I plopped into a chair, waiting for him to finish.

Sitting there for a few moments, I noticed all the cool memorabilia he has on the walls, from the cases we've closed over the years. He slipped a note to me across the desk, but I could barely make out the chicken scratch, so I looked at him, shrugged, and whispered, "What?"

"Dude, you smell like shit, and I'm going to be on this call for a bit. Go shower, then come find me." That was harsh. Okay, I just self-checked; maybe he was just spot on.

"Okay, I'm going."

I guess going more than thirty hours, a few different high-sweat environments, a federal prison, and a shoot-out will have you sweat profusely. I'm trying to explain the fact that I smell like an old-ass high-school gym bag that's been in some kid's trunk for four years.

With a cup of java in hand, hot shower washing away the stench of the day, I was making my way back into the real world, working through the reality of the day that happened yesterday. Watching Frank save my life, work to help me pull it off, saving another agent, and dealing with a gunfight in a chemical company headquarters yesterday felt more like an eighties action movie than a day in the life of Neil Baggio.

Today, on the other hand, is coming full circle. I'm tired as shit, the bad guy got away, he's got plausible deniability to make it out of this shit show with minimal to no damage, and we have little to no leads. This is what I'm used to dealing with, a pile of wood, someone asking for a shed, and no nails. That's my life, but somehow I keep building sheds that stand the test of time without nails.

All cleaned up with fresh clothes pulled from my go-bag that I keep in the car for such an occasion. It's a nice pair of David Bitton buffalo jeans, a 47 Brand Tigers T-shirt, and a beat-up Tigers hat. Throw those together with my navy blue Chuck Taylors and I'm looking slick. Or a Detroit version of Magnum PI, sans mustache. The past couple of weeks I've kind of let myself go in the hair department. It's getting a bit shaggy and I had to tuck it back under the hat. I've got stubble turning into a beard. I shaved under the neckline and my lip. I can't stand hair there for some reason, just drives me nuts. All clean and ready to go, I'm sitting in Ken's office waiting for this revelation of bullshit that I have to pull off.

"Well, Neil, the good news is that we closed the case. Gaines is captured, and you can go back to bed."

"You serious? Finally a win?"

"Fuck no, I'm just messing with you, but your face was amazing. For like two whole seconds I saw what I can only consider pure joy."

"You're an asshole, but that was perfectly executed. For that, I can't be mad. What do we have? Actually, give me a rundown of what we *don't* have."

"Well, we have almost no leads; Gaines and his security guy, Bryan; are ghosts; the bank as expected is a waste. That's who I was on with earlier. I've already booked Nicolette and Terrance on flights to Grand Cayman to take care of that."

"So what's next for us? Look into subsidiaries locally, do it the old-fashioned way, find their distributors, talk to street gangs, and round them up."

"Yep, it looks like old-fashioned street work is going to be needed in this case. As for Grand Cayman, why don't you and I go? Leave everyone else here. Maybe we can tell everyone it took us a month to figure everything out."

"Don't laugh; find a way to get Maria down there and I might take you up on that. Speaking of which, Father Roberts has a missionary trip he wants me to go on. I think I might invite Maria, thought it might be fun for us. I think it's in South America somewhere. Her linguistic skills would come in handy."

"Also, seeing her dressed in small clothing 'cause it'll be hot and sweaty wouldn't hurt you either, would it, Neil?"

"I wasn't thinking about that at all, but now that you brought it up, I can't stop. Thanks; you just brightened my day. Speaking of Maria, TJ said you spoke to her."

"Yeah, she and Mike said hit them up when you are moving; they want to circle back and plan out an attack and the next steps."

"I guess that's what I'll do."

I hopped in the old muscle car and got to driving. I don't think I've told you yet, but I'm currently driving a 2008 Dodge Challenger SRT. I didn't get it new, 'cause I figured I would mess it up. If it already had some damage to it, I wouldn't feel so bad. I had one of the guys take it to his buddy's shop to do a custom paint job on it. It's navy blue with a white stripe down the middle with a BCI decal on the backside about a foot in diameter. It almost looks like the SRT decal replaced with our company letters; it's pretty sweet. The racing stripe and company letters were surprises. I just wanted Detroit Tigers blue. I'm a bit of a homer, what can I say?

The car is the most comfortable thing I've ever driven. It's not even about the speed, though it's fast as shit, it just hugs you perfectly and rides so smooth. I got it shortly after Maria and I broke up and I think I did it because I missed her Corvette so much. I probably missed more than that, but what can I say? It was a way to take back a bit of control and get that speed back.

The drive downtown toward the FBI field office was a nice change of pace since Maria and I are dating again. Normally if I were going down there, I would have a pit in my stomach, afraid of what it would be like down there when I pulled in, knowing the agents would look at me in two lights. The guy who caught Cappelano, but at what cost? Not much has changed in Detroit, though many are now working toward making a difference, especially in real estate. A mogul is buying up property all over, making changes for the better. Sometimes it takes a big wallet to fix a big problem.

Pulling into the office felt good, though the problem was going to suck all the way. Trying to track down someone who is hiding out in the hood, while not wanting to be found, and has access to large sums of untraceable funds through his street gang connections and drug money. It all depends on which way he wants to go with this. One plus side to this shit show is that George is still there at the security check; he always brightens my day.

"George, what's up, brother? How're the grandkids? They in high school yet?"

"Actually, Neil, one of them is a freshman. Can you believe it?"

"Yes, George, you're almost as old as this building, maybe older," I said, joking.

"Very funny, even if it's true. Have a great day, Neil. Always good to see your face around here. Even if it usually means bad news."

"You have a point there, George. Talk to you later."

I never thought of it that way; it's not like the bureau calls me in for cake and candles. When I'm down at the FBI field office in Detroit—or any city, for that matter—it's never good news. It's always to consult on a case that has gone horribly wrong. Or it has so much red tape that they don't know how to work through it. That's where Neil Baggio and the BCI team hop into action.

"Hey Jen, nice to see your face as always."

"Neil, don't you 'Hey Jen' me. What's this, I hear you and Maria are back together?" Shit, news travels fast.

"I'm here for the Gaines Chemical case, I'm not sure what you're talking about."

Just as I said that, Maria walks out and gives me that come hither look, grabs me by the belt, and yanks me down the hall. Jen gave me the most judgmental look and said,

"Sure, Neil, nothing is going on."

Okay, so we are probably going to suck at hiding it this time around. Now people know we dated previously, so there's less at stake. We handled the breakup professionally, and that's always the biggest concern when there is a workplace romance.

"All right, Neil, I'll have Maria catch you and the others up to speed." Mike was leading a small group in the conference room.

"Well, it's pretty simple; we found where Gaines is hiding his offshore money. It's in the Grand Cayman, and that's where Neil's team comes in. As for the other leads, well, we don't have shit. That means we are going to go at this old school. Any questions?"

"Hey, all of you pups out there, you young ones, do you understand what we mean when we say 'old school'?" Mike's giving everyone a hard time. The room looked lost.

"Mike, let me help with this one. All right, everyone, what Mike is talking about is going off-grid. You can't simply use the Internet, or source intel from the web to track him down. You can try, but if he's hiding out in the hood, you're not going to get camera footage because what little exists is a closed loop. You're not going to get credit card activity because he has access to cash, lots of it through drug deals. He is off-grid, a ghost to the way you're used to operating. We are going to have to hit the streets, talk to CIs, and track him like a wounded animal." Shit, I'm tired.

"All right, get with your leads; we will have what sectors you will be working in. We have to look at this city as a grid and work through it section by section. We are also working with the local PD, but don't expect them to be too helpful. Many of them think Gaines is Robin Hood."

COLLOQUIUM

After that quick meeting, Maria, Mike, and I walked down to his office to go over my company's approach to tracking down Gaines. This way, we can ensure that we don't step on each other's toes and don't waste time crossing the same path. Mike finally has his office set up. The past couple of times, his office was still looking like mine—white walls, plaster, and not much else.

"Mike, look at you. Finally, all moved in. You had Bob's old office, took you a while to remove the look of state senator wannabe from here, then it was white walls for a while. Now it fits you."

"I was going for 1980s retro neon sheik. Do you think I pulled it off?" Mike said, laughing.

"I'm not sure what that is. Neil, do you have the faintest idea?" Maria was lost too.

"I think it's Mike's idea of a joke. Am I correct in that assumption, Mike?" I know I am.

"Yeah, all right, back on task, let's see what we have to cover. Maria, for being tired and a prisoner for a few days, looked amazing as usual. Neil, one long day, and you look like shit. Is sobriety bad for you?" Mike started laughing.

"Okay, that was pretty funny, and I still drink, I'm just not relying on it as much. You know me and my routines, I'm replacing a nightcap with a night heavy bag routine."

"Okay, are you guys done acting like two kids sitting on the back of the bus and ready to get down to business?" She knows this is how we work; it's what makes the shit days worthwhile.

I spent a good thirty minutes covering all the stuff we would have to do. I may have left out all the backhanded, shady stuff they would need done to ensure they would have some plausible deniability. I didn't tell them that I had to send my guys down with twenty thousand in bribe money just to ensure they would be able to get the intel they need. You might think, *Where are they getting twenty thousand in bribe money?* It's those speaking tours and the book deal I really don't want to do, but I'm willing to listen to now. The funds would come in handy for this case and others.

"All right, well, it's safe to say you left out all the fun stuff that we enjoy your services for. We greatly appreciate it, Neil. I don't know how you keep finding ways or funds to keep doing what you do, but we appreciate it."

"I pad my expense report a ton, and your accounting department doesn't seem to mind," I said with a smile.

"I'm the one that signs off on those. I haven't seen anything too crazy. You should see the things our agents try to pass off. We had one try to expense car washes on their trip."

"Hey, man, when you're on a budget you need to control all the dollars you can," Maria said with a chuckle.

"She's making sense, Mike; I'd say the next expense report might have my car insurance on there."

"Very funny, Neil. Let's get these teams organized and hit the ground. Time to track this prick, or at least narrow the field."

As we walked out of the office, Maria looked at me and noted that this shit was going to take a long time. We talked for a few minutes about what we thought was going to happen. She thought they had a shot at tracking him down quickly. I thought this was going to be long and drawn out unless he was going to turn himself in. The only way to pull this shit off was to track down where he is, or where he was if he turns himself in.

"Maria, as I was saying, if I were Gaines, I would turn myself in on my own terms and control the message."

"I still don't think he's going to turn himself in as you think, but you have a better track record than I do, so I'd have to follow you on this one."

"I think it's more along the lines of convincing his head of security to let him go. He has many options on how to spin this, though to us it's going to be ill-conceived bullshit, many will believe it. The courts won't have to believe it, just the plausibility of it, which gives more than enough reasonable doubt. It's annoying, but you have to respect it a little bit."

"I don't have to, but I see your point. I'm going to be stuck here most of the day organizing and keeping an eye on the teams we have out there. Keep me updated on what you and your team find backchanneling your contacts."

"Will do, Maria. Mike's right, you know."

"About what?"

"You look great. Hopefully we can get together tonight."

"Unless I'm stuck here, I'll probably be sleeping at your place. I'll make sure to bring a change of clothes this time. Makes it more efficient."

"Sounds good, cutie. Have a great day, good luck."

"You too."

Like that, the day was off and running. As we had alluded to in our meeting, this could be a marathon. These kinds of investigations rarely take days; they take weeks or months. Guys such as Gaines can hide out as long as they want; the key is what angle he wants to take. If his sister comes back from South America to run the company or the board announces a new CEO quickly, I think we'll know his endgame. I can assure you he's in communication with them or someone on his board daily.

28

Brock the Boxer is seated in back at his usual table.

At least Nicolette and Terrance have gotten some sun, but overall, this week has been a long waiting game. Let me give you the rundown of what hasn't been achieved since I walked out of the FBI field office last week in downtown Detroit. For starters, Maria never made it over to my place that night; she was in the office until midnight or later. They had issues with their field agents staying on task, getting sidetracked, and following leads on other cases. It's human nature to be working a case that you've put your heart and soul into, only to be pulled off on some wild goose chase, find a lead, and not run with it.

With a week of little to no intel from the bureau except a long list of places he isn't at, or probably won't be, they put most of their eggs in my basket. That of the theory that he is going to make a mistake. This is the old wait until they make a mistake strategy, which often works out with people such as

Gaines, especially when you have no other move. I'm still holding out hope for the old turned-in or released-by-his-captors move. I think he's just waiting for the right moment.

As for the BCI crew, we are turning up leads; we have been back-channeling and found a decent amount of intel in an underground fight going on. It's not so much underground as it's off to the side of a legit fighting group in Detroit that fights some of the best fighters. The thing is, if you want fights, you need reps. If you always wait for a sanctioned fight, chances are some of your guys aren't going to get the losses they need to find that fire or the experience they need before it's too late. Training can do only so much. Coaches preach it all the time, the game experience is needed, you can only count on practice so much.

What have we gained, how did we get it, where did we get most of it from? Those come down to a few integral people on our team. One being Christian, whose little brother is working up the ranks in the fight world locally. He used his connections to get us into the underworld; that, mixed with my celebrity, made it easy for us to work. People around Detroit know my reputation of picking my targets, meaning I'm not about going after small fish, I set my sights, and that's who I focus on. If I see a local drug dealer, I'm not going to give him shit, I need his intel, his crew of dealers as setup eyes telling me what Gaines's crew is doing. Without that, I'd never been able to operate in the fashion I have over the years.

COLLOQUIUM

When I left Maria's office, it was Thursday afternoon, and she had hoped we would get together that night, but as I explained, that didn't happen. What did happen was her working late and Christian calling me.

"Hey Neil, guess what? I think I have a lead that might help us out. It's a long shot, but it's better than anything we have working right now."

"I'm all ears. What do you need from me?"

"I need you to sit down with a local drug dealer, kind of a big deal out here, listen to what he has to say. If we help him, he'll help us track down and be the eyes and ears of gathering intel on Gaines and his operation. He wants him out of the game as much as the next guy."

"How'd you get this intel, this guy lined up? If you don't mind me asking."

"You know how my brother is a fighter. Some of the off-book fights he does with the guys to make extra cash and get reps are at a club owned by this guy. He's been on a winning streak lately and was able to get the ear of the man. He knows the case I'm working on, asked if he could help, so we brainstormed and came up with this. Sometimes our best friend is the enemy of our enemy."

"Smart man, Christian, also well played. Where are we meeting?"

"Why don't you swing by and pick me up from the warehouse; if we pull up in your ride it'll look better anyway.

Then we'll head down. His club is off Eight Mile, you know, where all the great ones are."

"Sounds good; see you in a few minutes. Let me change to be a bit more presentable."

"Ah, you're going to put on your clean T-shirt and hat."

"Shut up, it works for me."

Out the door, I grabbed a cup of coffee just to be safe. With a clean shirt and my favorite Tigers hat on, I was ready to go. I was rocking my jeans, with a nice button-up. It was casual but not too casual; I didn't want to be off-putting. I may have driven a little over the speed limit getting to the warehouse quicker than normal. This was the first sign of positive force we had in days, and I was excited. I didn't want to call anyone or tell anyone, didn't want to risk jinxing it. As I pulled up to the warehouse, Christian met me outside before I even came to a complete stop, and he was in the car.

"Let's get going, it's getting late, and we need to make sure we get there before Brock gets too drunk. Otherwise this meeting will be much harder to handle."

"Brock, that's who we're meeting with. Brock the Butcher, that two-bit hustler turned psycho?"

"Neil, I know what you're thinking, but do you want to get Gaines or not? It's the lesser of two evils. From we can tell, Brock doesn't have the manpower or the cash flow to handle the output Gaines is cooking. That means utilizing him, and his eagerness to crush the competition is our best bet at tracking Gaines's movements."

"I'm not saying it's a bad idea or a bad plan, I'm just not a fan of the guy."

Let me explain to you what this guy Brock is about and, more importantly, why they call him the butcher. It's not because he's killed so many people, though he's done his fair share of street gang violence. Brock is a big fan of DMX—that's the nicest way of describing his personality; the guy even growls when he talks sometimes. I've met him a few times, but I rarely gave him the time of day; he was a two-bit hustler back then working his way up. Now he's got a bit of street cred to his name, and he's pulling weight. This should be interesting.

As for the nickname Brock the Butcher, it comes from a night he shot up a warehouse, thinking it was a rival gang's hideout. only to find out it was a meat locker for a meatpacking company. No one knew what happened until a day or two later, when the news reported the meatpacking company had to destroy thousands of pounds of meat because of bullets and shrapnel spread throughout the warehouse. The name isn't to instill fear. It's to make fun of him a bit for being an idiot. The gang hideout was in the same district, but he shot up 1701, and the address they were at was 1710.

"He goes by Brock the Boxer now. He's been training, hoping in the ring, and beating up punks, trying to get a new rep. He's a decent fighter, never going to make it, but at least he's trying."

"I'm not going to call him the boxer, but I'll allude to it if it helps."

"You know the game, just don't call him a butcher."

We pulled into the club, which was built into an old warehouse, not uncommon in this part of town. It's cheap, lots of space, and easy to make it what you want. The square footage is massive, similar to what we did at BCI. The club is called Rocko's, but most people call it Rocko's on Eighth. Which is odd because there is no other Rocko's. When you walk in, it has a nineties strip club feel to it. Lots of mirrors, dark lighting, and plush seating that makes you question whether you should. You know the seats, when you go into a dark bar and wish it were vinyl or plastic, maybe leather, but not fabric, and not velvet, anything but velvet.

This place is covered in it, the seats all over are red and purple velvet with that theater lighting, so you don't trip with the near pitch-black lighting they keep the place at. The bar is pretty sweet, though; it runs the length of the place and is usually tended by two to three bartenders with a spiral staircase that runs up to the second-floor balcony bar. The setup is pretty sweet. I'm not sure who's idea that was, but it's a great touch for a shit bar.

In the back is where all the action is, the second half of the bar, where they have the boxing matching and cage matches, depending on the night. I'm not even sure how they swap out the rings, but they do. We quickly made it past security, as they recognized Christian. We talked about my car and were escorted by a few servers that were dressed very scantily— somewhere between ring girl and go-go dancer.

"Here you guys go. Brock the Boxer is seated in back at his usual table. Can we get you something to drink?"

"Thanks, ladies. I'll take a light beer, anything will do. Neil will probably take something straight. Neil, what do you need?"

"I'll take gin on the rocks with lime. Tanqueray is fine if you have it."

As they disappeared into the dark, hazy aether, Christian and I looked to Brock, saw him sitting there with his girl and a few guys from his crew preparing for the next fight. I couldn't help but notice Brock was wearing boxing shorts and boxing shoes, as if he were going to, or already had, fought for the evening. This guy really is trying to change that tag to his name.

"Brock, how's it going? As promised, I present to you Neil Baggio."

"Neil, I appreciate you coming down here on such short notice, and dressed up. I know how hard it is to get you out of a T-shirt. Rumor around town is that's all you ever wear. I feel honored to get you out here dressed up."

"Well, Brock, I felt it's the least I could do if we were going to find a way to work together, find common ground. The least

I can do is look the part of someone who is coming to do some business."

"I like your style, Neil. Let's get down to it." Brock was smiling like an idiot.

"This is your place of business, your home. I'm here at your disposal. It's my understanding we have a common interest in bringing down Gaines. How can I obtain your help in tracking him down?"

"I need you to get some intel. Essentially I need you to steal some evidence for me from the FBI evidence locker." Hell, no. I need help, but not like this.

"Well, Brock, I'm not sure how me helping you prevent a federal prison term and bringing down your top competition is a quid pro quo."

"A squid did what?"

"That sounds more like a double win for you. I was thinking, you needed to find a way we can build trust, but not that big. If you need more, I can go on my way, you have plenty of guests, I'm not going to waste your time."

"No . . . no . . . no, slow down, Neil. I was just testing you. I got a better idea. How about we go a couple of rounds in the ring? If you can make it to the third round, I'll consider you hard enough to work with us. Before I get into the ring with you, I'm going to need you to fight one of my young fighters."

Wait a minute. Does he not realize I've been boxing since I was a kid? My dad taught me how to throw a jab before I took my first step. I can remember watching old fights well before and way more often than any children's movies. I'm game; the hard part is going to be when I get in the ring with Brock the Broken Butt Butcher, I don't kick his ass.

"I'm game. I guess I can just take my shirt off if you don't mind one thing, though. Can I make a request?"

"Sure. What is it?"

"Mind if I go out to my car to grab my wraps and gloves? I'm not a big fan of using someone else's wraps and gloves, it's just not sanitary." He looked confused and a bit caught off guard.

"Sure thing. Anything that makes you feel comfortable in there."

It took about twenty minutes for me to get ready, and there was a fight going on. Eventually I ended up in the ring with some twentysomething kid weighing maybe twenty pounds more than me. The one thing I should have going for me is that he should underestimate the shit out of me. Even though I'm a federal agent who happens to carry his own wraps and gloves around with him.

"Neil, you don't have to do this." Christian didn't look worried for me, but about what I was going to do.

"Christian, you're a good man. I got this. I'm a little concerned, since I'll be boxing in a cage, but hey, I can adapt." I'm pretty sure that's not what he's worried about.

"Neil, you know that's not what I'm concerned with. I'm worried you're going to get competitive and jack some people up in there. You need to put on a good show. I'm not saying you need to take any face shots, but you can't be knocking people out either."

"You're no fun right now, but I hear you. I'll do my best rope a dope. I hear you loud and clear."

"Thanks. That's all I'm asking."

All wrapped up and ready to go, gloves on, mouth guard too. Luckily, something else I had in my bag: using someone else's mouth guard or a new one unformed would have been nasty and dangerous. No headgear; I decided to keep on my Tigers hat, just flipped around. This means I'm rocking sneakers, jeans, no shirt, a hat on backward, and boxing gloves with wraps, not the traditional tape job.

"Neil, just so you know, I bet a thousand dollars you can't knock this guy out in the first round. He's never gone done in the first round; then again he's only fought in a handful of fights, but still." Brock thinks he's funny.

"Sorry for what's about to go down, then Brock; if I were you, I'd change your bet to me knocking this kid out."

"I love a cocky prick, my kind of man." Brock looks like a coked-up rooster right now.

As the bell rings, I start sizing him up, making my way around the cage, circling and jabbing. Creating distance and pace, working on my footwork, trying to figure out how I was going to function in my jeans and sneaker ensemble. It's not the usual getup when boxing, especially a youngin. I'm trying to use it to my advantage, throw the kid off, make it look like I'm having trouble when I'm not. Trying to set him up for combinations later. A good forty-five seconds into the round, the kid came at me aggressively. Thinking he might catch me, I sidestepped and hit him with a quick one-three combo, dropping him to the mat. I have a strong left, always have, even as a kid, but my jab-to-hook combo is deadly.

As a boxer, there is no feeling quite like hearing someone hit the mat like a sack of potatoes. There is a very distinctive thud when someone drops to the mat out cold, and this kid hits it hard. There is no way he's getting up; I can tell you that. When I hit him with the jab, he turned just enough to the left, expecting a cross, and put up his guard looking for a big punch from my left. When I circled to my left and gave him a rocking hook, he didn't have a chance. Back in the corner, fight over, Christian gave me the look of death, but the coked-up rooster was smiling.

"Dude, that shit was amazing. I've seen enough, plus I switched my bet, so you made me some cash. Call it even; let's talk about what we can do for you and how we can help you bring down Gaines."

"Think you can get me a towel and a drink to help me get over the sweat I worked up in the ring?" Obviously I was kidding.

"Neil has jokes. Christian, this guy is funny, and he's a great fucking fighter. Let's relax, enjoy the next fight. Its Christian brother, he's a beast. Not sure he can handle your left, Neil, but he's a beast."

"If he comes from the same stock as Christian, he can probably fuck me up. Those boys may be from the city, but their country strong." Those dudes are just naturally jacked.

After going back and forth talking shit a bit and sharing some war stories, which I'm sure was mostly bullshit, the two of us finally got down to the brass tacks of what we were going to do. We talked through utilizing Brock's crew as eyes and ears on the street, some of his younger guys without street cred to keep tabs on Gaines's guys trying to get back to his new central hub. At the end of the day, the drugs and the cash have to get back to somewhere.

We are going to use Brock's guys as a way to track it down, find a pattern, and find out where he might be hiding. It's not foolproof, but seeing some ghetto street kids hanging out isn't going to look suspicious. An FBI agent or random painter's van might give off a vibe that is going to scare off the people we need to track back to Gaines and his crew.

"Okay, it sounds like we have a plan, we have an understanding, and I'll work to lay down some cover for you as a thank you for helping out."

"Neil, thank you. That's the appreciation I was looking for. Thank you for understanding the risks involved."

"We both are looking to get him off the streets, but you are risking a war. I got your back as best I can, Brock."

"Thanks, Neil."

"Have a good night. I have to get up early to work and grind on this case."

"Mad respect for that left, bro. Keep training."

Just like that, Christian and I finally made our way out of the club at two in the morning. His brother's fight did go well. He finished the fight in the second round, keeping up his status as a top fighter at the club. The three of us made our way out and headed back to the warehouse, where I dropped off the brothers so they could leave. My night was done, I had boxed in jeans, won over a drug dealer, and now it's time to head home to my girls and crash.

29

I know it reads like a bad movie.

Well, last night got us some eyes and ears; right now I have two people in Grand Cayman. Time to check in with them. I'm barely awake, lying here in bed, TV is on, but volume is low enough I can fake that it's not on, fake that it might be a dream and get back to curling up with the girls. All was going great, and then Maria came bursting in, waking my ass up. At least she brought coffee and a breakfast burrito, so all was forgiven.

"Neil, wake your lazy ass up. I know you're tired, I know you don't want to get out of bed, but shit, man, I'm here with breakfast burritos, early enough we might even have some fun if you get your ass going and take a shower. You've got sweat and bar funk all over you."

"How do you know what I did last night? I didn't call you, I didn't want to jinx it, I also didn't want to wake you up."

"I've learned to check in with Ken, almost like he's your mother. Since I had that long talk with Sheila and we made nice, I've learned how to manage the Neil Baggio experience."

"So Ken gave you the rundown of everything that went down with Brock and me? Christian really crushed it last night."

"I heard you crushed some guy's jaw. That's my man, being a badass." As she leaned in and kissed me.

"Wait a minute, what the fuck. When did you talk to Sheila?" I mean, I've fantasized about them together, just not as friends talking shit about me.

"Yes, I reached out to her before I decided to give you another shot. She convinced me you were worth it. She also gave me advice for surviving your best and worst habits."

"That was very nice of her. Remind me to thank her."

"Preferably with something simple like a card and not the Neil Baggio backrub and a shower," Maria said, laughing.

"Fair point. I deserve that dig. Now that you're not an ass, just like making me squirm. I'll hop in the shower now, meet you at the table for coffee and burritos, my lady."

"Sounds good, you smell so bad. I mean, it's kind of sexy, but damn, you stink."

As I made my way to the shower, coffee in hand and a sexy girlfriend giving me shit, a man could get used to this kind of wake-up call. I really am lucky to have the amazing women in my life outside of BCI. Sheila and Carol Lynn are why I stay grounded. I can already tell my daughter is going to be a driving force in my success, pushing me to be better at every turn. Maria is always showing up when I need her. Even when we broke up, we were there for each other as colleagues and friends. Now knowing Sheila looked out for me, and Maria reached out to Sheila—these say a lot about the two of them and the impacts they have on me.

As usual, the water is hypnotic, this morning just like any other. Slows down my thought process, trying to work through the information we have and how we can utilize it. I think I have a way to get Gaines moving, make an action, speed up the process, but it might take more cash than what I sent Terrance and Nicolette down there with. I guess we'll find out; then again, the two of them are very resourceful. That's one thing I learned in Warsaw: watching them develop into key members of our team was their ability to adapt.

Nicolette especially had an uncanny ability to adapt to her surroundings, think on her feet, and think of the long game. She wasn't always about the short-term kick, but willing to invest, think about planting the seed, watering the plant, and waiting for the sun to bring to light the hard work she had put in. Terrance is a bit more of a brute, but he's a calculating one. Willing to be patient and outwait his opponent, similar to a great hunter. He's also a great wingman; he trusts the process and the team members around him.

COLLOQUIUM

Out of the shower and in the kitchen, Maria was sitting there on the phone. From the sound of it, she was talking to someone at the office. Judging by the way she's dressed, though, she's not going in today, or if she is going in, it's a casual day. She's not rocking sweats, but for Maria, it's casual. She's wearing jeans, a cute red top, and some heels with a jacket. I'd go into details about the jacket, but I'm sure I'd make it sound like something out of a bad eighties movie than a fashion magazine.

"Hey Neil, sorry about that. I didn't even see you sitting there. How long have you been in the kitchen?"

"Just a few minutes, Maria. I was enjoying the rest of my coffee just waiting for you to finish up."

"I was talking to Ken this morning and following up with Mike. We are hitting dead ends all over. As usual, you seem to be coming up with the best leads, even if they are long shots. What do you think you got out of last night? And do you think you have any chance of getting anything out of the bank in the Grand Cayman?"

"The bank is going to take some work. Nicolette and Terrance are already in the middle of a plan that should show some fruit before long. As for last night, that was a different story. Brock the Boxer, as he is trying to go by now, is going to help us. He wants Gaines out of the game, so helping us get to him is in both of our interests. We just have to keep the heat off of him for a little while."

"Seems like a fair and usual trade-off for something like this. Brock isn't a big fish, though he likes to think he is. He doesn't have the capacity to think big enough. Gaines, on the other hand, wants to take his shit globally." Maria is right.

"That's the scariest part of it all, and he can probably pull it off if we don't step in."

"I know, Neil. I also know we often put a ton on your plate. The bureau, me, even Sheila. Ken and I were talking about it: everyone gets that *wait and see what Neil is going to come up with* mentality."

"Well, almost everyone. We have a great team, and we're building people like TJ, Christian, and Nicolette, who are starting to form their own paths. They may not be carrying as much weight as I do, or even Ken, when we were working in the field full--time, but I can see their potential. Especially Christian; he's got that innate ability to keep going where others stop."

"You mean he's got the inability to sit still like you?" Maria said, smiling.

"Unlike me, he can focus for long periods. Being a sniper has taught him that."

"Well, why don't you give me a quick rundown of what's going down in Grand Cayman. The official off-the-books version, not the on-the-record bureau version."

"Okay, but this might take a moment. Grab a fresh cup of coffee as I give you the rundown."

Well, as you know, we sent Nicolette and Terrance down right away as soon as we realized this was going to come up. Honestly, we thought if it wasn't needed, Terrance needed the break and Nicolette could force him to relax. It was a win either way for us. When they landed, within an hour of checking in Terrance started doing recon and tracking the movements of the bank manager. Nicolette was pleased to find out that the bank manager was married and cute, meaning he probably has an ego and some leverage points she could work on if it came to it.

Within the first twenty-four hours, they found out that the bank manager also had a tendency to stay out late and drink at one of the local bars hitting on the tourists. Nicolette, keen to this, slid into his routine nicely. Dressed to kill, she casually introduced herself, laying the groundwork to run into him later. I know it reads like a bad movie, but guys, especially guys like this, can be extremely cliché. They are frequently put on their job because their father or someone close to them got them there, they didn't earn it, so they are easily impressed. They also don't take their job seriously, which makes them easy marks. You make more money than you need at a job that takes little to no work and you live on a gorgeous island. Beautiful people come to escape life regularly and you have a tendency to start to believe your own shit.

Taking what they've learned from us and life in general, Nicolette and Terrance set the bank manager up with the oldest trick in the book. They got him drunk, took incriminating pictures of him, and played nice with him. She spent a few days playing with him, meeting up with him on minidates, being cool. She only asked me one time what to do with this guy. I told her for now, to make sure she can control him when the time is right.

That's what Terrance and Nicolette did to perfection. She worked him, keeping herself at arm's length, just stroking his ego, letting him on, thinking he was getting somewhere. She always laughs at how often the guys that get the least will give up the most in those situations. She's been heard saying more than once, "Just do the math, bro." It's a good life point in any relationship, business, or friendship.

"So let me get this straight, Neil. You have them down they're manipulating some guy so that you can get more info out of a banker, but you haven't done anything yet with him?" Maria is impatient.

"Slow down there, Maria. Nicolette and Terrance, with the help of TJ's team, were able to plant a virus on the manager's computer, which allowed them to gain access to the files we need. That being said, it's still not going to help us a ton because it just points back to more shell companies. That is why I haven't done much with it. I think we are going to have to use what we have, the leverage, to create a problem that Gaines has to solve, that will get him out of hiding."

"What do you have in mind? Does it involve the destruction of an automobile?" She's got a point.

"No, Maria, for a change it does not." At least not currently.

"How do you plan on getting him out of there? Do you have a plan yet? Or are you waiting for the right moment and time for you to think of one? I understand the irony of me just saying we all put a lot on you, and now I'm badgering you to solve this case."

"It's okay. I think I have an idea, but I want to simmer on it for the day. Maybe hit the heavy bag for a bit at the office. I think it's an idea, but not sure it's a good idea. You know, like a jump- to-conclusions mat or a pet rock. I mean, they were ideas, yes, but were they good?"

"Okay, I see what you're saying. I'll give you some time; you've earned it." she said, laughing.

"Thanks."

"When you are going back to FCI Milan? I notice it has been a few days since you've been to talk to Cappelano."

"I'm going today, actually; I want to talk to him, run my psych breakdown of Gaines with him and see how he feels after a few days to think about his interaction with Gaines."

"I am reviewing old case files and bank records we have on Gaines and Gaines Chemical. Attempting to see if I can find a connection to their subsidiaries that we might be missing. There are so many transactions, it's getting insane. Is it okay if

I use the basement office to set up shop? I need to get out of the office."

"Go for it. Look for mundane but repeatable transactions like $450, $350, or $550. If they are small but consistent from one account to another, chances are they are connected."

"Thanks, Neil. Never thought of it that way."

"It's transferring small amounts of money you hope no one notices. Doing it so often you repeat similar numbers, presenting a pattern."

"Have a good day, as good as you can get with Cappelano at the prison."

"Thanks, Maria. I'll try."

Fresh off a great way to start the morning, with your sexy girlfriend waking you up, breakfast with her, and knowing she'll be there waiting for you when you return. I can't complain. Except for the fact that I'm going to a federal prison where someone just tried to kill me a few days ago. Also, dealing with Cappelano, a man who tormented me for years, fun times. Other than that, it's a great day. Can you sense the sarcasm?

30

Don't worry, I would never label you as empathetic.

The ins and outs of my routine now when I arrive have changed a little bit. Without the warden, I can streamline through checkpoints. The guards that are left who remember me have a look like I took their father from them. Some are happy, but many are pissed. I'm sure the difference is which ones were on the take with Gaines and his crew along with the warden and which ones aren't. Some of them might as well hang a sign around their neck that says they are henchmen. They crack me up; it's like seeing friends on either side of a divorce pick sides—you can see who is for which side. It's obvious as shit.

Sitting in the room, Frank was making his way in, with a new guard walking him down. This time he didn't take his usual time waiting at the door. I would assume after our interaction with Gaines the other night, he doesn't want to waste time. There's too much to talk about.

"Neil, glad you made it through that ordeal. How did everything turn out? Were you able to succeed in freeing your colleague and arrest Gaines?"

"It's a little complicated, which is why I haven't been here for a few days, as you will soon come to find out."

"Neil, when is it ever clean? It's always complicated and a pain in the ass. The only time it's simple is when it's low-level bullshit. Oftentimes that's beneath you; that's the stuff the local cops deal with, not investigators like you."

"I appreciate the compliment, I think, but let's get into it."

The next twenty minutes, I spent catching up Cappelano on the case, what happened, and where we are currently in tracking Gaines down. I may have left a few details out, such as making Colby shoot a fish tank for no apparent reason. I tried to keep it to the pertinent facts of the case.

"You did all the work, risked your life, arrested the asshole, and now he's in the wind, with plausible deniability and a way to get off from most if not all the charges. That's a pretty rough deal, even for you, and you had to chase my ass for years." Cappelano is spot on with this one.

"Exactly, Frank. It's a rough one, it's a pain in the ass. What can I do, waste time and dwell, or deal with it?"

"Good point. What can I help you with? I'm assuming today is going to be less about our past and more about the present."

"We're still going to go over some things, but I did want to bounce an idea off of you, let you play the role of Gaines. See how you might react to a scenario, see how it plays out."

"Set the scene a bit, I know what happened, but what is the current state of play?" Frank loves the details.

I set the tone, explained to Frank that Gaines has gone underground, utilizing the cash I'm sure he has stored up with stash houses and the street drug game. He doesn't need to touch his legitimate money. I also mentioned that the longer he is off the grid, the less likely he can come back and use the victim card, which Frank agreed with. After a few minutes of back and forth and a little bit of convincing, I got Cappelano to play along. He isn't a fan of doing anything outside of our world, and I was as surprised as anyone that he helped the other night when everything went down.

"Now that you have the details of what's going on and where his head is, I think the plan is to cut off his money, all of it, as much and as quickly as possible. Force him into action, to call me or someone out. When you mess with the money, it's easy to rattle the cage. As long as he's flush with cash, he's in no rush to act."

"I agree with you; if you find a way to cut off as much or all of his funds financially within a quick, coordinated way, it will force him to act. It should affect his ability to operate in the shadows. Still, it cuts out his influence on the gangs and other thugs in the underworld. Money is power. No money, no power."

"I guess the next step is to organize it all and figure out just how to pull that off. I have a few ideas. Luckily, I'm surrounded by smart people."

"Neil, you know I'm not going to agree with people at the bureau being smart—a few of the people you have trained, maybe. At the end of the day, it's going to fall on you. It usually does. Don't you notice people wait for you to act?"

I already know this. Telling me, reminding me, or making me aware of it doesn't make me feel better about the situation.

"Why do people keep telling me this? Do you guys think it makes it better?"

"Neil, I think we're bringing it up because we care about you, and we know it's a terrible burden to carry. I was not empathetic, merely pointing out you're the smartest one in the room and you can't count on others as much as you think." Frank was adamant.

"Fair enough, don't worry, I would never label you as empathetic," I said, laughing.

"I would hope not. Back on task and Gaines, I do think you need to make a bold move. It worked with me; it's the only way to get the attention of someone like Gaines. He has all the cards right now, playing with a stacked deck. It's time for you to pull out a big stack of cards and even the field." Did Frank say I made a good play on him?

"Now that we have that out of the way, let's get back to the reason I'm normally here. The cases, the time you left the bureau. Those first six months, I should have the case files you were asking about soon enough. We can work on the cases, but for now I would like to focus on the first couple of murders following Tony and your nephew. There is still one I know you're leaving out. I can tell when you're lying, especially by omission."

"Good deduction, Neil. I'll tell you what: I'm going to give you three different scenarios, and if you choose which one is right, I will go into depth about it for you. If you guess wrong, we go back to talking about the case you're on."

"Okay, I'm game for that, but you have to keep each case description to under a minute, none of this rambling on bullshit to drag out the day." Frank knew I was onto his game.

"All right, I see you are trumping my card with a bigger one. Let's dance, Neil."

Frank sat there quietly for a good ten minutes, then he told me to get out my watch. He will keep them brief for me. He started going into depth on three murders; two are fictitious, one is true. The first murder he described was of a gas station attendant he met along the highway just outside the border of Michigan and Ohio. I'm familiar with the area, and if it were at night, as he described, this could be plausible. The second murder he described was of him picking up a hitchhiker for the mere fun of it, then killing the man. The final murder he described was that of a woman he met outside of a Denny's late at night.

My instinct says to go with the gas station attendant because he claims it was late and the middle of nowhere. The fact that he gave little to no information on the second murder has me intrigued. My guess is that he hopes I think he was lazy in creating a murder, not trying to hide one and skip over it, get fixated on the details of the other murders.

"You killed the hitchhiker, except your story was bullshit. You picked him up because you wanted to tell someone what you did, someone you know wouldn't tell anyone. Not to mention no one would trust anything they say; they would just think they're nuts. My guess is something happened like he said something or did something that triggered you, and you killed him."

"Look at Neil, learning so much from me over the years, though I have to give you some credit for inherent ability. You were correct in your assumption. I was hoping with the minimal details, you would gloss over it."

"I didn't say that." At least I didn't say it out loud.

"No, but you were thinking it. That's the logical reason to pick that murder over the other ones."

"Okay, well enough about why I picked that one over the others, let's focus on the details of the murder. Why did you pick him up? Then why did you kill him?"

Frank went on a long story about needing something to fill the time. He was getting bored. I noted that he was lonely trying to distract himself from murdering his nephew. Frank then continued to describe that homeless man in a fashion that made me think he was a folk singer touring the country and who was out for an adventure. Eventually, while driving, he just didn't stop talking, driving Frank up the wall. Eventually the combination of stink and endless talking put Frank over the edge.

Frank explained that the murder was done quickly and aggressively, out of anger. He said that the man just wouldn't stop talking. In my notes, though, I wrote that the anger and guilt of killing his nephew overtook him, causing him to act on this man in his car. Frank took out his misguided guilt and aggression on this homeless man, putting his guilt into each swing of a tire iron.

"Well, Frank, that was a great story, and I will add it to the notes. I will try and be back this week, but I have to focus on tracking down Gaines and making this move."

"I guess this is so long, farewell, and see you tomorrow. Good luck. If you need me, you know where to find me."

Like that, I was out and back to the Rubik's cube that is the Gaines Chemical problem. Taking a story that started off with Erin getting kidnapped, then Maria, and ending in a shoot-out where we captured the bad guy. Only to end with a sour taste in my mouth when I found out he got away. If you're wondering why we haven't followed up with Erin, there's a reason for that. There were a few items that were found when she was debriefed. For now, she is in witness protection until we get this case under wraps. That means we are going to keep details on her where she is on a need-to-know basis.

I put my stuff in the trunk of my car and noticed the sun going down on another day. As the cool December night was setting in, I couldn't help but realize that Christmas was only two weeks away. I had Maria back in my life and a psychopath to track down, and those mean shopping to do.

I do have one thing going for me. When I get home, I'll have Maria waiting for me, probably with my basement torn to shit, but she'll be there just the same. I shot her a text message letting her know I was on my way home. She replied with "About damn time!"

31

That's what Christian said. I just wanted to hear it from my man.

Walking in, I noticed that the girls were out back; the radio downstairs was jamming; and from what I could tell, Maria was definitely comfortable. She was dancing around my basement in a hoodie, some shorts, and socks. It was her version of risky business in the Baggio basement. I walked up and grabbed her, she screamed loud as shit, but when I gave her a kiss she quickly melted into my arms.

"Hey Neil, fancy seeing you here. Did you like my dancing?"

"I don't know what got me more—the dancing, or your use of my closet."

"Sorry, it was getting late, and I wanted something a little bit more comfortable."

"After a long day, I needed to come home to something like this, just you are running around my basement, all cute and hyper."

"Well, I aim to please; I have found a bunch of maybes for businesses connected to Gaines's main holdings. I also found a couple of companies they do business with that they send maintenance payments to. There doesn't seem to be any services from them, simply payments. I feel they warrant a look. I have our agents looking into them as we speak. How'd your day turn out?"

"Went okay with Frank, but I got some confirmation on what I think needs to be done to flush Gaines out of hiding. It's going to take a group effort with my deal from Brock, the bureau, and our team at BCI."

"What do you have in mind?"

"You can loop in Mike, but keep it hush—I don't want anything formal until we're ready to roll."

"Understood. Is it really that off-the-handle nuts, even for you?"

"I'm going to need you to freeze his assets, even if you think he's just going to win within a week in a court of law. Then we are going to hit all his stash houses and burn those bitches to the ground with Brock's help. When Gaines moves all his money offshore we are then going to have a banker move it to a new account, to scare the shit out of him."

"That's vindictive and maniacal; I love it. This is why so many people put their trust in you. It's the big picture you see. Not just the individual move, but the way to motivate someone to do what you need them to do."

"It's just about paying attention to what got them to where they are, the totality of it all. Weighing the risks and rewards to their current actions and finding a leverage point."

"If it were as easy as you make it sound, there would be countless others that would do it. For example, most cases are closed because of simple facts, but you have an uncanny ability to get people to roll over, make a stupid decision that you can capitalize on."

"Thank you, Maria. I appreciate it."

"One other thing—are you going to tell me how the fight went last night?" Maria was flirting with me, and it was cute.

"It wasn't much of a fight; the kid went down quickly. I don't think he even made it to two minutes into the round."

"That's what Christian said. I just wanted to hear it from my man." She started laughing.

"Stop giving me such a hard time. So, what are we up to the rest of the night?"

"I figured you could help me clean up and organize down here. Then we could go up and roll around a little bit. Since I know you can box, maybe you can show me your wrestling moves."

Maria and I cleaned up downstairs, which was chaotic. It looked like someone left their seven-year-old unattended in the basement to color for a good hour without supervision. There were papers everywhere. With everything cleaned, and a little bit of kissing and foreplay, we finally made our way up to the stairs, but not before she tried removing my clothes.

"Maria, can you at least let me get to the bedroom? First, we need to let the girls in. They've been outside for a while, and they're freezing."

"Oh shit, I didn't realize you didn't bring them in."

As soon as I brought them in, they ran to the fireplace, where Maria had left it running. Maria followed suit and gave them the attention she was giving me. I decided to use my newly found freedom to sneak in a shower, get cleaned up, and relax from a long day. With the shower running and steam building up, I made my way into the shower.

"Neil Baggio, you're not getting out of this so fast."

"What are you talking about, Maria? I'm just trying to clean up for you before we get dirty."

"Cute play on words, but not cute enough. Get over here and kiss me."

And like that, Maria dropped a kiss on me that sent me back to middle school. Toes curled up, my brain turned to mush, and all thoughts wiped clean. It could also be the placement of her hands, but that's for me, not you. She shoved me into the shower, made some flirty comment, and before I knew it, I was joined in the shower by Maria, just like the first time she stayed the night.

"This brings back memories, doesn't it, Neil."

"I am a sucker for you wet in my shower, that's for certain."

Then again, what guy isn't a sucker for a gorgeous woman covered in the soap in his shower. She is crazy, my kind of crazy, and this just puts me over the edge. Maria is brilliant in so many ways; the way she attacks a case stays on it like a huntress stalking prey for days or weeks on end. She will not lose sight of what's in front of her. Where I get a bit impatient, irrational, and like to push the envelope, Maria is by the book. Though I do feel I am rubbing off on her, I think she is going to start pushing the envelope the more she hangs around me.

"You always know what to say to the ladies, don't you, Neil."

"In my defense, once they're in your shower, it's more about not messing up than anything else."

"Fair point." Maria chuckled.

"Hey Maria, while you're in here, let me take this moment to corner you."

"I like where this is headed."

"Sorry, you might not. Did you go get your eval yet, see the head doc after your ordeal? I know you're strong-willed and say you're fine. The thing is, anytime you have to deal with that kind of stress nonstop and fear of death, it's got to weigh on you."

"I'm going tomorrow; actually, first thing in the morning. Thank you for checking up on me."

"I care, always have. Even when I was doing that crazy off-book shit in Mexico that pissed you off." Maria gave me a look of death and rolled her eyes.

"I get it, I did then, and I do now. Still, it didn't make it easier to trust you for a while. "

Maria and I just sat there, water rushing over us, having a little therapy session. Talking about our fears from those days. What drove us, kept us strong, and the moment when we saw each other the courage that was lit inside each other. We both had a feeling that everything would be okay. There is something to just enjoying the moment, sitting there quietly, even if it is in a shower with your lady and talking, expressing your fears.

When you go through something like that, almost losing your best friend, colleague, and girlfriend all rolled into one person, one event, it can drain on you. Being that person who is strong-willed and determined, being thrown around like a helpless rag doll takes its toll on you. It can make even the greatest agent have confidence issues. I'm worried about her, even if it's not today; one day it will come to the forefront and hit her head-on.

"I know, the key point is that you're going to have your conversation tomorrow. I want to make sure you're okay. It's a ton to process in a few days, then come the questions. You know the routine, this isn't your first rodeo."

"No, it's not. Let's get out of here and get some rest," she said with a smile and soft look in her eyes.

"We've only been in here twenty minutes. You know how much I love my thirty-minute shower, but I can adapt for you." I smiled.

"Oh Neil, thank you so much for sacrificing those ten or so minutes for me."

Out of the shower, in my favorite shorts and rocking my hat on backward, I noticed that Maria was staring at me. More like enjoying the view than anything else, but she looked like someone smitten, that's for sure. I was sitting on the bed, going through the case, going through what I talked about with Frank, double-checking my notes. Maria had the news on, Channel 4. Christina Moore is touting some shit again; I'm sure it's a misguided story.

Wait a minute, misguided story, off-target—

"FUCKING BROCK!"

"What?" Maria jumped.

"The Butcher, that fucking dumb piece of shit. He just gave me a clue I needed."

"I feel like I'm not working with the same deck you are." Maria looked perplexed.

I got up, ran across the house, and sprinted down the steps, with the girls on my heels, all three of them. Maria, Danielle, and Jackie were chasing after me, trying to figure out what the crazy man of the house was doing. This reminds me, at work,

I'm surrounded by a ton of testosterone, but at home it's all estrogen, women galore. I wonder if I did that shit on purpose, or if I subconsciously set my life up that way for balance.

Okay, back to why I'm standing in the basement with my Detroit Tigers spring training shorts, Tigers hat on backward, and nothing else. Just standing there, looking around, looking for something, but I can't find it. *Where is it?* I know I saw that shit around here somewhere.

"Neil, what are you looking for? I can help you if you just let me know what you're looking for."

"I almost found it. Give me a second, I don't know what it is, but I'll know it when I see it."

"You're lucky your track record allows you to act like a—"

"Found it! Schmitt's Meat Packing! Fucking Schmitt's! I knew it!"

"That's the business with random transfers all the time but nothing from them to Gaines's businesses. I was telling you the bureau was looking into it. What does Brock have to do with this?"

"This is the meatpacking district he shot up. Gaines and his crew aren't over there, but they are close by. If I remember correctly, he flipped the last two digits of the address and shot up the wrong place. That's where Gaines's crew is hiding, I bet you anything."

"What's the next move, then? Do you have anything you are going to do, anything you have planned?" Maria knows better than to think I have a plan.

"Maria, I'm going to get dressed, head into the office. I'll call Christian to meet me there, and have TJ get to work on cross-referencing the information to find the right address for us to do some recon on."

"You mean, right now? What are you going to find out at eleven at night?" Maria knows the answer.

"Maria, really?"

"Yeah, that was stupid; most illicit activities happen late. Just like Mama used to say, nothing good happens after midnight."

"Exactly, Maria. Plenty of good things happen; they just lead to bad things often," I said with a big-ass grin as I kissed her.

"You're really proud of yourself, aren't you, Neil?"

"Yup!"

Like that, I ran back upstairs, ladies trailing behind. This time Maria chased more aggressively, and when I got to the bed, she tackled me onto it. For a good two minutes I was getting my ass kicked by the ladies of the house, but I didn't mind it.

"Hey, I'd love to stay and wrestle with you, but you can't mess with progress, you know that."

"I know, Neil, but you know I can't join you. I have my meeting in the morning. I have to lay low, keep my mind clear."

"I wouldn't want it any other way. You need to take care of yourself if you feel the need to get out and hustle, go to the office, and give TJ a hard time. The guys there aren't used to seeing a hottie like you. It would be fun."

"I'll keep that in mind if I get cabin fever. I feel safe here with your girls and knowing Sheila is down the street and your warehouse is close by." Maria gave me a big hug and a kiss.

"I'd say I won't be late, but we know that probably won't happen. If you need anything and can't get ahold of me, you know TJ and Ken are just a phone call away."

"Thanks, Neil. You're cute when you are trying to be ultraprotective."

"Have to be. As Gaines said, always protect your queen."

Like that, I quickly changed and made my way out of the house. I shot Christian a text to meet me at the warehouse and gave TJ a heads up for what info I was going to need. I didn't drive too fast on my way over there; I knew Christian would need time to get there and TJ would need time to pull the info. I just took my time, drove with the heat on, windows down, and started thinking through the case. I kept coming back to the idea of Gaines talking about a chess game. I thought it might help if I draw it out, map out our moves, what he did, what I did, how each of us countered each other. Might help me figure this shit out, always remember to protect your queen.

COLLOQUIUM

I texted Ken to get a guy on the house ASAP, keep an eye on Maria to be safe. I didn't want her to know, though; I just want her to be safe.

32

Drunk and stoned street dudes aren't the most punctual.

At the warehouse, I was sitting there with TJ for a solid fifteen minutes when Christian pulled in. TJ and I were going over the old footage from the meat plant shoot-out, sifting through all the data we could from when he did that. It was only a few months ago, but Brock has quickly raised in the game. He took that anger out on a lot of people, which led to his rise in the streets. TJ had found the address, we believe. Only one way to find out.

"Hey Christian, did you bring your gear? It's time to have some fun, raise a little hell. Also, did you reach out to Brock to see if we confirm it's a Gaines location if he's game to help us with it?"

"Yeah, Brock is game, he said he can get there in ten to fifteen max. He'll have a crew of guys ready to go if we call him. To be safe, I'd say we give them a thirty-to-forty-minute heads up. Drunk and stoned street dudes aren't the most punctual." Christian has a point.

"I'll let you keep up the communication with them. I'm going to poke my nose around the building and tick some people off. You're going to cover me with that big old rifle of yours."

"Neil, I'm always game for your crazy-ass shenanigans, but don't you think we should have a few more people come with us? I know Terrance and Nicolette aren't around, 'cause they're in the GC, but we have other great people."

"Christian, you know how I am on ops like these. I'd rather roll light and controlled than heavy and unpredictable. If we get into shit, you call in the cavalry of thugs followed by BCI and the bureau. We got this." I think.

"Okay! When are you going to explain to me what you plan on doing with all of those flash-bang grenades?" Oh, he noticed.

"What, these? Nah, I'm not going to share that. But that's also because I haven't figured it out yet."

"That's the Neil honesty we've come to know and love. Breeds great confidence." Christian has jokes.

"It's gotten me this far and kept me alive this long."

"Sometimes I feel like you're our Ricky Bobby!" TJ lost it on that one.

"Christian is killing it tonight, really bringing the heat. Damn, son, did I call your mom fat by accident or something?"

"No, I'm just trying to lighten the mood, Neil. Let's get going; we want to get out there and see if your hunch is correct."

Christian was following behind me as we made our way out to the warehouse district where Schmitt's was shot up a few months ago. Their address is 1701, and we needed to head over to 1710, scout it out, and see what we can find. It's hard to get away with playing dumb when you have a recognizable face. Especially when you are walking around one of these places, but I still like to try. You can always hope for the uneducated idiot youth of America.

I don't mean idiot, like dumb, lacking intelligence, more in terms of lacking the willingness to connect to the news or current events. I feel that being an idiot has so many levels. We have smart dumb people all over; for example, look at our politicians. Plenty of them are lawyers, they passed the bar exam, but they say and do so much dumb shit.

As we got closer, I saw Christian pull off and make his way to a neighboring street so he could get up on top of a different building. Christian drives a big-ass Ford F-350 truck, turbocharged and lifted. You may ask yourself why, but when it comes to two- and three-story buildings, it comes in handy with a small ladder easily stowed away in the back. He also put an HVAC company logo on the back, so it doesn't stand out if he's on a ladder to a roof. People question it less; they just assume someone is working on an AC unit. Yes, at BCI, we really do think through stuff this much. From the painter's van for surveillance and Christian truck, thinking ahead is what gives us an edge.

"Christian, let me know when you are in place. I found a parking spot in the alley a block over."

"I can see you. I'm up here; give me a second to get in place and find a good vantage point."

It took Christian just a few moments to get in place. I began walking toward the building while he started scoping it out. While he was scanning the building, I walked around the neighboring businesses looking to see what was open, what was closed, getting a feel for the neighborhood we were working in. He said there only seemed to be movement in the southwestern corner of the building, to which I replied, "Huh?"

"Christian, does it look like I have a compass out here? You see me, you see the building, where should I go?" I said with a light chuckle.

"Now you're joking; I see how it is. Okay, it's on the opposite side of the building from where you're at. The opposite corner, if you walk around and turn left, you'll see the light on, it looks like a loading bay."

"Got it, Christian. I'll get a better look."

Making my way around the building, I noticed the distinct sound of rap music—loud as shit, too—coming from the building. Not surprising that some gang bangers are listening to loud music at nearly midnight. Oh no, we should call the police on them for a noise complaint, although that shit would be funny. I could see the bay, but I could see only so much. Christian needs to make his way around and look from over here.

"Hey Christian, are you circling the perimeter for a better view?"

"Luckily, these buildings are stacked on top of each other and close. I'm almost over there, I'm just hoofing it. Give me a second."

"Let me know when you see what I'm seeing. We need to take a few pics of this shit. I can try with my phone, but no way the camera is picking this up. Any ideas?"

"There is a security camera on the building across from the bay at the other building. It's not pointing that way. Maybe you can get over there and turn it, then TJ can hack into it to keep an eye on the bay from there."

"Shoot him a text, the address is 1695. I'll figure a way to get this shit turned."

I had to find a few items to stack up, but luckily there was a crap ton of trash in the alley. Barely able to reach it, I said fuck it, jumped, and started jerking the camera a bit one way to another. Then I head Christian chiming in my ear.

"Neil, what the hell are you doing? TJ said you're way off base. You need to bring it back a bit."

"I need more direction than that."

"TJ said you're at eight o'clock; you need to be at eleven. Does that make sense?"

"I think so. How about now?" I wiggled as slightly as I could to square it up.

"TJ said you're good; now you just need to get down without anyone hearing you."

I let go, fell to the ground, and landed on what can only be described as an aluminum can that had combustible air of some sort in it. I made a loud-ass sound similar to a balloon being popped, if the balloon was made of light metal and in an alley across from a place where a bunch of bad guys with guns were.

"Nice, Neil. That was gentle as a feather gliding to the ground."

"Your sarcasm is duly noted. Keep an eye on the loading bay. Is there any movement, or are they jamming too loud to that shit music?"

"Hey man, don't you dare call Jadakiss shit music, I mean they aren't listening to the best hip hop imaginable, but it's not crap." I didn't peg Christian as a rap guy.

"Fine. I'll stop judging the music for now, but I'll be talking a ton of shit about it later."

"You're insane, Neil. It's just you and me out here, you're a sitting duck, and you're cracking jokes."

"I know. I see movement. What do we have? Is that who I think it is?"

"It is. That's Gaines's head of security, Bryan. Any sign of Gaines anywhere?"

"Well, I don't see any of his cars, and there are definitely no cars out there that give off the comic book villain ride. So I doubt he's here."

"I have a crazy idea that might just work. Call Brock now, also make sure to cover my ass when they get here. I'm going to kidnap that little shit when the gunfire starts, then we can question him and drop him off at the FBI field office when we're through with him."

"You really are crazy, but then again this shit will probably work. I just texted Brock; he said they're ten minutes out."

The next ten minutes felt like it took almost thirty minutes; it was brutal, but that's because it took thirty minutes. These idiots got lost. This Brock guy is really struggling. We even told him it's where he fucked up last time. Come on, man, get your drunk and stoned ass in the game.

If this were a movie, the guys would be running around, doing flips, and shit shooting; it would be epic. This isn't the movies, this is real life, this is Detroit at nearly one in the morning, and I called one group of drunk and stoned dudes to take on another group. If I don't get shot, it's going to be a miracle.

"I see them pulling up; keep your head down, Neil, they are—"

"Making an entrance. I hear them bumping their tunes and shooting bullets in the air. Hopefully they don't empty their clips before they get here. These guys are real pros; we work with the best teams at BCI."

"Neil, you're crazy. Let's just survive this shit."

"I got this, don't worry. I'm going to make a move on the building; cover my ass. They are about to pull up. The best way to nab this guy is to be behind them when the shooting starts."

"This is a bad idea, Neil, But then again, all your shit ideas seem to work out."

With the confidence of Christian oozing out at immense levels, I was ready to go. I sprinted up to the side of the building where there was a window open. Previously it had guys standing by it, but at this moment they were a little preoccupied with Brock and his guys shooting at their warehouse. I think a five-year-old who was nearsighted and had an issue with being frail would have had a better chance shooting at these guys, but I'll take it. Neither side is hitting anything. They are just shooting all over the place, hitting cars, buildings, and other random shit.

"Neil, where are you? I see Bryan heading out the back."

"I'm right behind him. I'm letting him lead me out of the building, head toward your truck. Let's get ready to toss him in the back of your truck. Make sure you have your zip ties handy."

"You crazy bastard!"

Christian was running and yelling at me at the same time. I think at one point he was yelling at me in Polish. It's something he picked up on the case we took that had us in Warsaw for some time. Bryan made his way out of the back door, no one in sight, he was running like a roach when the lights are turned on.

"Hey Bryan, where do you think you're going?"

"Neil, what the fuck, I should have known this had you all over it."

I reached back, punched him in his ribs, then again in his stomach. When he bent over, I uppercut his ass with all the anger I had from him getting Gaines out of that mess. Bryan hit the ground, partially with it. The combination of the hit, adrenaline, and his head on the ground caused him to pass out. I guess I have to carry his ass from here.

"Christian, you better get to your car quickly, 'cause I've got Bryan on my shoulders like he's a lost sheep. I don't think I'm going to make it all the way over there, especially around the building."

"I'm in the truck, coming around now, just a throw-in in the backseat, I'll pull away, tie him up, and we'll meet up. Just tell me where."

Christian made his way around the building as I made it halfway to the back where he had parked. I used up a lot of leg strength, trying to ensure I got away from all the shooting. As he pulled up, I opened the door, threw Bryan in there, and closed the door.

"Christian, pull the truck against the building. I'm going to climb up and use the roofs to get around the check on the loading bay and then get to my car."

"What's there to look at?"

"I won't know unless I check it out. Get out of here, start heading toward Orchard Lake. I'll tell you where to meet me."

"Where?"

"I'll text you the address. See you in an hour."

Christian pulled his big-ass truck to the building, allowing me to climb up easier. As I made my way around the rooftops, I saw him pull off, and I began to make my way toward the scene of the chaos we just created. Brock and his guys were gone already. From the looks of it their cars were not damaged too badly, no parts left behind, I don't see any large pools of blood, so that's good. As I looked into the bay, you could see the guys regrouping. From the looks of it, no one from their side took a hit.

Seriously, all that shooting and no one took a bullet anywhere? Not even the pinky finger or big toe? I'm not one for encouraging violence, but proper shooting technique is a necessity; think of where all those other bullets went. The only plus is this area was vacant when we pulled up, and there isn't a house for miles out here. I bet you Brock is out there talking shit like "They shot them motherfuckers up" when in reality all he shot up was the concrete, a garage door, and a few walls.

The sad part is, almost ten minutes after the shooting started, and there still isn't a cop in sight. I bet no one even called the cops, figuring what's the point? As I sat on that shit thought that just entered my brain, I finally made my way over to the alley where my car was. Dropping down, much quieter than before. Which was useless because my car isn't so quiet when it starts up. I'm a block away, but still it's loud as shit, especially in this alley. Time to head toward Orchard Lake. I'll text Christian the address.

"Neil, this address is your old high school. Why are we going there?"

"I have a key to the boatshed for the rowing team. We may have donated a new building for them. I had a key made for just an occasion. Just in case."

"I'll see you out there shortly."

"I'll catch up to you. Let me know if you see any cops since you're ahead of me."

"So far it's clear. See you soon."

33

My mom taught me rule number one when you run with
someone like Gaines.

In the boatshed, with Bryan propped up on a chair, Christian and I were talking. We could see Bryan was beginning to come to. We were arguing over whether we should hide our faces. I said he already saw me, so it doesn't matter, plus who is going to believe him? We just need to find the right leverage on him.

"Christian, I'm telling you, it won't be a big deal. We'll be fine, just roll with it. I have a feeling he's about to serve us a big-ass curveball."

"Really, Neil. What makes you think that?"

"Nothing, other than to Gaines, this is a big-ass chess game. We need to think like that. Take pieces off the board for him."

"Okay, I'll follow your lead."

Bryan was groggy but started coming to. He swayed a bit in his chair and fell over. He just laid there, mumbling a bit, kind of pissed too. I cleaned him up next to the chair; I didn't even have the decency to pick him up. I just left him there, figured it would throw him off a bit. Have you ever seen anyone put the suspect on the floor next to the chair in an interrogation? Nope, but they will, you'll see: they'll learn from Neil Baggio.

"Neil, what the hell do you think you're doing? What was this stunt? Hey you, bro, I'll double whatever Neil is paying you. Shit, I'll triple it."

"First of all, I don't even pay that guy, I don't know who he is." This is going to be fun.

"We weren't arguing just a moment ago, we were introducing ourselves. I'm a big adventure fan, answered an ad, here I am. This is some fun shit, it's so real." Christian is having fun with this.

"You guys are crazy. What the hell do you want with me, Neil? Gaines is the guy you want, not me." Bryan kind of has a point. I'll take both.

"Well, Bryan, you're only partially correct. See, you are key to Gaines's bullshit defense of claiming you kidnapped him."

"What the fuck are you talking about? That's bullshit, I didn't kidnap him, he asked me to rescue his ass. Where did you hear this shit about him claiming I kidnapped him?"

"His lawyer on TV, minutes after you saved him from being arrested."

You could see Bryan's head trying to work through what we were telling him. He knew it sounded like something Gaines would do, he knew that I was plausible as shit. Christian and I kept up our shenanigans and finally got Bryan so pissed he started to come around and ask us what all this shit was about. I really didn't know; I was just trying to get him to a place where he would stop being defensive and get curious.

"Okay, I give up. What's it going to take to get out of here, or at least get these things cut off of my hands. You know I have a girlfriend; she's going to be worried about me."

"I'll tell you what—do you and your girlfriend feel like taking a vacation together? Maybe dipping out before this case goes sideways and you get stuck with everything?"

"I'm listening, that's all I can tell you." Bryan was open-minded but still mad.

"I wouldn't trust him. I say we just put him in one of these boats and let him float around the lakes for a while." Christian has a good idea.

"Although that would be funny as shit, I don't think to give him pneumonia is what's needed here. He knows we want his boss, that's the leverage he has, but it's also the card we have."

"You guys know I can hear you, I'm sitting right here." Bryan was getting impatient.

"Okay, I need to get you off the board, out of the game, to put pressure on Gaines. You've got one choice and one choice only. You cooperate with me and the FBI to make an announcement, make it look like you turned yourself in or got arrested, I don't care. Either way, we need Gaines to know he can't use you as his scapegoat."

"If this is going to save my ass I'm all in, my mom taught me rule number one when you run with someone like Gaines and the gang bangers I work with. Cover your ass at all times and take care of number one at all costs."

Bryan is starting to get on board; he realizes he has only one smart play, and it's not to back Gaines at this time. This is a time-honored tradition of crime-solving: find a guy below the guy and turn him. In this case we aren't turning him just yet, though he will quickly learn that if he turns state's evidence, that's his best option.

"I'll make the call to my contact at the FBI and get everything set up." My girlfriend.

"Christian, you can cut off those ties, let him get up and grab a seat. I think there's some water over in the corner over there behind those benches." Christian went and grabbed his water.

"Okay, guys, so what's the next move? I get out of town and lay low for a while?"

"Not quite that simple—you can run forever, or you can turn state's evidence on Gaines and get off easy, take a vacation for six months."

"Wait a minute, when you said 'vacation,' I thought you meant a real vacation. Not prison." Bryan is playing catch-up mentally.

"Bryan, let me walk you through this. You have committed a handful of felonies in the past two days alone. It isn't going to be hard for us to tie you to others. If you want, I can go to the warehouse right now, ask your guys who want to save their ass by turning you in, and see how many quickly raise their hand."

"You don't have to rub it in, I get it. I'm essentially screwed either way; at least with you, I have a shot at living and getting out of jail before I'm fifty. I guess we go with your plan."

Christian looked dumbfounded; he thought this was going to be much harder than it was. I figured it would go one of two ways. He'd either roll over, which he did, or he'd double down. After watching him run out of that warehouse like a scared cat, I figured he would break like a wet napkin. While Christian was keeping an eye on him and having a friendly conversation with him, I dialed Mike first; no answer. I guess I'm going to have to wake up Maria; I hope she's not too pissed.

"Neil, it's after one in the morning. Is everything okay?"

"Maria, I have some news that might make you mad, followed by news that will make you smile. Why don't you wake up, grab a cup of coffee, take a shower, then call me back."

"Neil, what the hell. Just spit it out. What dumb shit did you do that ended up working out?" She knows me so well.

"Long story short, I may have help Bryan escape the warehouse he was at and now convinced him to turn state's evidence." If I don't say 'kidnap,' she isn't obligated to testify that I ever did.

"So you helped Bryan, free himself from his own warehouse with his own men?" Maria is figuring it out.

"Yes, ma'am, that is God's honest truth. Christian was there to ensure we were safe and followed protocol. Less about the how, let's get down to the what's next. Bryan wants to turn state's evidence on Gaines for a reduced sentence."

"We need to call Mike immediately, probably get Bryan down to the field office, at least a safe house." Maria was wide awake now.

"He's calling on the other line, I tried him first, but no answer. Get some rest. I'll call you in the morning."

"Neil, are you going to be okay?"

"Yeah, we're good. I have to take Mike's call. Talk to you later, Maria."

Once done with the quick call to Maria, I followed up with a short call to Mike. He was quick to wrap his head around what I was saying. He needed to call a judge in the middle of the night, secure some paperwork, and go from there. He asked if I had somewhere to hold Bryan over for the night. We had three options: in my opinion, we could go back to my place, my warehouse, or stay here in a dorm and crash for the night. Here being the easiest option, it's my high school, which might have you wondering how we are going to stay there. Well, they have dorms, if you remember from the case that brought me back here in the first place.

"Hey Christian, you can get out of here if you want. I'm going to keep Bryan here to lay low off the grid for the night." They both looked at me, confused.

"In the boatshed, really? There isn't anywhere else we can hide him?" Christian asked.

"Yeah, I'm with your buddy. There isn't a hotel, or someplace else we can check into?" Bryan was fighting back disappointment.

"Don't worry, we're not sleeping in the boatshed. We're going to the dorms. We'll pop in on the RA, a teacher I'm friends with, to get a key they keep for the visitors' rooms."

"I still vote to go to a hotel." Bryan really wanted that room service.

"Bryan, we have two choices: come willingly, or I can knock you out again."

"No need to get angry, Neil, I'm just a bit whiny. I'm getting hungry too." Bryan has a good point. Even I'm hungry.

"Christian, can you run and find us something to eat, even if it's junk from fast food somewhere? Bryan, I'm assuming at this point a burger or a taco will work just fine."

"Yeah, just get me something to eat. I don't care what it is."

Like that, Christian headed out to find us some grub, while Bryan and I hopped in my car and drove around campus to the dorms. It was almost two in the morning, and I know Rich is going to be pissed. Hey, what's a guy going to do? I spent more than a hundred grand on that case, then I turned around and donated a building to them. Walking into the dorms, Bryan kept looking around in awe. For someone who went to school there, I sometimes forget how beautiful it can be, especially blanketed in white snow. Here goes, Rich is going to lose his shit on us, thinking we're some kids.

"Who the hell is knocking on my door at two in the morning? It better be good; someone better be close to death!" Rich was pissed.

"Hey Rich, it's Neil. I need the keys to one of the visitor rooms for my friend and me."

"Neil, you aren't in any trouble, are you?" Rich handed me the keys.

"No, we just need to be off the grid until the bureau can get some paperwork to bring him in. I was already on this side of town, figured this is a safe place."

"Always a safe place; a son of Orchard Lake is always a son. We are family, even though I want to kill you right now. Just put the keys in the mail slot when you head out in the morning."

Rich was a paratrooper in the army and served almost ten years. He was also a graduate of St. Mary's Prep. A lot of students make their way back to the school to give back, teach, and inspire other young men to do great things. He's also one tough bastard: he kicks a lot of kids into shape, straightens them up. That's what he's great for, though he's always there too, no matter what the issue, these kids know they can count on Rich. Shit, I'm counting on him, and I graduated back in the early thirties. I'm kidding.

"Thanks, Rich, we'll be quiet, just need to lay low and head out in the morning."

"If you need anything, you know where to find me." Rich smiled and closed the door.

We made our way into the room. Not sure what Bryan was expecting, but he was pleasantly surprised. The rooms are set up for studies, double bed, elevated with desks underneath. They're clean, inviting, and full of Orchard Lake St. Mary's swag. They're designed for when students come to visit the school. They want to see what the dorms are like; its marketing material in the form of a room.

"Neil, this isn't half bad. I have to hand it to you. All I need now is something to fill this stomach, and I'll be ready to crash." Bryan looked exhausted, not surprising.

"Christian texted me a minute ago when we were walking up. He'll be here in a minute. He said he found an open burger place, so he got us some burgers and some fries, plus a couple of drinks."

You could see Bryan licking his lips; he was ready to eat. Some of us eat when we're stressed. I know it used to be a big problem I had for years, then I turned to drinking, now I hit a heavy bag and drink an absurd amount of coffee. I don't even think it's about the caffeine anymore, I think it's the mental state it gives me holding a cup. Like a doctor coming to save the day, Christian knocked at the door so softly I ripped the door open quickly to scare him.

"Dude, way to knock with authority." He didn't enjoy my joke.

"Come on, man, here's your food. You guys going to be good for the night? And Neil, you're sure you don't need me to stay?" Christian was double-checking, as he always does.

"Man, you've done more than enough. Go get some rest, we'll be good. I'll let you know what happens in the morning."

"Thanks, guys. It was a pleasure meeting you, Bryan. Sorry it was under these circumstances."

"Me too, but hey, it's the bed I made. I need to deal with it. I knew someday it was going to be this or a box in the ground. I'll take this."

I'll give Bryan credit, this guy is taking it on the chin, really seems to be playing the role. He's playing it a little too well, though; I hope he doesn't bolt in the middle of the night. I'll have to do my best to stay up all night or sleep light. The burgers and drinks hit the spot, I didn't eat the fries—I forgot they were there. I was too busy inhaling burgers. Eventually I wasn't hungry and moved on. Bryan, on the other hand . . .

"Hey Neil, are you going to eat your fries? Just in case I don't get to eat this kind of grease inside, I'm going to get my fill." Good point.

"No problem, man. Tell you what, we can grab a nice breakfast in the morning."

"That would be sweet. For now, I'm going to lay down and get some rest." Bryan rolled over and passed out.

"Night."

I guess I'm going to get a quick shut-eye Bryan isn't dumb enough to try to leave, make a run for it, is he? I guess I'm about to find out. As my eyelids kept getting heavier, I found myself fading into dreamland, thinking of the case and how we're going to make a move on Gaines. I had slipped into a deep sleep; you know the ones when it feels like five hours, but it turns out to be fifteen minutes? That's what happened, I was out like a light quick when I heard a large thud that sounded like someone slamming a bat into a wall.

"Hey there, buddy, it's not nice to sneak out on your friend Neil. He brought you here to make sure you guys were safe."

"I don't know what you're talking about. I . . . I was just looking for the bathroom." Bryan is a horrible liar, especially for a bad guy.

"You mean the one in your room that's easily visible isn't good enough for you? See, it looks to me like you were trying to dip out on Neil while he was sleeping." Rich is my guy.

Oh, did I forget to mention to you that I texted Rich when we were heading to the dorms? That's why he didn't get too mad when I knocked. He also followed behind shortly after we came in, probably talking to Christian a few different times but not letting Bryan know. I figured if we let the birdie think he can fly away, then grab him again, he might realize the totality of his situation a little better.

"Thanks, Rich. Bryan, get your ass in here. I'm not dumb enough to think you're not going to try to escape. Rich is going to sit out there and keep an eye on the door so we can get some sleep. You can either come back in here and catch a little bit of sleep, or you can fight with the angry army guy who has a bat."

"I'll take the option that doesn't include getting knocked unconscious again." Smart boy, Bryan.

"Rich has a pretty mean swing too. He's won softball MVP multiple years in the faculty game. Good choice, Bryan."

Finally able to sleep, knowing we have just crushed his will and shown him he's stuck, I'll get a good three hours. It's enough to function in the morning, especially if I get my coffee on an IV drip, I'll be good to go. Now it's time to crash, time to fall asleep.

34

Long day, need coffee, what the fuck.

You ever have one of those days where you feel like you're going to cross paths with a black cat while walking under a ladder on Friday the thirteenth? Holy shit, the day feels that way already, not because I slept for shit, just something in the air. It took me a minute to get moving. At least my roommate is still here. Bryan is a heavy sleeper. I ended up kidney punching him to get him moving, not enough for damage but enough to wake his ass up quickly. Once I was up, I took a moment and called Mike, got the rundown for how the morning would go. He told me to get Bryan there by eight thirty this morning before the craziness ensues. Now I just have to get him up. Damn, he sleeps heavy.

"Holy shit, what was that?" Bryan woke up, startled. I wonder why.

"No idea, I'm just sitting over here minding my own business. How'd you sleep?"

"You sure you didn't just kidney punch me? Damn bro, I guess I deserved some cheap shot after trying to ditch you guys last night. I promise I'll stop trying to run."

"No, you won't. That's okay, it's in your nature, it's why you're a bad guy working for a crime boss wannabe."

"Wait a minute, Gaines is more than a wannabe, he's running so much all over this city. You don't even know the half of it." He's an idiot. Why don't you tell me?

"Gaines is a hack; he reminds me of some guy that read too many comics growing up. I know he's not a two-bit hustler, but he's no kingpin either."

"I guess we'll see when I lay it out for the FBI what they think of him. I helped him build that empire. If he thinks he could toss me to the wolves, take the credit, and walk away, he has another thing coming. I'll give him all the credit; let's see how he feels with all that weight hanging around his neck." Damn, he's getting fired up.

After getting Bryan riled up, we finally got on our way. I got him to the car and led him on, told him we were going to breakfast. I wasn't a complete asshole. I took him for some breakfast. Coffee and a breakfast burrito, the best way to start the day on a budget. I'm not sure Bryan was feeling me, though I'm quite positive he was pissed.

"Dude, you said last night that we would go to a great breakfast this morning. You had my hopes up."

"Bryan, dude, bro! Did you forget that little bit of information where you tried dipping out last night? That's when your great breakfast downgraded to a drive-thru kind of morning. You're lucky I'm even feeding you and not making you eat out of a vending machine downtown."

"Neil, shit! Why do you always have to be so blunt? I get it, but damn."

"Bryan, I don't have time for wasting, not on this case, not with Gaines, not with anyone. Too much going on, just get your story straight and remember the more you sing, the less you sit in prison. It's a pretty simple math equation. The more you give, the more you get."

"I get it, I get whiny, and you remind me of the fact that you're not handcuffing me and throwing me to the cops. I should just quit while I'm ahead."

It took me giving him a hard time all morning to slowly break him down. My hope was that by the time we get to the FBI field office, he'll be ready to talk. If I were to puff him up, fill him with a great breakfast, and make him feel like nothing is going on, he would walk in the office feeling like he's in control. This morning and last night are about showing him he's no longer in charge. The only way he can impact his future is by being cooperative.

As we pulled up to the FBI field office, Mike and a team of agents were waiting for me. The scene was a bit odd because Mike made it sound like he wanted this quiet, with a limited number of people. I didn't even see Maria there. Come to think of it, her car wasn't in its usual spot, either. I didn't see it on my way in. Something odd is going on here. I told you the day is going to be messed up. I can just tell.

"Neil, thanks for bringing our esteemed guest to us. Have a great day."

"Mike, what gives, man? I did all that work for what? Now you're kicking me out?" This isn't like Mike at all.

"Neil, time to go, talk to you later," Mike said, gritting his teeth and gesturing toward the corner. Then I realized why.

"Okay, peace."

Like that, I took off driving as fast as I could without making a scene. I didn't peel out, but I drove out of there fast. I knew Maria would have an idea of what was going on, especially since she wasn't even there. From the looks of it, Mike is trying to insulate Maria and me in this case. Which means his bosses from DC are probably in town putting pressure on him. Shit, they better not fuck this up as they did with Cappelano. Gaines is no serial killer, but he's a psycho causing plenty of death and destruction with drugs and his gang affiliations.

I tried calling Maria, no answer, tried her again, no answer. I guess I'm going to have to call Sheila; I need to talk to someone, get myself to come down from this manic state. When I get like this, I can go off the deep end, not drinking or anything but doing rash shit. For example, a few years ago, as a newly minted private investigator, I came across a cheating husband, but not just any cheating husband. This kind finds a way to divorce his wife and try to leave her with nothing because he has the lawyer and the money.

He was also connected, so the fact that he kept getting busted with hookers and blow kept disappearing. The rumor is that I may have surprised him at one of his favorite shit motels with his shit girl, took a bag of coke, and might have to shove it up to his ass. Now before you get all weird and think I stuck my hand up this dude's ass, nope. What happened is I came into the motel, kicked the door in, found him in missionary, real fancy, on top of this girl. So I thought quickly, grabbed the bag of blow I saw on the table, and with the end of my gun, I may or may not have accidentally slipped, allowing the gun to force the drugs into his rectum.

Again, that's the rumor, but I cannot confirm nor deny the allegations. I can head home and keep calling people until I get there. Maybe I can try Ken, ring . . . nope! Shit, this is getting annoying, I'll give Maria five more minutes, then I'm calling Sheila. I don't want to run to Sheila every time, it's not fair to Maria, it's not healthy, but it's what I've done for so long.

"Neil, sorry I missed your call. I was finishing up with Mike, he said you seemed pissed. He wanted to assure me he is only trying to protect you and me. Calm down, come home, and we can talk through it." Maria is being stern with me like an angry mom, but I need it.

"I'm almost home, I'll be there in ten. I'm just pissed a bit, I did all that work, what am I missing? You know I hate being blindsided, especially by you FBI fucks!"

"Neil, first of all, you fuck this FBI agent, don't insult her. You know the game, that's why you lead the life you do. Come home, we'll hit the heavy bag and work through it. I'll get your wraps and stuff ready, I'll even lay out some shorts and a shirt."

"Make it a hoodie, I need to sweat, I need to clear my mind." Maria is always on it.

"I'll see you in a few minutes; I'm going to crank the radio and clear my mind. Work through this shit. Just tell me it's not that shadowy asshole Gracin; I think he still blames me for his daughter." Even though Cappelano did that shit.

"Gracin is part of the group that's in town, it's the DC guys coming to pull rank. They think they can build a RICO case against Gaines with Bryan there now." Maria is gritting her teeth now.

"I'll be there shortly; we can talk shit then. I can hear your frustrations too."

It took me nearly fifteen minutes to get there; I stopped for gas and a cup of coffee. Shit, the gas station coffee was cold and stale, come on. Told ya, it is one of those days, it has that hazy kind of shit day to it. I took an extra minute driving through the subdivision, thinking of what Bryan can give them, what he can add to the case, simply a witness, someone to point in directions? Then I started to think about Gaines saying over and over that this is a game of chess. It kept repeating in my head. Sometimes you have to sacrifice a key piece to win the game. I can't think this is over, I can't get fixated on Bryan.

Back home, I pulled in slowly, thinking I could catch Maria off guard, but she was waiting for me in front of the house. Standing outside with a hoodie on and one of my Red Wings winter caps. She looked so cute. She had the girls out in the back—I could hear them barking. When they're outside when they hear me pull up, they bark to help me find them.

"Hey cutie, I dig the hat." Maria does look cute—cold, but cute.

"Neil come here, give me a kiss, we're both pissed, but I know you're fuming." She gave me a quick peck.

"Let's go inside, let the girls in, and talk this out as I hit the bag."

"Sounds good."

With the girls inside, feet clean from the wet backyard, and a cup of coffee in my hand, I made my way to the basement. Maria was already down there, moving some papers around that were stacked up. She's been going above and beyond lately, and I'm worried. She's always been the confident, leave-me-alone type. Lately she's been nesting, planting at my place, which I don't mind at all, but I still worry. I grabbed my wraps and started my prebag routine.

"Hey Maria, I don't understand what's going on. I mean, I get the DC office bullshit, but why now, why the RICO case, and how did they get out here so quickly? Who tipped them off?"

"That's the thing. Apparently they've been in town a few days working on their case, trying to track down Gaines themselves, and they were leaving the field office in Detroit out of it. They thought you and I were too close to it." Maria had this disgruntled look on her face.

"Mike has to be pissed. I know he didn't look happy when I pulled up, but he knows this case is going to get taken from him, going to get trumped from him." Maria rolled her eyes.

"You have no idea. One of the reasons Mike loves working with you in Detroit is that it usually keeps prying eyes away. They just like the results and don't want to deal with you."

"Hey, now!"

"Don't get me wrong, Neil, he likes you, respects the shit out of you, but he enjoys the perks your shadow casts, as we all do." She's got a point.

"Okay, I got you there, I can see that. But why now? Why haven't they gone after Gaines before? It's the kidnapping case that elevated it, brought the threshold over the RICO statute so they could nail him with it."

As we're talking, I'm working through it, hitting the bag, hitting each spot, focusing on my footwork with each thought. Allowing the anger from one shit issue to rise up from my toes, through my core, and out into the bag as I snap each punch. Maria was feeding me, getting me riled up a bit. I think she was enjoying watching me hit the bag, especially once she told me to take off my shirt since I was getting sweaty. That's when the morning turned on a dime.

"Hey Neil, come over here, give me a kiss, you sexy, sweaty beast of a man."

I'm not one to keep an attractive woman waiting, so I leaned in and kissed her. At first I played a little coy; it was fun. She got mad at me, even hitting me in the shoulder, calling me an ass. Then I leaned back in, kissing her passionately. It was one of those moments, the one like you had in high school with that first date, when you really start getting into kissing and you finally let yourself go. We were lost in each other for the next twenty minutes, kissing, playing, and enjoying each other's company to the fullest. I was always told you can tell plenty without telling all, and we all know what happened.

Lying flat on the floor, the two of us panting like the girls after a run, we just started laughing. Giggling uncontrollably. We realized it doesn't matter what the feds do, I can still do what I do best, be me, piss off the authority—that is, until the result is what they want.

"Is that what you had in mind when you made me take my shirt off?" Maria looked at me softly.

"You know exactly what I wanted, and you followed suit properly. Well done!"

"Shit, you make it sound like I just performed a good trick for you. Does Neil get a treat now?" I said, joking.

"Shut up, asshole. I'm getting cold over here. Either lay on me and warm me up or let's go upstairs."

I went upstairs with her behind me, yelling, but I thought it was cute and funny at the same time. I went into the bathroom, turned on the shower, and got her all warmed up. While she was in there, I got changed and made my way back into the basement to clean up the mess we made, along with reviewing a few cases files Maria had organized. The ones she had on the wall and the file she had organized had lists of subsidiaries along with businesses that didn't fit their industry. For example, if you're investigating an oil tycoon company and for some reason they keep buying large quantities of sandwich bags, you'd want to figure out why.

"Okay, wiseguy, I see you've calmed down. It's almost noon, and we have no plan?" Maria was fishing.

"I have the semblance of a plan, I have an idea that I know will work. I'm also partly thinking that Gaines is just trying to buy time for one last big-ass score, one to flush his secret bank accounts."

"You mean the ones you know about in the Grand Cayman?"

"Yup, it's time to call Nicolette and Terrance, get them ready, coordinate with TJ and bring in Brock the Boxer, but we might have to give him C4 after watching him and his crew shoot last night."

"You want to give a street thug C4? Even for you, that's crazy!" Maria was getting high- pitched.

"If you saw how bad they were shooting and hear me out, you'll want them to have bazookas."

35

Maria rolled her eyes so hard I thought she sprained her neck.

It took me a solid hour to get coordinated with Nicolette, Terrance, and TJ, working through the plan, what they need to accomplish by the end of the day, and where we needed to be logistically. TJ gave me a list of properties he's positive are the stash houses for Gaines's operation. I have two other calls to make. One is going to piss off the FBI so badly, but I really don't care right now. This is about getting Gaines behind bars. Most importantly, getting his cash.

They don't see it; they don't understand it. Guys such as Gaines will do a ten-year stint in prison knowing they just pulled off five hundred million and have plenty of stuff stashed all over. To them, it's also about building the street credit for a fifty-year run at this, not some small-time shit. He's building an organization to keep the legitimate company rolling without him; that's his board. He's also building an underground board to keep an eye on his shit if he ends up in prison.

"Okay, Neil, walk me through this one more time. I'm still a little confused about what you're doing."

"Well, I gave the team in Grand Cayman the game plan to move all of Gaines's cash to a new account that we control."

"Stop right there. You're going to simply steal millions, maybe hundreds of millions of dollars from a drug lord, and you're just smiling like you're talking about ordering a hot dog."

"It's not really a heist, it's moving some digital numbers from one account to another account with the help of someone in the islands. Let's get back on point, that's only part of the piece. The next step is to use TJs list, the confirmed locations with Brock's guys, and call my buddy at the DEA to raid a shitload of houses."

"No, you wouldn't do that. Neil, plus who do you know over at the DEA that's willing to step on the FBI's toes on a case this big?"

"Someone who doesn't care. Senior Sergeant Jordan Meeks, he's crazy as shit, crazy about busting drug dealers." Maria rolled her eyes so hard I thought she sprained her neck.

"Neil, he's crazy, legitimately crazy. I sat by him at a fund-raising function once. I could have sworn up and down he was blown out on something, but everyone just said, 'No, that's Jordan.'"

Jordan stands about 6 feet 2. He's put on a little weight, but in his prime days he was a rocking 220 pounds, solid and ready to go. As he's gotten older, a bit crazier and off his rocker, I can think of no one better to call than he to get the troops riled up, start raiding stash houses. and seize a shit ton of drugs. Not to mention, the DEA, especially around here, needs a win. Whether they get Gaines doesn't matter; if they take thousands of pounds of drugs and money off the street, it's a great PR win.

"Maria, I know he is. Why do you think I'm going to call him? I need someone as crazy as he is to call in the cavalry to bust all those stash houses."

"At least you know what you're getting; you're not going in blind to his crazy ass."

Jordan is what we call a medicated-functioning agent. He works his ass off, but after two failed marriages, three kids he pays for but doesn't see, getting through the day is brutal on guys like him. But the system needs hardened assholes like Jordan. He may be a bit of a mess, but you have to be crazy to run into a meth lab with a fully loaded gun.

I remember one case where I heard him and two agents busted a meth house when Jordan came in. He had a lit cigarette in his mouth, causing the majority of the evidence to burn up, along with the house and the neighbor's shed. If I correctly remember the neighbor's cats took it pretty hard too. They survived, just going to have a bare spot for a while.

"That's the point, I know exactly what and where I'm going with this. I need help from you, though. You need to convince Mike to freeze Gaines's assets for me at a very specific time to make all this work. He can just say he accidentally turned the paperwork in too early."

"I'm pretty sure that I can get him to do it, but we're going to need a better excuse than oopsy!"

"Fine, I'll work on that part, but get on the phone with him and tell him he has to get the ball rolling. I'm going to need Gaines's assets frozen by tomorrow sometime. We are going to put the squeeze on ASAP." I'm done fucking around.

"While I'm on with Mike committing career suicide with him, what are you going to be doing?"

"Calling our buddy at the DEA, setting up a meeting so I can give him all the intel, tell him what the plan is, and get him fired up. I don't think a call will do, I need to get there, get in his face, and get him riled up."

"Here we go again, Neil."

"I know, this is the best part."

Maria got on the phone with Mike, trying her best to get him to understand what I was asking, and I was asking it. I know it's hard to understand sometimes. As Cappelano said, I'm often the smartest man in the room, especially in these instances. I'm starting to see what he was talking about; it can be a burden. Always seeing things ahead of or differently from your colleagues, they simply have to trust you. They have to find a way to understand it, but they can't.

As I called Jordan, I realized that this was going to have to slow down when I talked to him. Within the first couple of minutes, he was so hyper talking to me, it was like having an excited dog ready to fetch. I just needed to wait for the right moment to throw the ball to him. He was on board with what I was selling, I just had to meet up with him to give him the intel and get organized. I told him to meet me at the warehouse in thirty minutes so I could get him the intel. I'll also see if I and a few other guys from my team could tag along to question some people.

"Okay, Neil, Mike is going to do his best to pull this off for us. He said you brought home Cappelano, you've helped the bureau countless times, he'll do what he can, but he can't make any promises. He might need some cover to pull this off. Any ideas?" Maria looked concerned.

"That's good that he's on board, but I'm not sure how I can give him cover. Maybe we work the DEA angle and hope the FBI gets upset and wants to one-up the DEA in the news cycle."

Don't get me wrong; the day-in, day-out grinders of these agencies don't think this way. They simply want to get the bad guys off the street, make their communities and their country safer each day. There are those at the top, the brass, the leaders that want to keep their spots. They know that it's a popularity game. If someone else is doing something big, eventually the question gets asked, Why not us?

"You're going to bank this whole thing on the ego of men in powerful positions? That does sound like you, though." Maria smiled.

"Is it really that far-fetched? It's going to take some work, some hint dropping, and some coaxing to ensure that people play their parts. If Gracin is in town, I know he'll take a meeting with you, perhaps me, even if it's off the record to talk, but it can be a way to bring it up. Then we keep having key people in the office, such as Mike, dropping a hint to freeze Gaines's assets. Maybe get the press involved to help us get public opinion going."

"You know I'll back you; you always see the field differently than most, but it's an advantage."

"Thanks, Maria. I've got to head to the office to meet up with Jordan to get him squared away, then have him and Ken coordinate at the office. After that I'll call a few contacts in the media to get the ball rolling on this. It's already in the news every day, and might as well fan the flames we need."

"Not a bad idea. I'm going to head into my evaluation, should be a few hours. I'll message you when I'm out." She leaned in, gave me a kiss, and went on her way.

"'Bye, Maria."

As we both left the house, ready for the day ahead, I was thinking about the many moving parts I had to work ever so carefully together, just as a composer masterfully bringing in different instruments at different times. It starts with hitting Gaines in the illegal drug game where it counts, his cash. Then we force his hand at his company, trying to get him to move his cash offshore, where we bankrupt him. Checkmate.

I know it seems simple in my head. But even as I say it out loud, I realize how crazy it sounds, but hey, it beats sitting around and waiting for something to happen. I became a bit impatient driving to the warehouse, not surprising, so I reached out to Larry, my news contact. I told him what I needed, just waiting for a response.

Though texting can be efficient, it can also be horrible for someone as impatient as I am. Pulling into the warehouse, I saw Jordan outside with Ken. I should mention that Ken can't stand Jordan; Ken just doesn't have the patience for it. It takes a special kind of person to deal with Jordan, or people like him; you have to be understanding as well as have a long rope. It's similar to dealing with me; the difference is I have some self-awareness of my craziness.

"Neil, heck yeah, nice of you to join us." Ken chuckled sarcastically.

"Sorry, guys, didn't realize Jordan would get here so quickly." I really had no idea.

"I wasn't too far. When someone says they have enough evidence to take down multiple stash houses in one swoop, you listen." Jordan was eager, just like we need him.

"Well, let's go inside my office to go over everything. I'll have Neil grab you the packet from our team. If you're on board, we can send the information to anyone you want us to." Ken flipped the switch and was on point again.

Ken is the ultimate salesman, not just for our company but also to our clients and the people that work for us. He is always finding new ways to keep the client happy, ensure they get what they requested, and he works his ass off to ensure that we do everything spot on. When it comes to the gray area, it's only a handful of us. Christian and I lead the way. Ken keeps this place running tight; that's probably what drives him nuts about Jordanl—he's wilder than I'd ever been, and I already push Ken to his limits.

"All right, Jordan, as I told you on the phone, we have actionable intel from surveillance. Using confidential informants and tracking bank records to point you in the direction of five different stash houses. That the crew Gaines is working with is housing their drugs and cash."

"I'm confused on why the FBI isn't all over this. I'm okay with it. Just wondering." Jordan was second-guessing all of a sudden.

"Neil, let me interject for a moment. Jordan, it comes down to the FBI wanting to focus on a RICO case, they want to slow-play it and work their way up to him. I think it's a bad idea: we need to flush him out, damage his drug trade, clean up our streets, and keep their case intact. Normally I think Neil is off his rocker, but I think this is the best way to play it." Thanks, Ken.

"Neil, what is it you see that no one else does? I understand loyalty and Ken supporting you, and I want this big bust; I just want to make sure we're doing it right." When did Jordan get cautious, maybe old age? It gets us all.

"Jordan, I get hesitation when something of this size gets dropped on your lap. First, let me explain this to you as simply as I can. If you don't act on this by tomorrow, I will go around and burn or blow up all of these houses myself with the help of a rival drug gang." Where did that idea come from? I need sleep.

"Neil, Jesus Christ. I get it. You want to be all over this guy. He kidnapped your girlfriend, is doing irreparable harm to the community, I'm not sure what you want from me. That's a quick ask to put together a task force to accomplish this much this soon, but we can do it. Fuck it, I'm in!" There ya go, Jordan.

"Hey, I have a call I have to take. Ken, can you work with Jordan and get him everything he needs to pull this off? If I need to come down to their headquarters, I will." Larry was calling.

Jordan finally got into it, was on board, and needed help getting it across the finish line. This is where Ken excels, though; he has a far reach in this community and the law enforcement agencies. With his military background as well as the guys we have on staff, he can get to almost anyone in any agency with a good, friendly handshake to where we need them to.

"Larry, thanks for calling me back so quickly."

"Neil, you only call me when it's huge news. What can I do for you?"

"Well, I need a story run, even if it's just an editorial piece that someone talks about at the end of a story you're already doing about the Gaines Chemical case."

"You have my interest; that case is leading almost every local station right now. What do you have in mind? Is it new and can I get a quote?"

"I'd prefer to keep my name out of it for now. If you want to say an agent close to the investigation is concerned, that's an option. I need to encourage the FBI brass to speed up the process of freezing Gaines's corporate assets. They have all the paperwork in, preapproved; they just need to file it and act on it."

"Is there a specific time frame? We can use that, it's a different angle, and it'll ruffle some feathers at the FBI office to get them to call us. Do you have anything else for me?"

"I'm working with the DEA to pull off a massive bust. If we pull it off, I'll text you details so that you and your team can get in there and report on it. It's the least I can do." Back scratching.

"Neil, you always were good at playing the game and making sure that you keep us owing you one." Larry is right.

"I just know the role the media play, and it's a necessary one. If possible I try to utilize it, especially in cases such as this. Thanks, Larry. I'll email you the details shortly."

"Thanks, Neil. As always, we love working with you."

Off the phone, time to head back into the meeting with Jordan and Ken, wrap it up, and get Jordan rolling. This case is about to turn on its head: we need to get moving and push Gaines to the limits; it's our best shot at flushing him out. I took a quick minute to text Maria to check in on Erin's status; I'm worried about her. Gaines has far-reaching friends just as we do; I hope he hasn't made a move on her.

"Okay, guys, are we set for tomorrow?" I'm an optimist.

"Neil, I just got the info. Ken is sending it to my superiors; give me a day to try and pull this off. You know we act fast, especially with this many drugs and cash involved." Jordan was ready to roll.

"Okay, Jordan, I've had TJ email everything over. We will have a courier bring hard copies within the hour, and we can be there for a briefing on a dime if it's needed to carry this across the goal line." Ken was playing salesman of the year.

"Thanks, guys, I'll be in touch later today. As soon as I get some feedback from the team, you'll be the first to know."

"I appreciate it, Jordan. You too, Ken. Thanks for organizing all this so we can act on it."

Just like that, I walked out of the office and made my way to the bunks for a quiet place to check in with Mike, Maria, and Nicolette. That's when I noticed I had a few missed phone calls, not surprising with all the stuff going on the past thirty minutes. One was from Maria, telling me that Mike reached out to her. The text read, "Erin and her detail are missing. Agents en route to look."

36

Like that, I was in the house alone again with my thoughts. Not a great place to be right now.

This day keeps getting better with every passing minute; then again, I'm going to say I told you so. I called Mike, no answer, also no surprise. I texted him, asking him if it's okay for me to call Gracin and put some pressure on them to act. While waiting for a response I was sitting there in the warehouse, not knowing what to do; I almost looked like a lost child in a grocery store. I had so many things I wanted to do but didn't know where to start. I tried Maria a few times, no answer, I finally got a text from her, "Stuck on the phone. I'll talk to you when I get a second."

"Hey Neil, you look a bit lost. You good?"

"Yeah, TJ, I'm all right. I'm just taking a moment to sift through all the shit we've got to pull off on short notice."

"Just do what you always do best."

"What's that, TJ?"

"Slam a square peg through a round hole and make it work," he said, smiling.

"I needed that, thanks to TJ." I couldn't help but laugh.

"No problem, boss. Hit me up if you need anything."

I decided it was time to call Gracin, get him to back Mike's play—well, my play—on freezing Gaines's accounts immediately. We need to force his hand, the board will push him out, there will be too many variables for him to deal with, he'll have to come out of hiding. I called Gracin, only to get ignored; that wasn't nice. Let me try again, also ignored. All right, this is getting old. I'll call from one of the office phones; maybe he won't notice.

"Agent Gracin. How may I help you today?"

"You couldn't answer when I called you the first couple of times from my cell? Come on, Gracin, that's just rude."

"You're right, Neil, I should have answered, but I'm dealing with this case that you know is taking precedence over everything."

"Is it really? You're sitting on the biggest play you have to get him moving, and you won't pull it."

"What are you talking about, Neil? We're doing everything we can to build a RICO case, we even brought in extra help from DC."

"Is this so hard that I have to spell it out? You guys need to freeze his assets. What are you waiting for? This move will force his hand and get him out of hiding. I know the paperwork is there just waiting to be submitted."

"I can understand your frustration, but you know we have a way to do things. The slow way might not be your way, but it works." Gracin sounds like a machine.

"In the meantime, he keeps drugs on the street, cash flowing to his dealers and stash houses, and you just sit there." I'm really pushing him.

"Neil, you never could understand the subtlety of taking your time, being patient." Fuck this guy.

"Well, then let me end it on this note. Gracin, your daughter would still be alive if the bureau didn't pull this wait-and-see shit the first time I went after Cappelano."

That went about as well as planned, hoping Mike can walk him off the ledge. I took a moment to text Mike two little words: "I'm sorry." He just sent back a smiley face; he had to know how this was going to end. Dealing with Gracin is like dealing with a red-tape machine with legs. He finds a way to bind up the simplest of tasks; even taking a shit he could turn into a twelve-step process with three forms needing to be filled out in triplicate.

"Judging by the sound of that conversation, I see Gracin hasn't changed much." Ken stuck his head out.

"Yeah, he's a real prick still, but I was rude as fuck, so I guess it's a stalemate."

"Well, what's the next move? I'm heading down to the DEA to give them a briefing. Jordan already reached out, said they'd prefer to hear firsthand from someone that sifted through all the data. Since I put the file together, I figured I would take care of it and coax them to the finish line."

"Thanks, Ken. Then I guess that leaves me checking in with Nicolette and Terrance in the Grand Cayman and heading back to make sure Maria hasn't broken up with me yet."

"That's a good idea. As for Maria, I think you're good."

As quickly as he stuck his head out, Ken was gone on his way to brief the DEA on the stash houses. He even mapped out the most efficient route to do it; he is backing my play and doing his best to make it easy for the DEA to pull this off. Hence Ken has the reputation he does; it's built on solid planning and delivering in the clutch. With Ken on his way to their office, I hopped in my car, threw my stuff on the front seat, and peeled out, noticeable to the whole warehouse. Not my best moment, but sometimes we act irrationally and slam on that gas pedal.

Calling Nicolette, there was no answer; the same with Terrance. I'm starting to sense a trend here, no one is answering or picking up when I need them to. I know they'll be clutch when needed, but I'd like the mental clarity to talk them through it. I settled for a group text, which I'm not a fan of, but necessary. I let Terrance and Nicolette know the plan and the timing. It took a few minutes, but eventually I got a message back saying confirmed. It's not like them to ditch me unless it's for a good reason. Then again, maybe they are finally enjoying the island life.

About five minutes out, I was going to let Maria know I was on my way home but realized it was pointless now. As I pulled in, I saw her outside waiting for me again, but this time she wasn't so happy. The first time she looked cute and playful; this time she looks like I stole her kid's lunch money. Moma's pissed.

"Neil Leonardo Baggio, get your ass inside this instant!" Maria said loudly.

"Leonardo? That's not my middle name."

"That's not the point, Neil Michael-Angelo Baggio." Maria started to smile.

"Wait a minute. Are you just naming off ninja turtles now?"

"Maybe! I can't stay mad at you, though I want to. Our buddy Gracin called. He wasn't too happy with the way you ended your call."

"I know it was cruel, but he was his usual robotic dick self. So I gave him a dose of reality, the cost of waiting is the cost of a life." I know it was brutal.

"I understand why you did it, and it might have worked. He was ticked when he called me, but by the time I got done with him, he saw our side much more favorably."

"Once the press starts running the story, asking why and calling the bureau for comment, Gracin is going to be pushed over the edge. That should get us to where we need to be."

"Neil, do you ever get tired of playing people like this? I mean, it doesn't feel like you do it every day, just when the scenario calls for action. It's still a bit crazy to watch."

"Maria, it's not about playing anymore, it's more about getting them where they need to be; they just don't know it yet. Oh, hey, this is Terrance. I need to take this."

Maria and I walked separate ways, back to our routine. I spent the next ten to fifteen minutes talking to Terrance and Nicolette about organizing the transfer with the bank manager. They said they would get to work on it, they should be able to pull it off, no problem. The guy is a huge pushover who's scared shitless that his wife is going to find out he's been cheating. Oh, you have to love the guys that think they're untouchable, then run scared.

By this point in the day, after talking to everyone involved and pissing off Gracin, I needed to work out. I probably should have squeezed in a trip to see Cappelano, but he's going to have to survive for the day, probably two. If all goes well, I can get him a cellmate, his biggest fan, Gaines.

"Hey Maria, what are you doing? Maria? Where are you?"

I was calling to an empty house. It sounded like there was no answer back to me. I looked all over the house, looked out front and saw her car, which got me even more confused. Now I'm losing my shit. I'm getting all worked up, all the years of dealing with Cappelano have gotten to me. Those ghosts never go away, they simply hide for a while. I know he said he only kidnapped my family to scare me away, but it left a lasting impression. I guess I would say he completed what he sought out to scare me shitless. I noticed the girls weren't around either. I noticed the back door was partially open and went out back to find Maria on the phone yelling at someone.

"You don't understand, this shit isn't that hard to comprehend. Gaines kidnapped Erin, she's the only connection to all his shit with Bryan in prison. That means we need to get him in a protective detail ASAP; this case could blow up otherwise." Maria was lighting someone up on the phone.

"Hey, come get me when you're done." I leaned in and gave her a kiss.

"Okay, give me a minute," she whispered as she covered the phone with her hand.

Back in the house, I realized it's a waiting game for me. At this point I have all the kettles working. I have my team in the Grand Cayman getting everything ready to pull the trigger on, I also have Ken with the DEA giving them the briefing to make this an easy sell. All that are left is are the five- and six-o'clock news calling Gracin for comment. To increase the fire a bit, I texted Larry and gave him Gracin's cell, I also told him to lose it once he got his "no comment."

Down in the basement, I was sitting at the foot of the stairs in my usual uniform. Chuck Taylors, comfortable jeans, a T-shirt, and a hat on backward. I guess I could mention that the hat is a black Red Wings hat with a green emblem, from the St.

Patty's Day collection. My shirt, well, that's a bit of a different story, it's a vintage Green Arrow T-shirt. I know it's a look for the day, it's also a bit of foreshadowing to the rogue shit I'm going to be pulling over the next thirty-six hours to close this case. Trust me, by tomorrow night, if we do all of these things, Gaines will pop up somewhere and we'll be able to get him. I realized with all this shit going on, we're still waiting on an update on Erin, where she is, what happened, etc. I got an idea that is going to involve TJ.

"Hey TJ, I need you to do something. Throw a few top dogs on it."

"Sure, boss man, I love it when you sound fired up. What do you need?" TJ was eager.

"I need you to track down who was posted on Erin's detail last. Then I need you to dig through their financial records to see if we can find a connection or an in that Gaines might have used. Also, try tracing their phones, keep an active ping going, to see if we can find them."

"No problem Neil. I'll get you the info as soon as we have something."

"Thanks, TJ."

Off the phone, sitting downstairs, I'm still a bit hot under the collar. I started wrapping my hands, getting ready to put in some work on the bag. It took me longer than normal because I kept getting text messages from guys in the field. I took the time to talk to Christian, who was telling me about Brock and his crew. They think they have an inside line on where Gaines is, but I think it's just them trying to act like they have something. If they didn't check in regularly, they would be lost; they know we wouldn't be covering them anymore. Maria came down the stairs.

"Hey Neil, sorry about that. I was on the phone with the agent at the scene of the place where they were keeping Erin. It doesn't look good. All of her stuff is still there, but both agents' gear is missing. It looks like she was taken, either abruptly, but they would have checked in by now, or one of them was in on it."

"Who's leading the investigation? Anyone we trust?"

"Yeah, you're looking at her. I've been sulking around here long enough. I know it's only been a few days, but I need to get back out there. Give them hell today and tomorrow, I'll probably be swamped trying to track her down, maybe we'll cross paths tonight or tomorrow." She leaned in and kissed me.

"Be safe, Maria. I'm getting used to you being around."

"Aw, that's sweet. I'll call you later to check in. Have a good workout. I'm heading out to see what's going on with this case."

Like that, I was in the house alone again with my thoughts. Not a great place to be right now, that's when I do my most damage. I took a few extra minutes, worked on my wraps to get them right, I knew I was going to be hitting hard today. You might have noticed I rarely speak of gloves; it's not because I'm a badass, just that for some reason I really enjoy hitting a bag with only wraps. I think it's because when I'm out in the field, it's not like I can call a TV time-out and put on wraps and gloves before a fight.

I turned the radio to WRIF—good old 101, the best rock station around. They have been a staple in Detroit rock city, giving you the drive you need to keep going. A few combinations in, I noticed my phone chiming left and right. I was hitting the bag, one-two, one-two-four, working through combinations, and couldn't get that phone to stop. As I looked down, it was Ken sending me a text as long as an email; the best part is it's coming through out of order, always a blast. I did catch one important line in the middle, though.

"DEA on board for tomorrow, organizing as we speak. Call me in an hour."

37

I need to run and talk to fifty assholes. I mean bosses. I need to communicate with my bosses.

Two hours later and I'm still working on shit. I've been making my way around the house, doing work on the computer, taking phone calls and emails. Never took my wraps off, just kept them on, dipping into the basement for a few minutes to hit the bag. I was finding a rhythm after an hour. I might be able to keep this up all night, get the mind right heading into tomorrow. Ken and I kept playing phone tag. I missed his call a few times and he missed mine; it was getting a bit pointless. Then I heard someone walking in. I know it sounds odd, but I have people with keys, and they know to just walk in unless they see two cars in the driveway.

"Neil, I figured this would be easier than to keep playing phone tag. It's on the way back to the warehouse anyway. How's your day going? I see you're getting a good workout in."

"Yeah, Ken, I'm all over the place, working out, working, and running around the house. Maria went out to the safe house where they were keeping Erin. I guess it wasn't so safe after all." Poor joke.

"That aside, the DEA is ready to roll,. I figured by now you'd have messages or calls from Gracin. Didn't you have the news call him for a comment?" Ken knows me so well.

"He texted me about an hour ago, a crisp 'Fuck off.' I figured he got the message; now we have to hope it hits home. I think it will; it's just a matter of how quickly it'll get him to move his slow ass."

"Yeah, Gracin was never known for his catlike reflexes, especially in decision making. Maybe we can put together the ghosts of FBI past to scare his ass." Ken was smiling.

"Not a bad idea. At the end of it we just need to get him to cross that line; I feel he is so close. It's just going to take some nudging."

"In your case, it's showing, pushing, and perhaps a little kicking to get him through the door."

"I'll be gentle. I swear, other than giving me shit and telling me what I already know about tomorrow being a go, what else do we have?"

"When the DEA took our intel and started to work on it with what they had, they were able to connect four more stash houses they are fairly confident in. They said we can come along tomorrow if we want to ask some questions, see what we can find out." Ken looked tired.

"You look a bit tired, Ken. Long day dealing with the DEA?" Always is.

"It's all the red tape, hand-holding, and handshaking you need to do. It just drains me."

"I hear ya, Ken. I'm the same way. I can handle only so much."

"What's the plan for tomorrow, then? See what they can kick up on the raids, talk to some folks?"

"I'm thinking it's going to be the best thing we can do while trying to track down Gaines. With us pressing him on the drugs, the bureau pushes him on the chemical holdings, then we take it all away and force his hand."

"It scares me sometimes how well you can read a room, put together a plan with fifty moving pieces, and just sit there calmly like it's no big deal." Ken knows I get worked up; he's just giving me a compliment.

"You mean other than hitting a heavy bag multiple times a day to ensure I don't snap? I'd say I'm not as calm as people think I am." I can have my bad days.

"Neil, I love you like a brother. Your level of anxiety versus that of most people are at different levels. You get worked up as you work through it. You don't sit on your hands." Ken has a point.

"My mind is always racing, but hey, that's me."

"And that's why we all love ya, brother."

The brofest and rundown of the day went on for another fifteen minutes before Ken left. He decided it was time to get back to the office and organize the next couple of days, since he'll be working with me closely on this case. The DEA likes him, likes his approach, and that means we need to keep him tied to them. This will keep them happy and moving forward with the plan. The day is turning into night, and I haven't heard from Maria most of the day, left her a few messages, and we texted back and forth, but nothing major. They have no leads and no idea how to connect.

That's where I come in. We're already looking into the bank records, assuming one of the agents is dirty. It makes the most plausible sense Gaines has enough money to buy almost anything; it's not hard to think he offered cash to the agents. Maria and I may not be able to touch base, but as I was staring at my phone with no purpose, I saw Mike calling in.

"Hey Mike, it's Neil. What can I do for you?"

"At this point we're good, but damn Gracin can't stand you. He gave me the go on freezing his funds; they'll do it tomorrow morning as soon as the banks open." Thataboy, Mike.

"Awesome; things are starting to fall into place. We have the accounts in Grand Cayman covered, his holdings in Gaines Chemical covered, and tomorrow the DEA throws a huge punch into the side of his operations."

"Neil, you know this is crazy. Getting everyone to work this coordinated usually takes months of planning."

"You're assuming the DEA knows what you're doing and vice versa. I set the plans in motion as a separate party; that's what allowed it to happen. My ability to walk that line gives me the flexibility of a great composer with a beautiful sonata."

"Look at Neil getting all poetic. How about I hit you up in the morning or late when I get an exact time? Just let me know if you guys find anything helpful that tracking turned down. Unless you are going to try and play a bounty hunter and bring him in yourself, like you did Cappelano."

"Fair point I guess we'll have to see how the case goes. Hey Mike, have you heard from Agent Garcia? We've connected, but it's been pretty vanilla even for her, just want to make sure it's all good."

"Yea, she ran into some rookie mistakes out there and was playing catch-up at the scene. Also, it wasted their time tracking the whereabouts of the three missing people—Erin and the two agents."

"The chances of two agents on the take is highly unlikely. I hope they're okay."

"My thoughts exactly. I need to run and talk to fifty assholes. I mean bosses. I need to communicate with my bosses," Mike said, laughing as he hung up.

For now I can't do much. We have a waiting game until tomorrow. I still have my wraps on. Come to think of it, I've had them on most of the day, and since my hands aren't numb, I either wrapped them too loosely or I'm just getting used to being in them so often. With wraps on and time to kill, I went back to the bag for an hour. Thinking through the case, starting with the missing girl, Erin, and the protests, something still doesn't add up. Working through the idea that she was taken so quickly, then treated decently from what she said. The lack of stress she seemed to show after being taken, I feel we are missing something. I'll find it, though. With each passing combination, I feel the case breakdown, I sidestep, duck, jab, then hook. Working through a sequence, my mind starts to focus on the task, my footwork, and proper follow-through. This slows my brain down, similar to all the showers I used to take; it gives me a moment of clarity to find the missing pieces to the puzzle.

I remember in my studies learning about the Method of Loci, which allows you to store mnemonic devices in your memory, in a specific place for later. My mind notices more than I'm aware of most days; it's taking in ten times, if not more, information than the average person. I've been like this even as a kid, which is why I always got in trouble. The hard part is learning how to sift through it all, work with it; otherwise you just have a large pile of unusable crap.

Erin is connected to Gaines Chemical somehow, I can just feel it, I need to keep focusing on this, while I work through the rest of the case. Looking at the connection Gaines had with local street gangs to push his drugs, and build his empire makes sense for business. What seems another story is Gaines Chemical was hurting, hiding losses with drug money. Someone at the bureau would have caught it, though, you would assume. That is, unless he's using a shell company to make purchases from Gaines Chemical to fulfill his street orders and wash his drug money. I'm not sure he's smart enough, but he's definitely brazened enough to make that play.

Dripping in sweat, I realized it was time to stop, clean up, and go over these accounting files, maybe call the FBI agent who worked on it with Maria. I wish I could get her on the phone to walk through this. I also wonder where TJ is in connecting the agents to any dirty money.

Oh shit, Maria just texted me; she's going to call me in a few minutes. I guess I need to get this shower in, I took too long all day on the bag, I'm going to have to make up time in the shower.

I was able to get a solid twenty-minute shower in. Waiting for Maria's call, I figured it would be an easy way to keep myself distracted and calm a bit. Nights like this are usually hard; it's like being a kid before Christmas or a big trip, the anticipation builds and starts to drive you crazy.

"Hey Maria, I knew today would be rough, but damn, you guys been swamped with leads over there?"

"Shit no, the original lead on this case messed it up so bad. I don't want to get into it; right now I just wanted to talk to you, go over a few items and see how you're doing." Maria seemed exhausted mentally.

"Sorry to hear it, Maria Is there anything I can do to help?"

"Do you have some random lead you might be able to share?"

"I might have something, but it might also be pointless. Let me have TJ run it down before I add to you and your team. If it has actionable intel, you'll be the first call."

"Sounds good, Neil. I need to get back to this shit show over here. Call me if you get anything, Also I heard Gracin approved the account action. Nicely done."

"Thanks, Maria, I'll get my guys to work on this lead and see what it gets for you. I'll talk to you later. Stay safe."

"I will. I shouldn't worry, since I know my man will come to save me when it's needed. 'Bye, Neil, give the girls a kiss good night from me."

As soon as I got off the phone, I sent a message to TJ, walking him through what I needed him to check. He said it shouldn't take too long, since he has the case files from the protests, the disappearance, and all items tied to Gaines and the Monroe case. To ensure he hopped on it quickly, I expressed the severity of speed on this topic.

Here I am again, back to a quiet, empty house. Under previous circumstances I would call Sheila, especially when I'm bored, and chances are she'd come running over. I'm working on breaking that habit; if I want it to work out with

Maria, I need to break some of these habits. I decided to gather all the info I was reviewing, trying to connect the dots and sit in my study, also known as the front room, but hey, I made it look pretty sweet. With a fire going, the girls lying down peacefully, and me with a crap ton of work, I almost gave up five minutes in. Then I remember I have a nice bottle of gin in the cabinet. With a little ice and a lime twist, I should be good to go—that is, unless I fall asleep from just relaxing in the chair with the addition of the alcohol.

38

I guess we need to track her ass down ASAP.

Shit! What time is it? Where is my phone? Where did I get this blanket? So many questions in need of answers. I got up, noticed the girls bailed on me, probably when I turned the fire down. They're probably in the bed, taking up all the space, but hey, that's their job. I found my phone on the floor next to the chair, showing three forty-five in the morning. I also noticed my glass was damn near full still—melted, but full. I barely got a few sips in when I must have passed out. TJ texted me back saying he found something. He added, "Call no matter the time. It's important."

"All right, Neil, I found what you were looking for. It took a minute to figure it out, then a little bit of time to confirm it, but it looks like Erin and Bryan were either hooking up, working together, or dating. I have tons of text messages, phone calls, and emails going back and forth between them for two weeks."

"No shit. I knew there was something funny about this from the beginning. Do we have anyone at the bureau we can ask about? Never mind." I just noticed that the real reason the girls left me is Maria came over.

"Neil, never mind what?" TJ sounded lost, but that's partially my fault.

"Email me what you have, at least a *Cliff's Notes* version immediately, and get a file organized. I'm heading to the FBI field office to confront Bryan."

Before I could gently wake her up, Maria started moving around, noticing I was up and about. She rolled over a few different times fighting the urge to wake up. I wasn't bugging her, but she could sense me—okay, she heard my loud ass. I thought I was home alone, I wasn't talking quietly, which woke my girlfriend who's exhausted from work—that's right, boyfriend of the year material.

"Neil, who was that? Also, what time is it?" Eyes barely open, Maria smiled.

"It was TJ. That lead I was hoping to have for you just came through."

She stood up like a rocket. Apparently those words were the energy drink she needed to run up her spine and get her moving. She sat up at the end of the bed, went to the bathroom, and still didn't respond. I let her go with it in case she was going to fall back asleep. She made her back to the bedroom, lay down, pulled the covers on her head, and then I heard her muffled voice.

"What's the lead?" I could barely hear her.

"What are you saying, Maria?"

"WHAT'S THE LEAD, NEIL?!" I heard that one.

"I had a hunch that Erin and Bryan were connected somehow. TJ did some digging and found out they are; we just don't know how. We need to talk to Bryan, tell him that she's in trouble, it might be the only way we get intel we can use."

"Slight problem, they're moving Bryan at six this morning from our office to a holding facility. His lawyer requested it, and it got approved late last night. It'll be hard as hell to get anything out of him with his lawyer present, especially outside of our walls." Maria was back up.

"Well, I guess it's time to get ready, meet you in the shower in five minutes. Do you want me to go to the office on my own, so you can rest?"

"Neil, I'm not going to let you go into the office without me, especially after the shit you pulled with Gracin. Also, I'm not going to turn down a shower with you, even if we have to make it quick."

She raced me into the shower, ensuring she would get the majority of the hot water. Luckily, my shower has two heads and some steam jets, but like any house with plumbing, one is stronger than the other. It was quick in the shower, but we still were able to have a little fun and connect as a couple, not just agents on a case. I know it can be a cliché to have agents hooking up, but life and relationships are about proximity. In psychology class, they called it the proximity effect, which makes it sound fancy. All it means is, you simply can't date or have any relationship with someone you don't meet.

Maria and I chased each other down the freeway at four in the morning, her classic Corvette and my newer Dodge Challenger. We weren't going too crazy, but we were enjoying the open freeway with no traffic at this hour. Even the FBI field office was empty. By the time we made it to the building, Maria had made a call and found out where they were holding him in the building.

"Neil, once we get in there follow my lead, we need to do this quickly and discreetly. Don't even tell anyone why we're here."

"Got it. I'll wear a name tag with my intentions written under it," I said jokingly.

"Really, Neil, now isn't the time to play around." Maria smiled, though.

Once we got inside, it was a quick movement to track him down. Maria spoke to the agent on duty, then pointed at me, and they both laughed. That's odd; I wonder what she said. Whatever it was, it worked; the agent walked away from the door. At the same time, Maria and I entered a small room with a makeshift bed; it looked like an interrogation room sleepover and a cot. Bryan was lying there, asleep, until Maria woke him up.

"Shh, Bryan, don't scream." She placed her hand over his mouth softly.

"What the hell, why are you and Neil here in the middle of the night? Why are you doing it so quietly? You're agents, it's not like you're going to bust me out. Wait, are you going to bust me out? Hell, yeah." Wow, he got there fast.

"No, Bryan. We need to talk to you about Erin. We know you two had some form of a relationship. What we don't know is what kind. We have phone records and text records coming tomorrow, but for now, we know you guys were in contact as far back as a month before the protest."

"Why don't you ask her? She's the crazy bitch." Bryan looked scared.

"We would love to, but she's missing with both the agents assigned to keep an eye on her. Maria and I sneaked in there to get info to help track her down."

"Wait—she escaped from your protection? I knew it was too good to be true. She's coming for me, I know she is. You need to protect me." I didn't see this coming.

"Protect you from the socialite, activist, the girl that stands about five-foot-six small-fit frame, blond hair? That one?"

"Neil, you have no idea. I swear after getting involved with her, she's either an agent or just a plain old psycho." Bryan was legit scared.

"Wait, guy, both of you slow down. Bryan, that's great that she's nuts, we'll deal with that in a minute. Start with how you met, then work up to why she's loco." Maria was dropping some Spanish in there.

Bryan started explaining that they met in a coffeehouse. He keeps a regular schedule, so it's not surprising that when he looks back she was able to find him and come up with a way to get his attention. He describes their first meeting as one where she dressed to impress, played it just right, then met him the next day, accidentally walking into him. He got played hard; I just didn't think Erin had it in her.

He told us first he thought she was coming on to him to blackmail him with his girlfriend, but they're not married. He quickly realized she was interested in his work at Gaines Chemical. Mainly, what they are doing at two specific plants, eventually getting enough dirt on him to screw him over with Gaines. She used that as a way to blackmail him into getting the sealed documents she used to uncover their fraud with the city and state.

"Okay, Bryan, I get where she plans things out and is vindictive or calculating, but how does that lead you to believe she's going to kill you?"

"Do you remember the video footage that's missing from the security tape? From that loop, it's in my home office on a thumb drive in my sock drawer."

He said he realized it's not original, but he at least taped it to the bottom. It was his insurance in case she came after him. The footage shows her shooting a guard from behind, in cold murder before the protest and stashing the body in the woods. It will also show Bryan helping her throw the body in a security van, which is how she ended up in the warehouse. It was to lay low, not because she was missing. We found enough evidence and pieced part of it together, so she just went with it.

"Okay, so you have the footage that incriminates you and her, but that doesn't explain why she would bust out now." Maria was still a bit lost.

"I got this, Bryan. Maria, with him in custody, it's only a matter of time that we process his whole house and find the thumb drive, or he gives her up in general as a bargaining chip."

"Bingo, Neil! She's going for that thumb drive, and she's coming for me. I know it. If you see the footage, it shows how cold she is." Bryan looked like he saw a ghost.

"Maria, the agent, is making her way back. I'm assuming that means we need to get going. Bryan, we'll see what we can do for extra protection. Maria and I will talk to the lead agents ASAP but can't make any promises."

"I'll take anything I can get. Thank you, guys. I know I'm screwed, but that's better than dead. Among her, Gaines, and the street gang, I've got a lot of people wanting to kill me right now." He's got a point.

"Be safe. brother. We'll do our best."

Just as quick as we were getting in, we got out. We made our way to Maria's office to make a call to Mike, give him a heads up on what is going down, and see if they can add any extra protection. Without solid evidence, we can predict it's hard to get more money spent on a prisoner transfer, but at least we can try. Maria was on the phone with him for only a few minutes when she hung it up with some force.

"Apparently Gracin is leading the prison transfer, so you can assume there isn't going to be any changes to the protocol. You know he'll say something along the lines of, we are already set up to handle these variables." Maria was doing her impersonation of him.

"Well then, I guess we need to track her ass down ASAP. Can the FBI ping the phones of Erin and their agents? Or should I ask TJ to do it through our channels?"

"We've been trying to on our agents' phones for some time, but they're offline, probably turned off."

"I guess for now we head over to the warehouse. We'll be there by six thirty at this rate. That means we can get breakfast on the way, a cup of coffee, and get organized."

"You can, Neil. I need to stay here and work through this new lead on our end. Do your best today to find her. Remember, Bryan is getting moved out of here shortly. That means you need to get out of here before Gracin pulls in." Maria has a point.

"Okay, bye, sweets. Be safe, as usual." I gave Maria a quick kiss.

I damn near sprinted out of the building; I even took the stairs to ensure I didn't catch Gracin in the elevator. As I jogged out the door, I high-fived the security guard and yelled, "Go

Wings!" He hollered back, then I hopped in my car, heading out. As I made it to the exit, I saw Gracin pulling in. I slowly put my window down, watched him look over, then flipped him the bird. As I pulled away, I could hear him scream.

"Fucking asshole!"

I love messing with that prick; he deserves it. Then again, there is a place for the by-the-book approach. They take forever to do anything in the FBI. As I drove away I couldn't help but laugh because I'm getting them to freeze Gaines's accounts. I just got a text from the crew in Grand Cayman that they are set, they can move the funds within one-hour notice, maybe quicker, and I'm about to head out with Ken and the DEA to bust up a major drug ring in Detroit. These are the days when we earn our money. I do feel like one or two more huge curveballs are coming our way. The Erin-to-Bryan connection was just the first hanging curveball.

39

The best part was every bullet damn near shot him in the foot.

Well, here we are. Ken and I rounded up the guys and got them organized for the day, then we headed out to meet up with the DEA at the first stop. Our plan was to be fifteen to twenty minutes behind them; we're not in this for the gunfights but for the intel. We're looking to write our own after-action reports, interview witnesses, and track down Gaines and now Erin as well. Jordan and his team were ready to go, with agents stationed around three different houses. Ken had our guys scout ahead on the other ones in case word gets around that they are getting raided. If anything starts moving, we can get pictures as well as tails on it.

"Hey Jordan, we ready to rock today? It looks like you have plenty of agents."

"You can never have enough agents for raids like this. I wish we had more time to cover more of these as possible."

Jordan knows they will lose some stuff the farther down the list we go.

"If our intel is correct, this should give us the best shot to hit many if not most of these houses before they can reach out or get organized at the other ones." Ken always has a plan.

"I hope so, the intel looked good, was verified, and we even did some scouting to ensure it's as solid as it can be."

"Thanks again, Jordan; this was a huge pull at the last minute." It was massive.

"Thanks, Neil, it's going to do some major good."

Sitting there waiting for the raid to start, I decided to sift through my phone and emails. I probably looked like that jackass that's buried in their cell phone at church. I get it, time, and place, but I've got lots of other moving parts right now. I was shooting a text message to Maria to see how her day was going when TJ was calling me.

"Hey TJ, you know we're about to head into this raid. I'm assuming it's important."—

"Yeah, it is, I got confirmation that Gaines's holdings and business funds are all frozen. I'll keep an eye on his accounts in the Grand Cayman; I'll let you know if I see any movement. Also, I got confirmation that Bryan's transport is under way. I'll call you if I hear anything else."

"No worries, TJ. Hey, I need to let you go—Maria is calling on the other line."

"Peace." TJ hung up quickly.

"Hey Maria, what's up? Any movement over there?"

"Yeah, but not the good kind. Bryan's transport got hit, someone rammed into it with a Pontiac Fiero filled with some kind of accelerant. The second that car hit the transport it went up in flames."

"Are you okay? Did the person jump from the car?"

"I'm okay, just a little shaken up, but we lost three agents to the fire, and Bryan is dead."

"Witnesses have a female matching Erin's description driving the Fiero before she jumped and took off on foot. We have agents in pursuit, but no luck so far. This girl feels like a pro; I think Bryan was right to be scared."

"Let me get this straight: Erin rams a Fiero into the caravan, and her car catches on fire fast? Probably from the fiberglass frame of that car mixed with an accelerant, not a bad way to take someone out. Brutal but creative."

"I need to get back to this shit storm. I'll let you know if we find anything, but I doubt it. Please be safe, see you at home hopefully tonight, or tomorrow." Maria sounded pissed.

"Talk to you later, babe. You be safe, too. Glad you're okay."

I looked at Ken with utter disbelief. hat are the odds Erin's working for or with Gaines? Maybe it's unrelated and she's just tying up loose ends, but it's still a coincidence. Her involvement, taking out Bryan when Gaines needs him out of the picture the most.

"What happened, Neil? That call didn't sound promising." Ken's astute.

"If you mean finding out Bryan is dead and it turns out Erin probably killed him, and she's in the wind again, then yeah, I'd say some bad news."

"Shit. Well, that puts a bit more pressure on today to pull this off and track down Gaines." No shit, Ken.

"I'm going to text Christian to have him keep Brock and his crew in the loop in case we need to run down some stragglers. Also, to keep an eye out for Gaines. I still can't believe we haven't gotten a peep yet out of him."

"I know what you're saying, but we'll get there, hopefully not as long as some other cases, but you know we'll get there." Ken is right, I have to trust.

"Well, what can I say? I guess we'll find out more as the day continues."

The first raid was quick and simple. There wasn't much to be found, in regard to Gaines and what we were fishing for, but there were key statements given that helped us gather intel on the next couple of stops. We found out that the schedule for one of the warehouses we were going to hit in the middle might have to be moved up. I sent Christian and one of our other guys ahead to scout if anything was going on in the warehouse.

Halfway to our second raid. where the DEA almost came up empty until they found cash stashed beneath the flooring. One of the pieces of intel taken from the first raid was this second warehouse used to house a car bay where they did oil changes. There was a ton of cash hidden down there—the agents estimated close to twenty million. It's crazy to think that an organization would house twenty million in cash in an old oil change bay in the middle of the city. I guess you have to learn to adapt; it's not like you can go to the bank, but that's where Gaines was laundering the money back into his company.

"Ken, if there was twenty million in cash at the second stop, and Gaines is laundering his own money, how much is he taking off the streets in the illegal dealing?"

"With their volume and output, possible sales to other states and countries, he could be raking in close to fifty million a month. He can move an absurd amount of product."

"Wait—I thought you were going to say one to two max, and that's just built up."

Ken spent time explaining to me the sheer volume at which Gaines Chemical can produce drugs. Both legal and otherwise, the number is astounding, and the cash paid out is even more. That makes me wonder how much is enough. If Gaines has a hundred million in the bank, why risk it with street gangs and felony charges? I guess it's off to the next couple of raids, to see what we can kick up in the Detroit morning air.

Between the third and fourth raids, we're sure word got out on what was going on. Jordan and his team had seized more than thirty million in cash, guns galore, and enough drugs to fill my garage, floor to ceiling, front to back. I wish I were kidding, but they were hauling them away in evidence vans, and it took seven vans just to load them up and move them back to the DEA warehouse. The only reason we knew the word had gotten out is that my guys who had scouted ahead were watching people trying to head in and take out as much as they could. The only problem is that we have pictures of them doing it, and someone tailing the trucks they're using to move the materials themselves before the DEA raid teams arrived.

It was the same show over and over. The DEA would raid the place, people would run, and they would find a large stash of drugs and money, not to mention small arsenals of guns to ensure they could shoot plenty of concrete and random cars. I've never seen so many bad shots in my life; watching these raids and seeing so many DEA agents not taking any hits was a blessing but also sad. Those guys were brutal shots. I'm sure I saw one guy shooting with his hand up and gun on an angle, some shit he saw in a movie. The best part was every bullet damn nearly shot him in the foot, but he kept going, and kept nearly missing. I wish we had that shit on camera.

"All right, Neil, from what I can tell, we don't have anything to go on, but we put a shit ton of pressure on Gaines. I guess the next step is to follow up, regroup, and wait." Ken was recapping the day.

"Yeah, I'm going to call Christian and see where he is and what he has going on. His instincts are great, and he has a great knack for falling into shit like me."

"I've noticed that I think it's because the two of you don't have the same fear of doing stupid shit as the rest of us." Ken has a point.

"Thanks, Ken. Be safe today; I'll let you know if we find anything."

As Ken left and I got into my car, I sat there for a minute, engine roaring, the vents running loudly as they worked to defrost the window. I took a minute to relax, think through the day, all the different variables that came our way that I might not have given enough attention to earlier. I tried calling Christian, but no answer, tried him again and still hadn't gotten a response. Just then, Jordan knocked on my car window.

"Yeah, Jordan, what can I do for you? I'm about to head out of here. Do you still need me for something?"

"No, I just wanted to take a quick moment and say thank you. Today is going to go down in history. I wanted to make sure we got it on record that you and your team were a huge part of this."

"Keep me out of it if you can, it's not that I don't like the limelight, it's more than Ken and the BCI team did a ton of work on this, I just showed up at the end. I can't take credit for everything they did."

"You got it, Neil. As always, it's a pleasure, man."

COLLOQUIUM

As Jordan walked away and I rolled up my window, I realized I missed two texts from Christian. One was an address, the next just said three words:

Erin's with Gaines!

40

Christian shot through the can to perfection.

Let me get this straight: after all this work we put in, that ass clown Brock found him. By the time I got to Christian, he was across the street from a CPA's office, where Gaines and Erin were working to move money around; at least that's our guess. We only had Christian's scope to get a closer look, but he said you could see them handing over and signing papers to the CPA. I decided to call Nicolette to have them pull up and see what's going on.

"Nicolette, I know we had you keeping an eye on his accounts all day, but are you seeing any movement right now?"

"I'm not by the computer, but if you give a minute, I can pull it up."

"Thanks. We found him at his CPA's office, I don't even know how, but that doesn't matter right now. What do you see?"

"Yes, the account has already doubled; it looks like someone is writing money into the account as we speak. When do you want me to pull the trigger on moving it?"

"Let me wait until Gaines leaves the office and finishes the transactions; that way we can move it all out of his account."

"Sounds good. I'll wait for you to contact me."

Back to Christian, who's keeping an eye on everything, as usual. He mentioned that he made a trade, and that one he'll explain it to me. Apparently Brock had a tail on Gaines for days, but he was saving it as a trump card in case he got pinched, and we went back on our word. For a guy who comes off as a two-bit hustling idiot, he's got some skill in this shit. I still can't believe that Brock found Gaines before us, and now Erin is with Gaines. Something doesn't seem right. How did I miss this whole thing?

"It looks like Gaines and Erin are leaving. What do you want to do?"

"Call the FBI now and text Ken,. I know we have guys in the area."

"On it, what are you going to do?"

"I'm going to stall until they get here and piss him off. If I raise my left hand and throw something up, think you can shoot it for me? A nice display of *watch your ass* for Gaines and Erin."

"Yeah, you know I can, plus it will be fun to watch them squirm a bit." He means shit themselves.

"Well, no time like now."

Walking toward Gaines and Erin, I could hear them arguing about something, but it was hard to make it out. I was also texting Maria and Mike the address and some quick details—the more the merrier. Gaines was walking out with a bit of a swagger, knowing we hurt him but thinking he was going to have enough money to settle for many lifetimes. I quickly texted Nicolette that it was a green light.

"Hey bud, how you been? I keep missing you. I've been trying to reach you on your cell."

"Neil, my old friend, you know Erin. You should say hello."

"We'll deal with that later. Gaines, it's over, time to give up. You don't have any money left, your organization is crumbling, and now your company is going to be taken from you."

"First of all, no to the money thing, no to the organization, and that company will be pried from my dead hands before I ever let it go. Erin, can you do me a favor and kick this man's ass for me so we can go on our way?"

"My pleasure, boss. Should I kill him?" Okay, this Erin chick is a psycho.

"Tell you what. Before you kick my ass, maybe I can show you something first."

"What do you have in mind, Neil? I'm looking forward to watching her kick your ass."

"See that can over here? Check this out—I've got a really cool imaginary gun, and it shoots really big real bullets."

I picked up the can from the ground, looked at Gaines and Erin long, and tossed it high in the air. Christian shot through the can to perfection, and the looks on their faces were amazing. They both ducked, not sure how they thought that would help, they were standing in the open, but hey, you do what you do.

"Okay, Neil, I see you brought some friends." I have more on the way.

"You know what my favorite part is, we have your money too. It's all gone, man, you're washed up and useless. That's right, Erin, your boss can't pay you, he's broke as shit."

"Neil, you and the FBI may have frozen my corporate assets, but you know I have way more money than that." Oh, I love cocky guys.

"Gaines, tell ya what. Call your accountant over there, have him double-check your accounts, 'cause the money is gone."

Right then, Gaines pulled out his phone, called the man, and started talking to him. It took a few minutes because he was yelling at him. I'll be honest. It was a funny scene watching someone yell at another person on the phone when they were fewer than fifty yards apart. Judging by the look on Jason's face, I'm pretty sure he just confirmed there's nothing in his accounts anymore.

"He said there's only a hundred dollars left in the account, you cleaned out all fifty million from the bank account. I don't know how but I'll kill you, Neil, you'll see."

As Gaines was starting to rant, you could hear the sirens getting closer by the second, watching Gaines's head get lower and lower. Then, all of a sudden, he just started laughing; that's when I realized that Erin was gone. All I can do is hope Christian has eyes on her, and he's in pursuit, or one of the agents grabs her. At least we have Gaines, his money, and all the drugs.

Mike and Maria pulled up; as I watched an agent grab Gaines, handcuff him, and read him his rights, he started laughing again. He kept saying that this is just the beginning and muttering to always protect my queen.

"Neil, one of these days you're going to have to tell us how you keep ending up ahead of the bureau and their teams." Mike was thankful and perplexed.

"I take the buckshot approach, putting as many kettles in the fire waiting for the first pot to start whistling."

"Neil, any word on Erin? Christian said she was here, but we obviously don't see her anywhere." Maria looked a bit pissed.

"I don't know, Maria, but from what I have seen in the past twenty-four hours, I feel like Bryan was right, she was way more than what we thought. At this point, I can't tell if she was a bigger influence on Gaines or the other way around."

"Maria, Neil, hey, I know the two of you are always going to look at what you missed. You still need to get it straight. Between the two of you, we have taken out a massive drug dealer in the state and supplier across the country and even in Canada. This case took a bigger turn than any of us anticipated. Don't dwell on what can be, focus on what is." Mike has a point.

"I know, Mike, but Neil and I are driven by one thing. Ultimate success means the small big wins are great, but we can't seem to grasp it." Maria knows me well.

"I'm with her, I know it's too late to track down Erin. And without her bankroll, who knows what's going to happen?" Maria has a scent; she's not giving up.

"Maria, I have a feeling she's going to bother you, going to be a thorn in your side. But I'll be here to support in any way you need. Though I feel you're going to do this on your own with your own team."

"Neil, you know me too well. I spent the past couple of days hiding out at your place; it's time to get back at it and stop feeling sorry for myself." Maria looked the most confident I've seen her in days.

"Well, Maria, you got a clean bill from the head doc, they just want to keep up on you every other week to check in." Mike is always looking out.

"Thanks, Mike, but I think Neil just ditched us. He's heading over to Gaines."

I could hear Maria finish as I walked away. I was done with the small talk, the agent version of an after-case water cooler. I wanted to talk to Gaines, I'm certain he wants to talk to me. I'm also certain there is some bullshit he's going to say about how this is just the beginning of our relationship. He forgets I went through the same shit with Cappelano, so I'm a little worn out on the archnemesis routine.

It was a great feeling, though, seeing all the money, all the drugs, and the guy responsible for them taken off the streets. I do think this isn't it. I'm sure his lawyer will find some technicality, some way to get him back out; those rich guys always do. We took the money, removed his influence, and the hope is that he will remove his ability to beat this.

Seeing him sitting there was a great feeling, similar to winning the big game; there's a sense of accomplishment. It's not a feeling of joy, it's a relief. I've read enough stories from the most driven among us, such as Jordan, Jeter, or Kobe, to understand it's the thrill of the chase, the work put in that drives us. The feeling at the end of the rainbow is rarely fulfilling.

41

Every evil villain deserves to give their speech at the end of the movie.

As expected, Gaines was still jawing with some of the agents, talking shit, claiming I stole fifty million from him. They think he's talking about the money that was frozen, his holdings in the chemical company. What they don't realize is that we swindled the evil villain out of his bankroll. It did feel good to play a game of chess with him and crush him so quickly. It's time to get this over with; he's going to give me a speech and every evil villain deserves to give their speech at the end of the movie.

"Mr. Baggio, nice of you to join our little get-together over here. We have a few agents taking statements on processing me, and now you have graced us with your presence. How lucky we are to have the great Neil Baggio among us."

"I appreciate the introduction, but I feel it's you that deserves the introduction, the great narrator voice telling the audience what amazing feats you have pulled off. Drug kingpin in two different sectors, legal and illegal, friend to many in the community, an enemy to life itself."

"Neil, why so dark? We can simply talk. We are friends, after all, connected in our appreciation for a great chase and the need to understand the great mind that is Cappelano."

"If you say so, Gaines, I'm just glad this is over. Before you say 'for now,' I know this is not going to be the last time I hear from you, is it?" Gaines looked at me and smiled.

"You know you are a very clever investigator. However, I feel even you won't grasp the next steps in our relationship, but soon enough, you'll see. As for this conversation, we're done. I'll say hello to Cappelano for you." Wait, what?

"That's cute; you aren't going to FCI Milan, you're going to rot in a holding cell for some time. Knowing your lawyer, you'll end up in Florida somewhere at some minimum-security Motel 6," I said, laughing as I walked away.

"We'll see!" Gaines yelled.

He is adamant he's going to see Cappelano; I guess we all need dreams to believe in. I made my way back over to where agents were talking about the day and what went on about how Gaines felt he was some grand mastermind. Cappelano is a rare breed; to compare yourself to him is irrational. I know I like boxing, I'm decent at it, but I'm not comparing myself to any of the greats. I'm no Rocky Marciano, no Pacquiao or Mayweather. I'm just a guy who likes to box, but some of us take our dreams a little too seriously, I guess. The water cooler gang, as I have quickly named them, is hanging by my car. It's a group of five or six agents talking to Maria and Mike.

Speaking of teams, I wonder where Christian is; I decided to shoot him a text for his whereabouts. Lately, when I call, he ignores it; then again, he's usually on a case or doing surveillance. I think I'm going to change his name to Hunter or the Watcher, some cool moniker in the company since he's always got an eye on the lead suspect in a case.

"Hey Neil, that looked like an awkward conversation, even from over here. How'd that one go? Is he as crazy as Cappelano?" Mike was fishing.

"I don't know. I guess we're going to find out soon enough as this case plays out with the lawyers. He has this sense that he and Cappelano will get to visit soon in prison. They wouldn't send him to FCI right now, would they?" Now I was fishing.

"Neil, with Gracin leading the way and DC getting involved, I would assume they want him closer to their office, so I doubt it. You never know what kind of dirt he has on other people of power and politicians to get his way." Maria had a point.

"It's just going to be one of those weeks, isn't it, where we all sit and wait for the news on how this case is turning?"

"I believe so, Neil, I believe so." Mike lost his confident speech stature from earlier.

"Maria, are you ready to get out of here and head home, or are you going back to the office to keep up the hunt on Erin?"

"You already know the answer to that, Neil. I'm heading to the office to get a team together. I'm not losing another minute. By the way, where did Christian end up?"

"Maria, I wish I knew. I shot him a message to see where he is. There's no point in calling him, I know he's not going to answer."

"Let me know. I want to make sure he's doing okay, he's a great asset and an even better guy. I want to make sure all the team is accounted for."

We finished up with our water cooler talk at the Challenger, went our separate ways, and disappeared from each other's vision among the chaos of moving parts, police and FBI vehicles, and crime scene investigators. I climbed into my car, sat there for a moment, and something just didn't seem right still. I grabbed my notepad from the case, started sifting through chicken scratch. Sometimes I can write down a trend without realizing it.

I was still struggling with it, couldn't grasp his confidence, and it was a bit too easy. I started flipping, though, as if I had drawn an animation sequence across the pages. I need to talk to him longer, get a bigger interview with him. There is some depth to this case I'm missing. I understand the sheer greed portion that drives people like him, but there is still something missing.

Why not lose your shit on me for taking all your money, your drugs, everything? Unless there's an exit strategy I'm unaware of. Maybe he has a contingency somewhere that I don't see yet. I'm still sitting here, with the scene clearing up a little bit at a time. I need to check in with everyone. Also, why isn't Christian responding? I decided to text TJ and ask him to track Christian's phone. Next up is a conversation with Nicolette and Terrance.

"Hey Neil, what's up? Everything go as planned? We were all able to move the money to that account you set up. By the way, where is the money going, and what is it being used for?"

"We set up a charity to be run by a friend of ours we can trust. We're also considering giving the money to Gaines's sister in South America for her company's research efforts."

"I'm a bit confused. Can't she just give it back to him?" Nicolette was concerned.

"No, since it's a charity, we are going to work off of a grant system to support her. That way, if Gaines comes after the money somehow, he still has to go through us."

"I feel like you're still controlling the money. Isn't that leaving a sour taste in your mouth?"

"It does, Nicolette. I just don't know where else or what else to do with it at this point. It's better than it being wasted in a government slush fund for the CIA."

"That's true. We were able to pull it all out but had to leave something in there since we weren't closing the account. I thought one hundred bucks was perfect—a little poetic, too."

"I like your style. Hey, do you guys have a lead on where the bank manager is right now? Since this is over I want to ensure he's okay. We used him for the case, but I don't want him having lasting harm coming his way."

"We scrubbed the scene pretty well, but Terrance and I can look him up for you."

"Thanks, Nicolette."

Another conversation down that isn't settling my nerves, I really need to track down Christian and make sure he's okay. That will help minimize the issues I am having—that's a nice way of saying unsettling anxiety that I keep missing something. If I were Father Roberts right now, I'd probably tell me to calm down. I'm just struggling with closing a case quickly. I'm used to long, drawn-out slugfests that drain you like a long baseball season. I mean really, do they need one hundred and sixty-two games?

I guess I'm just going to have to go home unsettled, and lacking the closure I was hoping for. I picked my head up from my notepad, threw the pad on the seat next to me, and adjusted my hat. I realized that mine was the only car left. Everyone was gone; it was me and an empty parking lot. If no one is around, I'm going to peel out a bit, rip these tires up, and get some aggression out. Don't worry, I wasn't speeding through a subdivision, merely peeling out in a parking lot. Once home, I'll just have to hit the heavy bag, take a long-ass shower, and pour myself a drink.

COLLOQUIUM

COLLOQUIUM

42

That wasn't the end.

It's been a week since I peeled out of the parking lot. We eventually tracked Christian down, but it took almost six hours. A good friend of ours thought we might be looking for him and texted Ken. Christian was getting shit-canned at a local bar called the Village Idiot. He wasn't belligerent; he was just really wobbly. Ken and the guys made sure and got him and his car home safely; that's how we roll.

The last week has been stressful, to say the least. I finally called the publisher back, mainly for the distraction to start negotiating a book deal. Maria has been trying to track down Erin, but the case went ice cold a few days ago when they got word she crossed into Mexico. Maria's working on confirmation because she isn't one to believe stories without facts. We're still good, but life is always hard when both people can get wrapped up in cases and get pulled apart in different directions. I actually made it out to Cappelano two times this week and spent longer than normal time with him since my caseload is a little light right now. I needed the distraction. As Ken put it, I need to focus on that book.

In the case of the fifty million we liberated from Gaines's hidden slush fund, we are still trying to figure out what to do with it. If Gracin had his way, he would use it for a private fund to allow the FBI and other agencies to take on cases they might not otherwise go after. If you think this is just a literary tool, sorry, the government has been seizing assets, especially cash, since the beginning of governments and using it for their own gain. Then they rationalize it, claiming they're doing good with it.

In case you were wondering where I am currently, it's the federal prison FCI Milan, waiting for Cappelano. He's running late, was supposed to be here almost twenty minutes ago; this isn't like him. I guess I'll just sit here and review my notes for a few minutes.

"Hey Neil, sorry for keeping you waiting, but I was having a riveting conversation—a colloquium, if you may—with our mutual friend Gaines. He joined us here today."

"Wait. What the fuck are you talking about?"

"A colloquium is considered a conference, but it stems from the Latin, meaning to converse. I've been polishing up on my Latin since I have free time."

"I'll be right back; I need to make a call."

"I figured you might. Take your time, I have a whole lifetime."

I abruptly got up from the table, headed out of the room to the side area, where I can get a better signal. It's also where the guards do their smoke breaks. It's closed off, but it's a small area to get full services from that concrete prison for prisoners and cell coverage.

"Mike, what the fuck is going on? Why didn't anyone tell me about Gaines?"

"What are you talking about? I haven't heard anything. Other than the fact that Gaines's lawyer and the AG are working on some form of a plea deal. Gaines wants to save his family company, give his sister the coverage she needs to keep researching, or some shit like that."

"Gaines is here, at FCI Milan, in the general population. He just had a great talk with Cappelano."

"Wait. What the hell are you talking about? Let me get on the phone. You know this is going to take twenty phone calls, so if I get anything, I'll message you."

Like that, I hung up, didn't even say good-bye, I was too hot. I knew something was missing. Was he trying to get caught? Did he allow himself to end up here so he can learn from his hero Cappelano? Gaines is a planner, he's a thug, but he's a smart one. He's not like Brock, driven by instinct and primal drive. Gaines is cerebral, similar to Cappelano in that context; he's just not nearly as polished, or he doesn't seem it.

Maybe it's the fact that Cappelano worked alone for so long, which didn't give us any angles on him. Gaines essentially fell because of the people around him, the organization crumbled and brought him down; if he was solo, he might be harder to deal with. I can only assume I'm not the only one thinking this stuff: Cappelano and Gaines I'm sure will have this conversation. The next call I need to make is telling Maria, since I'm going to be useless to her for a few days.

"Maria, I have some bad news."

"We lost Erin, I know it. I don't need to hear it from someone else. We've already made it a case we'll keep an eye on, but it's no longer active. From what we can tell, she's out of the country anyway." Maria was frantic and jumpy; I could hear it.

"I wish that were the only bad news I had for you. Turns out that Mr. Gaines was able to get transferred into the general population at FCI Milan. During his trial he's going to get to talk to Cappelano."

"Wait, what? You have got to be kidding. You know what? I have an idea: I'm so burned out on all this shit I need a vacation. I know you need one worse than I do. Let's go somewhere."

"That was a quick change of subjects, but I can understand you don't feel like dealing with it. Mike is already on the phone, tracking down the details. As for the vacation, I've been meaning to ask you something but haven't had the courage."

"Shoot, you know I'm open to anything. I'd go on a vacation to Sarnia right now. As for changing the subject, I think I'm burned out on this case. I need a glass of wine and a quiet night before I can talk any more about this shit."

"I understand. I wanted to ask you, though, since we're on the subject. Would you like to go on a missionary trip with me and Father Roberts, do some good, and get some mental rest?"

"That sounds great. Want to leave tomorrow? Also, where are we going?"

"No idea. I'll leave that up to him, but I'll let you know. For now I need to get back into the room and talk to Cappelano. This is going to be brutal. See you at home, Maria, I hope."

"I'll actually be there; I'm grabbing a few bottles of wine and some Buddy's pizza, so I might be passed out with pizza stains all over if you take too long."

"I'll do my best to get home. Talk to you later, Maria."

I guess I can look forward to a good distraction. I'll just tell Father Roberts we need to speed up the missionary trip. Heck, I'll even pay for it, just to get out of here, get away from this mess, and clear my mind. As I walked back into the room, I noticed that Frank was smiling still, like he had accomplished something.

"Frank, what are you grinning over?"

"You . . . you're all worked up about two people you put in prison, as if we can do anything to you. We're locked up like animals."

"It's less about control and more trying to figure out the puzzle that is Gaines's mind; you know that. You've known me long enough to know I can get fixated on things. It's a strong suit and a curse."

"Neil, you need to relax; this Gaines thing isn't going away fast. The bureau does everything slowly, you know that. You might as well just let it go and deal with what is instead of trying to figure out how you got there in the first place. Not to mention, will it matter if you figured it out? So that wasn't the end when you arrested him. You should know someone with that much money and power isn't going down easily."

"Other than my own ego, no."

Cappelano and I tried our best to get back on the subject, go through the list of murders that he committed after his nephew Tony, and the homeless man, but we couldn't. I kept bringing up what was going on inside my head, the thoughts of Gaines, why Cappelano? We both realized after an hour of failing to get on point that we would take a break, I would leave for the day, and we would pick it up later. I had to get out of there, get my head out of the clouds. Hitting the shit out of a heavy bag to some loud music will help.

43

I'm the biggest fan of watching Neil squirm.

Well, this is it, I'm not sure how long it will be before Neil comes back and I'm not sure the next time I'll get to talk to you. I bet you wonder how that conversation went with Gaines, don't you? It wasn't long—not yet at least—we have time to catch up. Time to learn from each other. But he had a compelling argument, something that made me feel alive for the first time since being locked up in here. I guess you can say that Gaines gave me hope, especially in being able to affect the outside world again, one way or another.

"Mr. Cappelano, I presume, judging by the name on your chest."

"Yes, but I'm not much for the fanboys in here. Are you new to the block? First timer?"

"Actually, yes, but we've spoken before—quite recently, actually. Also, let me apologize for framing you for murder, attempting to kill you and Neil in prison."

"Mr. Gaines, I take it that you got your wish to make it to FCI Milan. You must have had some bargaining chip to pull that off."

"Actually, it wasn't quite as hard as I had hoped. I called a powerful friend, implied I would like to be here, and found out that Gracin, the lead agent on my case, can't stand Neil. I made it known that Neil would go nuts if I ended up here."

"That does sound like Gracin, making a poor decision simply to spite Neil. Such a shame."

"You're not going to run off and tell him, are you? I don't want him knowing how I got in here. I'm okay with him knowing I'm here, I just want to hold off on the why part for a little while longer."

"No problem; I'm the biggest fan of watching Neil squirm, try to solve the problem, and go neurotically insane."

"By the way, Frank, if I can call you that, I looked up what a colloquium is before I got locked up. Feel free to call me Jason, by the way. You said it was an interview in part, but the Latin translation leaves room for variance. I noticed many believe it to be more along the lines of a seminar. And that is why I am here, to be in your class."

"You want me to be your teacher? How do you plan on getting out of here?"

"I can influence just as much from in here as I can from outside. Not to mention the money Neil was able to take from me is pennies compared to what I have overseas in a Swiss bank account. It's attached to my sister's name and family, registered under a company name, so no one found it."

"That sounds intriguing; you do have a compelling argument. What do I get out of the deal?"

"I can get you anything we need on the inside and I will stay here as long as you need me to. I'll find a way so we can continue this interaction."

"You really think you're getting out of here?"

"I know I am. So what do you say, teach?"